Praise for *Graveyard Shift,*
Book 1 of *Lana Harvey, Reapers Inc.*

"*Graveyard Shift* is an impressive feat of imagination built on a broad knowledge of world religion. It's also great fun! No small accomplishment."

-Christine Wicker, best-selling author of
*Not in Kansas Anymore: The Curious Tale of
How Magic is Transforming America*

"Darkly comic and wildly imaginative. Angela Roquet gives us an afterlife we've never seen before."

-Kimberly Frost, best-selling author of
The Southern Witch Series

"Graveyard Shift is sacrilicious. Roquet's first book in the Reapers Inc. series will be a huge hit with fans of authors like J.K. Rowling and Neil Gaiman. I look forward to getting my hands on the rest of the series."

-Lance Carbuncle, author of
Grundish and Askew

"I love sci-fi and fantasy. Horror is also one of my favorite genres. I have had a lifelong love of mythology in all it many varied forms. It is rare to find a book that combines more than two of those with both a joyous wickedness and intelligence. Angela Roquet has managed it beautifully in her novel *Graveyard Shift*. She has artfully woven many different religions and mythologies into a believable afterlife."

-D.E. Cook, author of
Fairy Exterminators

by Angela Roquet

Lana Harvey, Reapers Inc.

Graveyard Shift

Pocket Full of Posies

For the Birds

Psychopomp

Death Wish

Ghost Market

Lana Harvey, Reapers Inc. short stories

Dearly Departed (in *Off the Beaten Path*)

Hair of the Hellhound (in *Badass and the Beast*)

Season's Reapings (holiday short story)

other titles

Crazy Ex-Ghoulfriend

Backwoods Armageddon

Blood Moon

POCKET FULL OF POSIES

LANA HARVEY, REAPERS INC.
BOOK 2

Angela Roquet

Copyright © 2012 by Angela Roquet

ISBN: 1479101257
ISBN-13: 978-1479101252

For my son.
If you believe in nothing else in this world,
I hope you at least believe in yourself.

CHAPTER 1

"Baseball is religion
without the mischief."
-Thomas Boswell

Gabriel always looked like he had just rolled out of bed. He wore the same dingy drawstring pants he always wore, and I wasn't even sure he owned a shirt. He shoved a handful of popcorn in his mouth and jumped to his feet, throwing a buttery fist in the air.

"Catch the ball, asshole!" he shouted at the muddy diamond below.

"You know they can't hear you, right?" I rubbed a hand over my throbbing forehead and groaned, almost wishing I had stayed home and studied. *Almost.*

The sun was annoyingly bright, and it had sucked up most of the moisture from an early morning rain, creating a sticky humidity that made breathing a chore. The air was heavy with the smell of stale popcorn and cut grass.

Josie was going to have an apocalyptic tantrum when she found out that I had pushed off studying to catch a baseball game with Gabriel. Of course, the ball field was conveniently located next to the cemetery where two funerals were about to take place for my last catches of the day.

Harvesting low-risk souls was a walk in the graveyard, especially after Grim's last assignment, hunting down a high-risk replacement soul to keep Eternity from deteriorating back into its former wilderness. The chaos that would have ensued, had I failed, would have brought on the Second War of Eternity. And only one man had been looking forward to that. Seth. Now he was on the run. At least, I hoped he was on the run.

Most expired gods embraced retirement and puttered around their respective afterlives like favored grandfathers. Seth wouldn't hear of it. But then again, he wasn't exactly favored in his realm. Probably because he made Hitler look like the Easter Bunny. The creep didn't care what happened to Eternity or anyone who lived there, and if he couldn't be king, starting a war would be just as amusing.

"Oh! How could you miss that?" Gabriel shook his head, bouncing around his tangle of blond curls. "You're not worth the crusty peanuts between my toes." He grunted and plopped down next to me on the roof of the concession stand.

"He is human, Gabriel."

"Well, it shows," he said.

I glanced over my shoulder and spied a small and weepy crowd filtering into the cemetery and congregating around the first death hole. "I better go get that soul before he's six feet under."

"And miss the last inning? Are you crazy?"

I raised an eyebrow. "You're shouting at people who can't see you, let alone hear you, and I'm the crazy one?"

Gabriel flicked his wings and folded his arms. "Do what you have to. I'm gonna stay here and keep an eye on number three. That home plate's been calling his name all afternoon."

2

"Well, number three can't hear that plate any more than he can hear you, pilgrim." I stood and swept the popcorn off my robe.

"Someone help!" A lady in the bleachers bent over a wheezing, elderly man and slugged him on the back hard enough to dislodge a lung. "We need a doctor!"

Gabriel looked up at me. "Sure you don't wanna stick around and pick up an extra commission later?"

"You don't see another reaper around here, do you?" I pulled up the hood of my robe and ducked down, hoping to avoid a confrontation with one of my coworkers. If wheezy there had a medium-risk soul, another reaper would be showing up any minute to collect it. I didn't want to get caught playing on company coin. Grim had enough reasons to send me to the proverbial guillotine.

"He's a low-risk. I can tell you that right now," Gabriel said.

"How would you know?"

"I saw him get out of his car. He has a Darwin bumper sticker."

"Oh." I relaxed a little. "If he's a low-risk, someone will be assigned to collect him later."

"Lana." Gabriel dropped his chin and gave me a look that paused somewhere between confusion and frustration. "He's right there, easy money, not to mention brownie points with Grim."

I scowled at him and tucked a black curl behind my ear. Gabriel was right. I could really use the brownie points, but he didn't have to go and spoil my afternoon by bringing it up. I seriously considered ripping out a handful of his feathers and shoving them in his mouth.

I glanced back at the man in the bleachers and inwardly groaned. It had been nearly six months since I'd harvested a soul from a body so freshly deceased. I liked my tidy routine, simply reaching in a coffin and caressing a body

3

that's already been cleaned and dressed and positioned just right. And I hated, hated, hated heart attacks.

I could already feel the man's eyes migrating towards the concession stand, ready to seize me with the helpless look of a puppy, right before it gets creamed by a bus. Like I could somehow stop it. He choked out his last breath and collapsed in the lap of the hysterical woman fanning him with a foam finger.

Several observers had popped out their cell phones. Ambulance sirens pierced the air. The umpire called a timeout, while one of the team physicians, a round man with swollen cheeks, hobbled up the stadium stairs like a wounded elephant.

"Gabriel, you suck." I scooted to the edge of the roof and leapt onto the stands.

By the time I reached the man, the physician had begun a half-hearted attempt at mouth-to-mouth, sloppily struggling to catch his own breath while trying to pump air into the dead man. CPR always looked so clean on television. What a crock. I cringed and looked away, blindly reaching for the limp hand dangling off the bench.

The result was unexpected. Fire zipped up my sleeve, and the wave of heat that followed shoved me flat on my ass. I rolled backwards, flailing my arm around like an idiot. I found my footing and jerked the flaming robe over my head before pitching it over the bleachers.

When I turned around, Gabriel blocked my view. His huge wings pressed outward to their widest span, glowing softly from his holy rage. "Lord of the Flies," he hissed. "Explain yourself before my patience gives way."

I rose up on my toes to peek through the gap between Gabriel's left shoulder and his wing. Beelzebub, the prince of demons, straightened his tie with a soft chuckle, keeping one hand firmly tangled in the leash attached to the soul I had unsuccessfully tried to harvest.

Beelzebub, or Bub, as his business cards said, was a handsome devil. I could give him that much. His suit was black, slick, and fashionable as ever. The collar of a silky red shirt peeked out around the edges of his jacket, enhancing the gold and amber flecks in his black eyes. His haircut was borderline edgy, longer than most businessmen keep it, and today he wore it slicked back. With his neatly trimmed goatee, he looked like a rock star ready for the grand jury.

"Gabriel, old boy, I thought you were on vacation." Bub reached into the breast pocket of his jacket and gently tugged out a small leather pad stuffed with papers. "Here's my registration and permits, not that you have a legitimate reason to request them."

Gabriel's cheeks flared as he snatched the leather pad and glanced over the tiny scribbling that declared Bub's possession and soul seizure a legitimate heist.

"Sorry about the burn, Lana," Bub said as I stepped around Gabriel.

"Those hideous robes aren't free, you know. And I thought this guy was atheist. What gives?"

Bub tilted his head to one side. "What gave you the impression he was atheist?"

"The Darwin sticker on his bumper."

"Ah. Must have borrowed the car. His son is atheist, but he's a Baptist. At least, he's Baptist enough to go to Hell for being a pedophile and a crook." He lowered his gaze at me. "And if you had completed the training Cindy requested of you, you could have avoided the scorching." He clicked his forked tongue at me.

"What training?" Gabriel wheeled around with a belligerent scowl. Crap.

I hadn't necessarily been lying to my friends. I just hadn't been filling them in on all the smaller details of my current situation. In order to secure Cindy Morningstar's vote for my placement on the Posy Unit, I had agreed to take a training course that would better prepare me for demon attacks. After witnessing the brutal death of Grim's second-in-command, Coreen Bendura, the training course didn't sound like such a bad idea. But between the classes I was taking at the academy and work, there was literally no time for anything else. I'd seen my boyfriend, Maalik, twice in the last month. Of course, his position on the Afterlife Council didn't help our relationship much either.

The Posy Unit wasn't even my idea. Horus, the Egyptian representative on the Afterlife Council, was blackmailing me into joining so I could do an illegal side job for him. He had even written up a placement proposal for the council to vote on, pissing Grim off even further.

Under normal circumstances, I would have told Horus not to let my scythe scrape him on his way out. I couldn't have cared less about joining one of the specialty units. In fact, I preferred my low-risk souls. But as it was, Horus claimed to know my newly discovered secret. I wasn't cast in the same mold as the other reapers. Khadija, the former soul serving on the secret throne of Eternity, had given me a unique ability, one that I only shared with Grim. The two of us could visibly see the potency of a soul. Not that the boss-man needed another reason to despise me.

My ability was a violation of the peace treaty between the gods. Reapers were not supposed to be gifted with any powers not sanctioned by the council. If word got out, it could mean a swift execution.

If that wasn't bad enough, I had also slain a lesser goddess last fall. It was in self-defense, but that would hardly matter to the council. Grim was the only one I had told, a decision I was still kicking myself for. It must have been shock that forced me into blurting out that horrid confession. At least he was just as horrified at the thought of anyone else finding out. Grim was an egotistical slug, but he still favored peace among the gods.

Bub shook his head at me. "Lana, Lana, Lana. You have less than a month until the placement ceremony. Cindy grows impatient." His light English accent had a seductive edge to it. I just couldn't picture him using that voice to command legions.

Gabriel was still frowning at me as he handed back Bub's papers.

"I'll figure something out," I mumbled.

"See you soon then." Bub snapped his fingers and disappeared with the soul, leaving behind a sickly yellow smog in his place.

"What training?" Gabriel tried to ask again, only to be cut off by a wailing sob from the cemetery. They were preparing to lower the first casket into the ground.

"That's my cue." I leapt off the bleachers and found my charred robe, the formidable uniform. I slipped it over my head and looked up at Gabriel. "I'll explain everything later. I promise."

"Sure," he grumbled and turned his back to me. Angels could be so pissy sometimes.

CHAPTER 2

*"The gods offer no reward for intellect.
There was never one yet that showed any interest in it."*
-Mark Twain

"Suck it up, Lana. You're not missing class tonight." Josie leaned her back against my front door, clutching her text book to her chest as she checked her watch for the fifth time. "Hurry up. Grace is handing out our final assignments tonight."

"Hooray." I leaned over my bathroom counter and resumed lazily applying my peach lip gloss.

Josie Galla was one of the very few reapers who I could tolerate being around. She was a century older than me, being of the seventh generation of reapers, which is probably why she had no problem ordering me around all the time. A no-nonsense attitude was her approach to everything. She applied it to work, school, relationships, and her personal style. She even sported a no-nonsense haircut that managed to look fabulous even when she haphazardly spiked it with gel, like she had done tonight.

On Monday nights, Josie and I went to the only class we shared, thank Khadija. The Wandering Souls course was taught by Grace Adaline, the only active first generation reaper. My mentor, Saul Avelo, had been a first generation reaper too. He was also one of the very few reapers who had died in the line of duty. That's not what bothered me about being in Grace's class though.

Craig Hogan, my creep of an ex, just happened to be taking the same course this semester. Had Grim not given me a special assignment last fall, Craig would have been happy to continue ignoring me like he had been for past the two hundred years. After our brief reunion at Coreen's memorial service, where I made it perfectly clear that I still detested him, he had seemingly given up on the notion of reuniting with me to further his career. I should have known better. Craig was the youngest reaper ever accepted on the Lost Souls Unit. The pride still hadn't quite found its way out of his system.

When he signed up for Grace Adaline's Wandering Souls course right after Josie and I had, I knew I was in for a round two. Craig and I had dated off and on throughout our initial schooling and for a short while into our apprenticeships. I knew the game he played. Hell, I used to be his practice dummy. Craig was the kind of guy who threw himself at a girl with his eyes closed, hoping he could play it off like fate had brought them together. Sometimes, depending on how much time he was willing to blow, the trick even worked. Unfortunately for him, there wasn't enough time in Eternity to make it work on me again. The semester was finally coming to an end, and the only thing he had managed to arouse in me was my gag reflex.

Josie led me through the academy doors like I was a high-risk, celebrity soul. She was determined to see me pass Grace's course, pairing up with me on every assignment she could to help balance out my lousy test scores. I already knew that if I didn't turn this final project into a masterpiece, I was doomed on multiple levels. I needed this course on my resume if I wanted my placement proposal for the Posy Unit to make it to the voting table of the Afterlife Council.

With that in mind, I pushed through Grace's classroom door and found Craig comfortably seated at a front table and chatting up two giggly colleagues of his from the Lost Souls Unit, Miranda Giles and Karen Durst. He had folded on fate and was now trying to play the jealousy card. No surprise there.

I paused with a mischievous grin, just itching to say something catty or embarrassing, when Josie grabbed my elbow and steered me towards a remote table.

"Wait until the semester's over, please," she said through gritted teeth.

I slapped my books down on the table with a frustrated sigh, drawing irritated glances from half the class, and slumped into a chair. Josie took the seat next to me and wasted no time as she reached under the table and pinched my leg.

"Sit up straight," she snapped. "Can't you at least pretend to give a rat's ass if you pass this course? I swear, if you weren't an apprentice of Saul's, Grace would have booted you out of here months ago."

"Yeah, yeah." I rolled my eyes and reclined back in my chair, daring her to pinch me again.

Grace was the last to enter the classroom. She gave her watch a tired glance and pulled the door shut behind her, flipping the bolt lock with an obnoxious pop that silenced us all. As if showing up late for her class wasn't humiliating enough. Josie and I had only made that mistake once. Grace showed no mercy as she berated us in front of our snickering classmates. After that, Josie began escorting me to class ten minutes early.

Josie wouldn't be making the mistake of signing up for a class with me again anytime soon. She was already on the recommendation list of Paul Brom, the instructor of the other class she was taking, the Art of Soul Hypnosis. Paul's class was a prerequisite for the Recovery Unit, while Grace's covered the Posy and Lost Souls Units. Josie liked to keep her options open, a quality she shared with Jenni Fang, her ambitious roommate.

I hated to admit it, but I was feeling more than a little guilty for not giving my all in Grace's class. I mean, she was the same generation as my late mentor. I'm sure that had helped her decision to fill out my placement proposal when Horus approached her. The hopeless stare she staked me with every time my mouth opened in her classroom didn't help mask her disappointment any either.

"All right, my little death merchants." Grace handed off a stack of papers to her apprentice. "Clair is passing out your last assignment, which will also serve as part of your final for this course. This assignment will require you to work with a partner. There will also be a multiple choice exam after your presentations, which will count for fifty percent of your final scores."

Craig's hand jerked into the air, not that he ever waited to be called on. "How many questions will be on this exam, and which chapters should we review?"

Grace sighed one of her bored, annoyed sighs, the kind I rather enjoyed when not induced by myself, and glared at Craig. "If you would have let me finish, you'd know by now."

I couldn't help myself. The snicker squeezed out along with my none-too-subtle commentary. "Moron."

Instead of the annoyed glare I was accustomed to, Grace's eyebrows twitched upward with a cruel sort of justice. "Lana, perhaps you could enlighten Craig here with your expertise by pairing up with him on this last assignment."

"What?" I sat up rigid in my chair.

"I insist." She pressed her horn-rimmed glasses up the bridge of her nose and gazed over the class. "In fact, I expect all of you to choose a partner you've never worked with before. It's a challenge you may very well face in the fields you're entering, so consider it a necessary challenge you must overcome in order to pass this course."

"But Craig's impossible," I blurted, sounding more hysterical by the second. That earned me another pinch from Josie. She had been right, of course. I should have kept my big mouth shut until the semester was over.

Grace turned her back to the class and began writing on the blackboard, not even acknowledging my outburst. She was resolved in her decision and of high enough rank that she didn't feel the need to argue with a peon like me.

Craig twisted around in his seat to give me one of his most charming, shit-eating grins.

"Think you can manage to keep your mouth shut now?" Josie snarled in my ear.

I huffed and leaned back in my chair, folding my arms in disgust... at myself. How, oh how, did I manage to get myself into these situations.

CHAPTER 3

"A man's got to believe in something.
I believe I'll have another drink."
-W.C. Fields

Josie gave me one of her full-blown lectures after class. Strangely, I wasn't bothered by it. Really, what could be worse than having to work with Craig? I was beginning to wonder if there was a vaccine for annoyance. Probably not. I'd just have to subject myself to Josie more often. Eventually, I would become immune.

Josie had also managed to find out about the baseball game I'd blown off her study group for. Kicking Gabriel in the feathered balls was at the top of my to-do list for the evening. Right after a drink.... or ten.

Purgatory was lively for a Monday night. I had a feeling it had something to do with Xaphen's new soul food menu. Even the nephilim were following their noses into the bar, thick with the warm smell of barbeque ribs and fried okra. Xaphen ran from table to table, filling pitchers and delivering plates of sizzling, southern-fried goodies. When he found a few seconds to take a smoke break, I saw him hang a help wanted sign in the front window.

I frowned into my empty beer mug and folded my arms over the scarred, oak table. The bobby pins holding up my dark mop of curls were threatening a headache, while the glittery trim of my dress scratched at my throat. I had to be the most depressingly dolled-up third wheel in the whole joint. Gabriel and Amy sat across from me, playing footsie a little too harshly to be mistaken for foreplay.

Gabriel's wings twitched and a patch of crimson blotches spread over his face, growing fiercer with each hissing syllable Amy spat at him. I had stopped listening when the conversation morphed into a personal attack on Gabriel's work ethic. I'd heard it all before, and my thoughts were tangled up in my own misery at the moment.

Maalik was over an hour late, which meant he probably wouldn't be showing up at all, and I would be getting the "work first, play later" speech the next time I saw him. Whenever that would be. The drill was getting old, but not the sex. I guess fifty years of celibacy will do that to a person. But the sex wouldn't be enough to keep us together forever. Eventually, some changes would have to be made.

"Don't you agree, Lana?"

"Huh?" I lifted my chin off my palm and stared absently at Amy. I was so beyond pretending to care about their mind-numbing soap opera.

I was still dumbfounded by Gabriel and Amy's union, as was most of Limbo City. They had made the headlines more than once in the local tabloid magazine, *Limbo's Laundry*. It was unheard of for an angel and a demon to date, especially an angel and a demon of their rank. Of course, Gabriel hadn't been too active in the field or in afterlife politics lately. He had become something of a drifter after the death of my mentor, Saul Avelo. His reputation followed him around like a flashing neon sign anyway.

Amy, on the other hand, was as ambitious as Gabriel was lazy. She was a president of Hell and commanded thirty-six legions. If that wasn't enough, she was also highly active on the Hell Committee and ran the Inferno Chateau, the hottest new vacation spot in Hell. It featured its own museum and volcanic hiking trails. She and Gabriel were definitely an unlikely pair. It was stranger still that she seemed to be a good influence on him.

Amy cleared her throat. "Gabriel should show more dedication to his career so he has a shot at a council position next term."

"What makes you think I want a council position?" Gabriel snorted and put his mug down hard enough to draw a few unpleasant glares from the neighboring tables.

Amy followed their lead with a glare of her own and dipped a manicured finger in his beer, sending the amber liquid boiling.

"Hey!" Gabriel jerked his hand away a second shy of a scalding.

"Well, it's been a blast." I stood and pulled my jacket on.

"You're leaving?" Gabriel gave me a look of panic. "Why don't you stay? I'll buy another pitcher," he offered, doing a lousy job of keeping the strain out of his voice.

Amy huffed and snatched her purse off the table. "I'm going to the ladies room. Have a nice night, Lana." She tossed her fiery curls back and stormed off, snapping her spiked tail around her ankles like a whip.

I whistled and shook my head. "Good luck with her tonight."

"Eh." Gabriel shrugged. "If I lay it on thick enough, we'll have some pretty incredible make-up sex later."

"More than I needed to know." I frowned. "Hey, I'm sorry I didn't tell you about the training course sooner."

Gabriel switched his spoiled mug with Amy's and finished off her cold brew. "No worries. I mean, becoming a demon-proof ninja is a good thing, right?"

"I guess." I laughed.

"Sorry I slipped up and spilled to Josie about the ball game." He actually blushed. Usually Gabriel was pretty good at keeping secrets. He kept enough from Peter.

"I'll make it up to her." I sighed and gave him a half-hearted wave as I left.

I tucked my hands in my pockets and kicked my boots along the sidewalk. Today had been a total bust. It felt like a divine sign that the week wouldn't be getting any better, but I tried to brush it off. Tomorrow was a new day. And hey, at least my hellhounds, Saul and Coreen, were waiting for me at home. I sometimes wondered if Maalik hadn't just bought them to keep me company, foreseeing all the long and lonely nights he would be standing me up.

Hushed snoring vibrated through the apartment when I entered. It broke just enough that I knew Coreen had woke to sniff the air and make sure it was only me. I tossed my jacket over a kitchen chair and dug a bottle of red wine out of the refrigerator. It was a Zeus special, over three hundred years old, and worth every single coin it had cost. I had planned on saving it for mine and Maalik's anniversary, but he'd probably have to work late anyway. I didn't bother finding a glass. It's not like there was anyone around to complain if I drank from the bottle.

I kicked off my boots and fell on the couch with a miserably fitting groan. Somehow, being with Maalik made me feel more alone than I had felt before he came along. At least before, I was okay turning in at night by myself. I didn't have any expectations about where my evenings would find me. I guess with the direction our relationship was headed, I still shouldn't have had any expectations. With Maalik serving on the council, it was nearly impossible for him to give me a definite yes or no for any occasion, let alone a simple date out to Purgatory Lounge. That didn't mean I was any less disappointed.

I sucked down a third of the bottle of wine and marinated in the rush of warm fuzzies that followed. This was my life. I was stuck back at the academy, which I hated, forced to work on my final assignment with Craig Hogan, whom I hated even more than the academy, freaking out about Horus's illegal side job, and dealing—okay, not dealing—with my mostly absent boyfriend. Oh, and babysitting the fragile soul that held this entire crap-hole together, I remembered as my gaze stumbled over the cardboard box sitting on my coffee table.

Winston was so not cut out for the secret throne of Eternity. The cardboard box was full of baseball cards, junk food, and dime-a-dozen trinkets, things Winston lovingly called his life support. The council was still patting me on the back for a job well done. I just wanted to forget the whole thing had ever happened. Winston wasn't exactly the cute little dying boy I remembered from the hospital I'd harvested his soul from. Not after Meng Po's potion. He was quickly becoming a bigger pain in my ass than his dear old ancestor, Horus. Tomorrow, after I got off work, I had promised to deliver his goodies as long as he promised not to sneak out and get himself into any trouble.

Winston didn't like being cooped up in his little palace, and I could hardly blame him. But his safety was top priority. After Grim stopped meeting his frivolous demands, he had turned to me. I could either bring him his box of junk every week, or cross my fingers and hope he didn't turn up missing. And as much as everything sucked at the moment, I really didn't want to be responsible for the Second War of Eternity. I was going to be in enough hot water once Grim found out I was still in contact with Winston.

Khadija had let me in on the location of his little hidey-hole just before Meng Po's special tea had wiped her memory clean, all thirteen hundred years of service on the secret throne. Unfortunately, the tea didn't have the same effect on Winston. He still retained all the silly desires of his modern life and several lives in between. He was like six annoying little brothers I never knew I had.

17

I stuck my tongue out at the box, downed the rest of my wine, and crawled in bed with Saul and Coreen. I was determined to smell like a hung-over dog for breakfast, just in case Maalik decided to show up. No need letting him think I couldn't have a good time without him.

CHAPTER 4

*"I do not believe in an afterlife,
although I am bringing a change of underwear."*
-Woody Allen

I awoke to the smell of bacon grease and frying eggs. It made my stomach so happy that I almost forgot Maalik had stood me up the night before. My feathered chef stood humming over the stove with a spatula in each hand, flipping pancakes and eggs simultaneously. I had to peel my eyes away from his butt, clad in nicely fitting blue jeans, before making a clumsy dash for the bathroom. I definitely smelled like a hung-over dog.

"Mission accomplished," I groaned at myself in the mirror. My mascara was crusty and my dark curls had tangled themselves into an unruly afro that I would have to tame after breakfast, when I could take half a bottle of conditioner to it. I slapped some cold water on my face and tissued off my expired makeup before fingering as much of my hair as I could into an elastic band. I peeled off my party dress and wrapped myself in a yellow terry cloth robe Josie had bought for me on our last shopping extravaganza.

Maalik was busy setting the table when I stepped out of the bathroom. I leaned against the couch, the unofficial divider between my kitchen and living room in the tiny studio apartment, and tried like crazy not to smile. I was still mad at him for standing me up again, but he had figured out some time ago that the quickest path to my forgiveness was a home-cooked breakfast. Who says eggs and coffee can't be foreplay?

Maalik turned around with a smile. His dark curls were pulled back in a low ponytail that trailed over his shoulder and down his bare chest, nearly touching one of his perfect nipples. I loved that he was comfortable enough in my crummy little apartment to walk around shirtless.

"I'm really sorry about last night," he began with a confident grin.

"But duty calls," I finished in a mocking sing-song, before snatching up a cup of coffee, presweetened to perfection by my groveling honey.

Maalik cleared his throat and had the decency to blush. "I rather prefer our quiet morning dates at home to the noisy dates in bars."

"Oh, me too. You actually show up for the morning dates."

Maalik's flirty grin drooped. He threw his hands up in dramatic helplessness. I sat at the table and picked up a piece of toast. I could be mad and still appreciate my apology breakfast.

"I don't really have to explain this to you again, do I?" Maalik huffed as he took the seat across from me and forked an egg onto his plate.

"I think I have it memorized by now. Why? Will there be a test?" I sneered and reached for the maple syrup. He beat me to it. The jerk.

"Maybe. If you keep this up." He dangled the syrup in front of me, pulling back when I reached for it.

I glared at him. "Why am I dating you again?"

"Because, I'm too sexy for my shirt," he sang.

I knew I was going to regret helping him update his music collection. But he did bounce around to more enjoyable tunes these days. So long, heavenly orchestra mixed tapes. Sometimes, if I could keep my eyes off his butt long enough, I even made a valid point during our arguments.

Four pancakes, six strips of bacon, two eggs, and a cup of coffee later, I was naked. Yes, that fast. I'm a sucker. What can I say? Maalik nuzzled his head between my breasts with a content sigh, while I sighed with frustration. The calm stretch of obliviousness that came after sex was growing shorter each time we were together, quickly giving way to the shame of being such a pushover.

I ran my hand up the back of his neck and through his damp curls. "When you don't show up, like last night, not only does it make me look ridiculous, but it hurts my feelings."

"Well." Maalik sighed, rising off me. "That didn't last long."

"What?" I raised an eyebrow.

"Your break from attacking me." He found his jeans, abandoned on the floor, and stood to tug them on.

"You can't just keep walking out every time I get upset over you standing me up."

"Lana." Maalik threw his hands up. It was a surrendering gesture I was starting to despise. "My hands are tied. It's not like I have a choice when it comes to the council. The best I can do is apologize. I'm truly sorry."

"I know." I closed my eyes.

Maalik sat back down on the edge of my bed and took both of my hands into his. "The placement ceremony is two weeks away, and Grim has us working overtime as it is. We still haven't come across any leads to where Seth or Caim might be hiding, but I'm certain we haven't seen the last of them."

21

I nodded.

"I'm sure after the ceremony is over things will calm down. We could take a little vacation. Maybe to Heaven or Summerland this time?"

"Sure." I sighed.

Maalik's wings twitched. He frowned and squeezed my hands tighter. "You should really be focusing on your studies if you want to be placed on the Posy Unit. Maybe we should take a little break, just until finals are over. I don't want to be a distraction."

I scowled at him. "Oh, really? Because we see each other so much as it is. You'd rather just not show up at all? Fine." I slid off the bed, wrapping the sheets around me as I stormed off into the bathroom and slammed the door, pressing my back against it.

"Lana," Maalik groaned through the door. "Lana, I have to go, but we'll talk soon, okay?"

I didn't answer. A second later I heard the front door shut. Only then did I allow myself to slide down the bathroom door and sob myself into hysterics.

You would think that being over three centuries old would give me an advantage in these situations, but I was really out of practice. Though I was sure that dating someone as unavailable as Maalik would have been enough to unravel even the most casual of lovers.

Before being voted onto the Afterlife Council, Maalik had worked part-time guarding the gates of Hell. As an Islamic angel, he was still quite loyal to Allah, so being stuck in Hell wasn't his idea of fun. He had high expectations when he moved to Limbo to join the council, but aside from our brief dates, if you could call them dates, he spent the vast majority of his time tied up in council meetings, hashing over the political turmoil of Eternity. Had I known what I was getting myself into, I might have resisted him a little more adamantly.

When I finally pulled myself off the bathroom floor, impatient knocking sounded through the apartment.

"Well, look what the cat dragged in," Josie said as I opened the door. "I guess Maalik showed up last night?"

"This morning. Help yourself." I pointed at the table. "There's plenty left, and I've lost my appetite. I'll grab a shower."

"Please do." She chuckled as she filled herself a cup of coffee.

Josie thought it was amusing, watching the newness of love take its toll on those who had previously sworn it off and gone celibate for decades, sometimes centuries. I used to find it amusing too, not so terribly long ago.

It had been at least fifty years since I'd been in a real relationship, but I didn't remember ever feeling this hopeless with my last lover. Of course, he had been a reaper. We eventually got tired of each other and went our separate ways. Maybe I just hadn't been around Maalik long enough to get tired of him yet.

Josie dated as effortlessly as she breathed. Her relationships were never terribly long, and she rarely grieved when they ended. She was currently dating my apprentice, Kevin Kraus. He was a new reaper, fresh out of the academy, and four hundred years Josie's junior. I'm not sure cougar covers a gap that wide, but they seemed happy together. Well, happier than Maalik and I seemed lately.

I sighed and hurried off to take a shower. Just because I felt like a hung-over dog, didn't mean I wanted to smell like one all day at work.

CHAPTER 5

*"Did perpetual happiness in the Garden of Eden maybe
get so boring that eating the apple was justified?"*
-Chuck Palahniuk

My mentoring class got out late Thursday evening, so it was pushing seven o'clock when I finally got around to visiting Winston. That meant I would only have to stay for a short while. Grim stopped in to check on Winston around eight, but I always made sure I was out of there long before then. It was the one thing Winston and I could agree on.

Coreen's memorial statue scoffed at me with her cruel, coppery features. I didn't like that Grim had used it as the new entrance to the secret throne. It was a constant reminder of the day I had been forced into leadership. Of course, Grim probably figured no one would think twice about him going to visit the resting place of his permanently lost lover. I had to be more creative with my efforts to visit Winston. Coreen and I hadn't been the best of buddies, but seeing her in battle had earned her a good chunk of my respect, even if she had been eaten alive by hellcats in the end.

I stole a quick glance behind me and pulled the hood of my robe up with my free hand. The cardboard box, stuffed to the gills with Winston's trinkets, was tucked under my other arm. I had even added in a few extras, hoping it would suffice him for two weeks instead of one. I desperately needed to free up some time to study.

Taking a deep breath, I flipped my coin and said the magic word. "Gale."

"Lana!" Winston was stretched out on a leather sofa with a punch bowl of cornflakes propped up on his stomach. He gave me a wild wave, sloshing milk everywhere. "You got my life support?" he asked, eyeballing the box in my arms.

"Yeah, two weeks' worth." I dumped the contents onto the coffee table while he retrieved another box from under the couch, his secret hiding spot. Some secret. I was beyond surprised that Grim hadn't found it yet. In fact, I felt like I'd been holding my breath for a very long time, just waiting for the day. There was really no telling what Grim would do when he found out about mine and Winton's little visits.

"Two weeks' worth?" Winston picked through the pile of trading cards and junk food, pausing on a bag of imitation faerie cakes.

I folded my arms and glared down at him. "I need a break, Winston. I've got finals coming up."

"Yeah, you do, and you better pass so you can get out there and find a replacement for me. I don't know if I can stand a hundred years of this. Grim's driving me off the deep end. I swear by the dog." He stuck his tongue out and panted playfully at me.

The secret throne of Eternity required an original believer of one of the major faiths to fuel it. It was the secret means by which Grim maintained the afterlife's boundaries and territories. Khadija, the previous soul who had served on the secret throne, had been an original believer of the Islamic faith and served for well over a thousand years. Grim's desire to keep his secret had nearly maxed her out. She became discouraged with Grim's reluctance and took matters into her own hands, creating me.

The Treaty of Eternity allowed Grim to create new reapers every hundred years to run his corporation, Reapers Inc. We were more or less glorified slaves. Sure, we were paid, but our career choices were pretty narrow. We could either work for Grim or work for Grim. The specifics of the treaty stated that no new deities were to be created, but we were still allowed basic immortality privileges. We could die, but we were more durable and wouldn't visibly age. The extra ability that Khadija had bestowed on me was a breach of the treaty. If the wrong people found out, it would mean my execution, or worse, war.

Winston finished tucking away his new treasures and slid his stash box back under the couch.

"What's Grim have you doing anyway?" I asked.

"Oh, you know I can't tell you that." He gave me a gentle grin, one that reminded me that an ancient child-king is still a king. "All you need to know is that it's exhausting, grimy work."

I shrugged. "Can't be too bad if you still have time to play with your toys and eat yourself diabetic."

"I'd trade you places if I could, trust me."

"Well." I glanced up at the clock on the wall.

"One last thing." Winston stuffed his hand down between the couch cushions to retrieve a copy of the most recent *Limbo Weekly*. "Read page six," he said, tossing the magazine to me.

I opened it and read aloud. "The Sphinx Congress is still searching for the missing goddess Wosyet and has invested in the aid of Anubis. Anubis has been issued a temporary license to search Limbo City with his jackals. All citizens are obligated to cooperate. If anyone has any information regarding the whereabouts of Wosyet, please come directly to council headquarters." I tried to give Winston an impassive look, knowing my flaring cheeks were a dead giveaway. He had been the only witness to my crime.

"Watch your back, Lana. You're my only friend in this place, and I have a feeling Anubis isn't the only one searching for Wosyet."

"You were there." I huffed. "It's not like I took her home with me."

"Just her head." His questioning gaze pierced me.

Okay. I'd forgotten about that. It seemed like a good idea at the time. Separating her head from her body seemed like a sure way to guarantee she wouldn't be coming back to bite me in the ass. Of course, I wasn't so sure giving it to Grim as proof was such a good idea anymore. But at least I didn't have to worry about Anubis's jackals sniffing around my apartment.

"It's been taken care of." I folded my arms and glanced at the clock on his wall again. Definitely time for me to go.

"Clean your axe with hellfire and holy water, just to be sure nothing gets tracked back to you." Winston gave me a short wave and flipped on the television as I left.

My paranoia went into overdrive as I reemerged in the park. Cleaning my axe was now at the top of my to-do list, with studying for my finals a close second. I liked Anubis, but I didn't think he would be handing me a get-out-of-execution-free card anytime soon. He was as dutiful as he was friendly. A good trait normally, just not right now.

CHAPTER 6

"Yes, I have my demons, and this is my way of exorcising them.
It gets them out- and better out than in."
-Naomi Watts

I had a startling moment of dread when I reached my front door. I could hear the shuffling of papers inside. Where were Coreen and Saul, and why didn't I have my axe with me? I tried to remember where it was inside, sure that I wouldn't have time to reach it. The couch? My closet? To hell with it.

I swung the door open and lunged inside with my fists up. Josie, Jenni, and Kevin looked up from my kitchen table in unison, text books and coffee mugs piled around them.

"Uh, surprise." Josie laughed nervously.

I relaxed and scowled at her. Cleaning my axe would have to wait.

"Study party?" I asked.

"Saved you a seat." Jenni patted the empty chair next to her. She had become obnoxiously friendly since Josie told her I was applying for a specialty unit, volunteering her tutoring services more often than I cared for. I had a sneaking suspicion that she had ulterior motives involving my future. She was in for a rude awakening.

I groaned at the scholarly mob in my kitchen and slid out of my jacket.

"No whining. We haven't even started yet," Kevin grumbled. His opinion of me had dropped somewhat since he found out what a crab the academy could turn me into. I was starting to get the impression that he wouldn't mind if Grim dubbed Josie his mentor instead of me. Well, my grouchiness couldn't take all the credit there. Kevin and Josie were dating. Another reason Grim would never assign him to her.

Grim was about as happy as I was about the extra class Josie had talked me into. It was tough for a mentoring reaper to change specialty units or join one at all, in my case, so early in their apprentice's term. The fact that I wasn't exactly qualified to take on an apprentice in the first place counted against me as well, especially among the reaper community's more ambitious members who would have gladly taken Kevin, the star pupil of his generation.

Kevin had been under the wing of Coreen Bendura, Grim's former second-in-command, until she met her end at the talons of hellcats. Grim hadn't so much as said he blamed me, as he had shown he blamed me by dumping Coreen's orphaned apprentice in my lap. He even volunteered to pay the tuition for the necessary mentoring class at the academy. Grim knew how much I hated school. Which is why I wasn't surprised at his suspicion when I signed up for an extra class and Horus nominated me for the Posy Unit.

Josie cleared her throat and picked up a pencil with a stern look. No baseball games to bail me out this time. I slumped into the empty chair and looked at the textbook opened before me. This was it. No more delaying. Focus, I told myself.

Jenni observed me with a spark of satisfaction. "Let's begin, shall we?"

"Where is the first place to look for a wandering soul?" Josie asked.

"The grave site," I answered. Good, easy stuff first.

"And the second?"

"Their last known residence." I smiled, perking up. Maybe this wouldn't be so bad.

"Third?" Josie asked with a raised eyebrow.

The answer hung on the tip of my tongue, but it disappeared as I watched my front door burst into flames.

"Hellfire!" Kevin sprang to his feet, leaving the rest of us sitting at the table with our mouths gaping open.

"On the menu," came a gravelling reply.

The door splintered inward, and a diva of a demon stepped into my apartment. Had she been any taller, she would've grazed the doorsill. Short caramel curls framed her angular face, drawing out her golden eyes. Ripped up jeans hugged her spidery legs, and a tiny leather vest squeezed her cleavage into brow-raising awareness.

Saul and Coreen were at my side in an instant with my axe. I picked it up and stood to face my uninvited guest. Jenni and Josie gathered their senses and stood, too. Josie armed herself with a chair, though I wasn't sure what good it was going to do against a demon. Jenni was closest to my open closet and quickly found my dusty scythe, discarded among the scarves and jackets. Kevin ripped out a kitchen drawer, scattering utensils over my checkered linoleum, and found the meanest looking steak knife I owned.

The demon took us in with a comical expression and then tilted her head back with howling laughter, giving Kevin just the right angle of her throat. He seized the moment and threw the knife, sinking it in her neck. I had to pat myself on the back a little. He was my apprentice, after all.

"Owww," the demon whined, narrowing her eyes at him as she delicately extracted the blade. The wound sealed itself as neatly as if Kevin had stabbed a bowl of pudding. We were fucked.

Before my horrified amazement had a chance to dissipate, the hag cinched her gaze on me and sprang, knocking away my axe as she pinned me to the floor and grasped my throat with one hand.

"Where is he?" she hissed, pressing a lacquered nail into the pit of my throat.

"Who?" I managed to choke out before she crushed my vocal cords. I clawed at my neck, trying to dig under her fingers. It was no use. I couldn't match a demon, not bare-knuckled. Desperation tore through my veins. I slammed the palm of my hand under her chin. She grunted as her grip gave way, sparing me one precious breath. It was all I needed.

Jenni stepped up behind the demon and smashed a vial of holy water into the base of her skull. She rocked over me, eyes wide with loathing, as a stream of bloody water glistened through her hair and burned a trail down her pale cheek before splashing onto my own. I turned my head away and gasped. Flames lapped up the walls of my apartment. My cute little kitchen was melting all over the place.

That bitch, I thought, just before passing out.

CHAPTER 7

"Although prepared for martyrdom,
I prefer that it be postponed."
-Winston Churchill

Meng Po's little temple on the coast was just the way I remembered it. Although, the last time I had visited it had been Josie laid up and drinking the abominable tea. It seemed odd for a grouchy old lady like Meng to live in such a tranquil place.

Meng's wrinkly jowls were looming over me as I came to, jarring me awake in record time.

"Sit still, girl!" she snapped, jumping back in surprise. She thrust a cup in my hand. "You drink now," she barked and darted out of the room.

I sat up and blinked a few times, taking in the dark paneled walls and decorative scrolls hanging in every corner. Dusky light filtered in through the bamboo blinds, mixing with the glow from the lantern anchored in the center of the room. I sighed, trying to remember how I had gotten there, and took a sip of tea. I immediately spit it back into the cup. Meng was trying to kill me. I was sure of it.

I set the cup on the bedside table next to a little bucket of daisies with a note from Josie, letting me know she would be by later after dealing with my insurance agent and salvaging what she could from my apartment.

My memory snapped into action and I groaned. "Well shit," I croaked.

My throat was dry, and a tickling sensation scratched its way down my neck with every breath I took. I reached up to touch the source of my pain and then thought better of it. Josie had wedged a little compact down in the greenery of the daisy bucket. She knew my vanity issues the same way I knew hers.

I tried to convince myself it was only whiplash or bruising, but it was a vain attempt. The smell of burnt flesh is very distinct. I snatched up the compact and angled my head back. A nasty, hand-shaped blister wrapped itself around my pearly skin. Just perfect. I'd have to find time to stop by Athena's Boutique and exchange my dress for the placement ceremony. I was going to need one of those evil queen collars to hide this sucker.

A soft tap at the door pulled me out of my shopping fantasy. Gabriel fluttered in, his face skewed with worry and anger. "What the hell have you gone and gotten yourself into? I take it this little event wasn't part of your training?"

"You think?" I jabbed a finger at my throat.

"Who did it?" Gabriel tried to keep a straight face, but his cheeks flared like he was preparing for the apocalypse.

"Gee, now why didn't I think to ask for her name while she was trying to strangle me to death?" I smacked my palm to my forehead.

"So, it was a female?" He looked surprised. "And obviously a demon. Describe her to me. I'm sure Amy will be able to figure out who she is and whose payroll she's on."

"I don't know." I shook my head, and then winced when my charred skin protested. "She had curly, dark blond hair and was super tall. Let's see. She was wearing torn up jeans and a leather vest, and obviously she packs a lot of heat in her hands. That's all I've got."

Gabriel frowned and let out an exasperated sigh.

I held my hands up. "I only saw her for a few seconds, and now I'm here."

"Let me see what I can do." He bent down and pecked me on the forehead before hurrying off to do his recon work.

My next visitor was an odd surprise. Bub looked a little less light-hearted than usual, which was saying a lot, since he had a pretty solid reputation for being a carefree playboy. He was active on the Hell Committee, but he made it look easy and seemed to go with the flow, never publicly contradicting his superiors. Even when he was working, he somehow made it look like he was at play. I couldn't imagine enjoying my job that much.

Today, he was wearing one of his flashy suits that barely passed for business attire and looked more appropriate for a Hollywood cocktail party. He set a dainty vase of pink roses on the table next to Josie's daisy bucket and rubbed his knuckles over the short whiskers on his chin.

"Daisies," he mused. "I should have known."

"How thoughtful of you," I said, fingering the petals.

"Well, well." He sat on the edge of my bed and reached out to delicately grasp my chin, rotating my face away to get a better look at my neck. He clicked his tongue a few times before pulling my face back around, locking his eyes on mine. "Are we ready to take Cindy's course now?" He raised an eyebrow.

"Yes." I pulled my chin away with a frown. "I'll have to take the next two weeks off work though."

"Of course you will. This training will be time consuming, as I'm sure you realize. And now that you have a secret demon admirer, it would be wise to stay out of sight for a while, until you're better trained to defend yourself. Take tomorrow off to rest, and then meet me at Hell's gate on Thursday. Say, around nine in the morning?"

"Sure." I folded my arms.

He retrieved a coin from his pocket and flipped it in my lap. "Don't be late."

Education was seeking me out with a vengeance this year. I could hardly stand it. My eyelids fluttered and I pressed my head back into a mountain of pillows.

"You've hardly touched your tea." Bub, unable to take a hint, didn't move from my bed. Having another demon so near wasn't exactly my idea of a good time at the moment, but I just couldn't bring myself to tell the Lord of the Flies to take a hike. So I decided to mess with him instead.

"Go ahead, try it," I dared him, cracking my eyes open to see if he would.

Bub tilted his head and cast me a daredevil of a grin. He picked up the cup and inhaled the rising steam. I smiled then, knowing full-well the nasty brew had no warning odor. Bub took a careful sip, swishing it around in his mouth for a good show, and swallowed. Now he had my full attention.

"No way."

"Your turn," he said, holding the cup out to me.

"Did you lose your taste buds or something?" I huffed, taking the tea from him.

"Oh, no. I taste just fine." He gave me a wink.

"Do you?" Maalik asked as he stepped into the room.

Bub glanced up at the angel and then back at me. "Well, this is a bit awkward."

My smile drooped and I sat up straighter before remembering I was mad at Maalik. "Is the council having recess?" I asked.

Maalik's gaze dropped to the flowers beside my bed. "No, I left early so I could come see you, but I see you already have someone to keep you company."

"I should be going. I'll see you Thursday, pet." Bub stood and straightened his suit jacket. He gave me a soft smile that crossed somewhere between sympathy and gloating before strutting out without so much as a nod to Maalik.

Maalik claimed Bub's spot on my bed. I folded my arms and gave him an unpleasant look. "You know, I think you were right."

"About what?" Maalik asked, gently placing a hand on my leg as he leaned in to examine my ruined skin.

"You're a distraction." I rolled my eyes up at the ceiling.

Maalik blushed. "You're still mad, and that's okay. At least you're safe now. You should drink your tea."

"I think I'll pass." I stuck my tongue out.

"Meng won't release you until you do, which is fine by me. I'm taking the day off tomorrow to be with you."

"Bet Grim loves that."

"No, but his concern for your safety compelled him to agree."

"Concern for my safety? Right." I rested my hand on his, deciding I just might forgive him for taking a day off. "So, are you going apartment hunting with me tomorrow?"

Maalik looked away. "I guess you could say that."

"I doubt the Coexist Complex will have anything available, now that I'm a demon-magnet."

"That you are. I suppose you'll have to take Cindy's training course now." He didn't sound happy.

"I'm taking the next few weeks off and making it a priority."

"Beelzebub will be your instructor, I presume?"

I nodded softly, trying not to smile. So he was jealous. If it meant he would take a day off work to be with me, then I could live with that.

Maalik picked up my tea and sniffed it. I almost stopped him, but part of me was still mad, so I let him take a drink. His brows drew together, but he didn't spit it out or gag. Apparently, no one could taste the crap but me.

"Drink up," he ordered, handing it to me.

"You've got to be kidding. It tastes like sewage." I took the cup and glared down into its murky contents.

"I have served in Hell for a very long time. Believe me, there are far worse flavors."

"And those flavors not heal you like my tea!" Meng snorted as she scurried into the room. She shooed her arms at Maalik, ushering him off my bed and towards the door. "You go now. Tea for Lana. I not make it for you or fly master. She need rest. Go!"

Maalik fluttered away from her flailing arms and gave me a short smile. "I'll see you in the morning, and don't worry about work. I'll let Ellen know you're taking some time off."

I gave him a little wave and waited for him to leave before testing the tea again. It was still horrid, but I dared not say it in front of Meng. Instead, I gritted my teeth and gave her a forced smile. Her eyes pierced into me, silently demanding that I take another drink. I did, but I couldn't hold the smile any longer. The stuff should have been reserved for torture chambers.

"Finish before bed, or you regret tomorrow." She tucked me in and turned to leave, facing yet another visitor.

Horus stood in the doorway, wearing a pristine blue suit and holding a meat and cheese basket lined with daisies. He gave Meng a charming grin, daring her to turn him away.

"She need rest." Meng threw her hands in the air. "All these men, in and out. Five minutes, and then I chase you out with broom. Yes?"

"Five minutes." Horus nodded.

Meng huffed and stormed out again, shaking her head and babbling obscenities in Chinese. Horus waited until her stomping footsteps faded before approaching my bed. He set the gift basket on the table, next to my growing collection of flowers. I frowned, realizing that none of them were from Maalik.

Horus took the chair instead of the edge of my bed. He seemed more guarded around me lately, but I could hardly blame him. He knew I was capable of slaying a deity. The only reason I was still in his good graces was because the deity in question had turned out to be a traitor. That and I was the only one who could help him free Winston from Grim's secret service.

I nestled down under the blankets and did my best to look fragile and defeated. It wasn't hard with a blackened handprint wrapped around my neck.

Horus took a long, sarcastic breath. "You poor thing. You should have expected Seth and Caim to retaliate. It was no secret that you were made the commanding reaper on Grim's big assignment after Coreen's death. Seth knows the soul is still somewhere in the city, and he'll stop at nothing to find him."

"He should be targeting Grim then, not me."

"Ah, but you're so much more convenient. Grim stays locked away in his high security office."

"So they plan on attacking me until Grim comes out to play?" I squeezed my hands into fists and glared at him.

"Don't let it worry you too much. Anubis is coming to town to take care of a few things."

I swallowed and willed my body not to start hyperventilating. My mind flashed back to my dirty axe. I'd be taking care of that just as soon as Meng released me. Horus sensed my panic and snorted out a cocky laugh.

"Ah, you read the paper. You don't really think he's coming to hunt down Wosyet's murderer, do you?"

"He's not?" I exhaled and slumped back into my pillows.

"That was just an excuse to bring the jackals. They'll be sniffing out the location Seth and Caim are using to infiltrate their minions into the city. The council is aware of this."

"Good to know."

Horus scooted his chair back an inch and gave me a more serious look. "I don't like that you have a certain measure of power unsanctioned by the council, but I'm willing to keep your secret and help you, if you will help me in return."

"It's not like I asked for this power, and I don't see why you feel so threatened by it. It's not much good for anything but evaluating souls."

"And killing deities," he whispered. "No other reaper would have been able to do that."

I sighed, regretting what I was about to confess. "I chopped her head off with an axe. I don't think any deity would have survived that."

"Is that what you think?" Horus looked thoughtful and then hesitated before he spoke again. "Had you been an ordinary reaper, your axe would have never penetrated her skin, even being the lesser goddess that she was. If she hadn't turned out to be a traitor, I would have, without a doubt, turned you over to the council."

"She was trying to kill me, Horus. Not to mention the fact that if she had succeeded, she would have taken dear Winston directly to Seth. I saved the fucking day, and I'm getting sick and tired of feeling like I should be apologizing for it."

"Winston?" Horus looked puzzled.

"Yeah, dummy. The soul."

"Oh! You mean Tut." Horus folded his hands in his lap and smiled.

"Tut? As in Tutankhamun?" I was dumbfounded. No freaking way.

"Yes, one of my favored descendants," he recalled fondly.

"But Tutankhamun wasn't an original believer. He just restored the old faith after Akenhaten tried to destroy it."

"Exactly why you need to find a replacement for him. I have faith that he can maintain Eternity for a short while. After all, you saw the strength and power in his soul. But it will not hold Eternity together half as long as the last one in Grim's service."

Horus glanced at the clock and stood to give a short bow. "Be careful, Lana. You're my only hope." He forced a politically correct smile at me and backed out of the room with as much grace as a cowardly god could muster.

What a mess I was in. I guess it was naïve to think my boring little life would return to normal after everything that had happened last fall. Was there really no peace to be found? Was I going to be caught in the crossfire forever? I had more than enough to think about, but at least I was safe at Meng's.

I grabbed the gift basket Horus had brought and stuffed a handful of cheese in my mouth before downing the last of Meng's tea in one agonizing swallow. Then I reclined back in the bed and prayed for sleep to come and drown out the whole miserable day.

CHAPTER 8

*"All actions are judged
by the motives prompting them."
-Muhammad*

"What are we doing here?" I pressed my cheek to the taxi window and raised an eyebrow up at the ivory towers of Holly House. Past a cast iron fence, holy water bubbled over the trumpeted horn of a concrete angel and spilled into a small pond encircled by clusters of milky-white carnations. This wasn't what I had in mind when Maalik said he would go apartment hunting with me. Holly House was way out of my budget.

"Well." Maalik cleared his throat and tugged at the collar of his robe. "Holly heard about your recent troubles, and she very graciously offered to rent you one of her condos."

"Oh, really?" I laughed. "She does realize I'm a reaper, right? My income doesn't stretch to this side of town. Let's go."

"There's Holly now." Maalik ignored me as he hopped out of the taxi. He held the door open, gesturing for me to join him.

"Don't go far," I whispered to the nephilim driver, slipping him an extra coin before gingerly stepping out of the car. Everything ached, from my toes to my ears. The itchy black turtleneck Josie had brought for me wasn't helping any either. I ran my fingers through my hair, wishing I had taken more time to tame the mess of ringlets bouncing around my face.

"Hello!" Holly fluttered over to us, looking as sweet as a cupcake. Her wings folded behind her, dragging a few feathers along the sidewalk like a glamorous wedding train. Her white cotton dress fell tastefully below her knees and gathered up at her throat where it fastened to a gold hoop around her slender neck. I was so underdressed.

I glared at Maalik. He could have at least suggested that I brush my hair. And blue jeans had to be against some dress code at Holly House. I folded my arms and sighed.

"Good morning, Ms. Spirit." I gave her a forced smile. I wasn't too comfortable getting all chummy with the council members. Until a few months ago, none of them would have given me a second look. Now I was dating one and being black-mailed by another. Shouldn't that have canceled out my ties with them somehow?

"Are you ready to see your new home?" Holly chirped.

"Well, this is just the first stop." I raised an eyebrow at Maalik.

"Let's go see it," he said a little too cheerfully.

Holly paused to frown at me, like she couldn't imagine why anyone wouldn't be thrilled to reside at the most immaculate and holy dwelling in Limbo. I met her stare, and she quickly pasted on her wide, campaign-winning smile before leading us through the courtyard with its sparkling fountain and tranquil gardens. She stopped at the glossy front door and punched in a code on the security box, decoratively disguised as a gothic cross.

If Jove had been a woman, I imagine more churches would have looked like the foyer of Holly House. White marble walls arched overhead, feeding into a thorny rose design that framed a giant bubble of a ceiling mural. Michelangelo had been thrilled when Holly invited him to Limbo City to paint his most famous masterpiece beyond the grave. The looming painting held dozens of feminine angels, all possessing dewy flesh and blushing curves, wrapped in flowing white ribbons. The image in the center echoed Mike's creation piece from the Sistine Chapel, except where Adam had once been, a sultry angel reached for Jove's hand instead, and a dove burst forth from the space between their fingertips.

I wouldn't say that Holly was full of herself, but she did resent how little her father acknowledged her in the bible, while inflating the status of a mortal like Mary. Images of the Virgin had been mindfully neglected in the foyer, elevating Holly's angelic mother as holy queen of the house.

"This way," Holly giggled, bringing my attention back down to ground level. She led us to the front desk where a husky nephilim in a sharp gray suit waited.

The nephilim were in awe of Holly, and they owed her a great debt as well. With her move to Limbo City, after being elected on the Afterlife Council, she created a surplus of job opportunities for her feathered brethren by opening Holly House. Though she was an angel-deity hybrid and the nephilim were half mortal, Holly felt she had an obligation to them. They were misfits, like her, and I suspected she related better to them than any other beings in Eternity.

The nephilim deskman glanced up from his paperwork and smiled at us as he extended his hand. "I'm Charlie. You must be Lana. It's nice to meet you."

"You too." I grasped his hand and gave it a firm shake. His fingers were thick and warm, undoubtedly holding enough strength to crush as well as greet. I could guess which talent Holly had hired them for first. Charlie plucked a key out of wicker basket and handed it to Holly with a bashful grin. His wings fluttered gently at her touch.

43

"Thank you, Charlie," she cooed, batting her eyelashes like a smitten school girl. I couldn't quite tell if Jove's rebellious daughter was playing footsie with the spawn of the fallen, or if she had discovered the secret to running a successful business. A happy employee is a good employee, or so I've heard.

"This way, please." Holly led us across the foyer towards the golden doors of three sparkling elevators. Hey, who needs wings when you can travel up in style? We loaded into the first elevator that opened and Holly punched a button for the tenth floor.

After meandering down a wide hallway lined with creamy beige carpets and gold-framed paintings of angels and doves, we came to the condo Holly had reserved for me. She slid the heavy key into the lock of the front door and stepped back, gesturing for me to finish the act, so I did.

It was a hazy dream of an abode. Light oak flooring stretched from the dining room into the sitting room, streaked with golden sunlight seeping in through a wide, arched window. A plush white rug framed the rustic dining table and its eight, that's right, eight matching chairs. A gray marble counter sectioned off the kitchen from the dining room, elegantly serving as a breakfast bar with four barstools that matched the dark wood dining set.

The sitting room, called so because it was too nice to simply be called a living room, held an engraved coffee table and a trio of white sofas, all positioned around a rug that matched the one in the dining room.

I didn't even want to see the rest of the condo. It was a trap. This was the sort of place deities stayed at when they visited Limbo City. In fact, I couldn't think of a single reaper who had ever lived at Holly House. Reaper's Tower was really the best apartment complex we ever had to hope for. This was all terribly wrong.

"Well, what do you think?" Holly whispered over my shoulder, sending the goose bumps a crawling.

I turned to face her with a sour look. "I think this is way out of my budget."

"But Maalik's paying for it." Holly said as Maalik gaped behind her. He hadn't expected her to spill the beans that quickly I guess. I would have kissed her for her absentmindedness if I hadn't been so furious at Maalik.

"What?" I injected enough venom in that single word to send him babbling for some ground.

"Lana, I—listen—" he stammered.

"You are *not* paying my rent."

Holly's eyes grew worried. "Perhaps the two of you would like some privacy. I'll be just outside when you're finished looking around."

She slipped out the front door without another word, while I was bubbling furiously with plenty of them.

"I will not be a kept woman. I am not a plaything you can appease with money. Just who the hell do you think you are?"

Maalik seemed to cower until the last sentence sank in. Then his back straightened and his gaze pierced me with a fiery conviction. "I am the keeper of hellfire! And if that is not enough to discourage a demon from harming you, then what else can I do?"

"I'm not staying here," I whispered as my eyes began to fill with tears. I finally had a day with him all to myself, and he had to go and ruin it.

"Lana," Maalik said softly, crossing the room to pull me into his arms. "I just want you to be safe. If anything happened to you..." His voice trailed off, but my overactive mind filled in the blanks with a harsh clarity. Sure, he'd be sad for a while, but he'd get over it. The people he surrounded himself with would never understand his grief over the death of a reaper, and they were the ones in charge. He probably wouldn't even take a day off work.

"I can't accept this, Maalik." I wedged my arms between us and pushed him back. "And if this place is so easy for you to afford, then why are you sharing that tiny flat with Ridwan?"

"I'm not home enough to enjoy a place like this, and I spend most of my time off work with you anyway, so what's the point?" He gave me a lopsided smile and slid his hands down the backs of my arms, trying to warm me.

I was trembling, but not from being cold. I was furious, and somewhere in the middle of our arguing, that fury had been penetrated with the throbbing awareness that I was exhausted and defeated.

Maalik reached his hand up to thumb away the tear running down my cheek. "Just give it a try. If you decide you don't like the place, you can always find another, *after* we find Seth and Caim. Is that so much to ask?"

"Fine." I sighed, looking down.

"Good." Maalik bent and kissed my nose. I felt like biting his off. "Josie's on her way over with a few boxes. Why don't you wait here for her? I'll go help Ridwan finish moving the furniture you won't be needing into storage."

"Ridwan's helping you move my stuff?"

Ridwan gave Maalik hell day and night for dating me. Luckily, Maalik had plenty of experience tolerating hell. I began to laugh, but then my jaw dropped as my brain retracted back to his first sentence.

"Josie's on her way over here?" I said through gritted teeth. "You weren't even planning on giving me a choice, were you?"

"Please, Lana." He pulled me to his chest and pressed his chin to my forehead. "Look past your pride for one second and understand how much I love you."

"I'm not sure love is the right word." I couldn't keep my voice from trembling. If he didn't let go of me and leave right that second, I had full intentions of screaming like a loon until he deemed me crazy and fled in terror. But just then, Holly popped back in.

"So," she said, "would you like to see the common areas and the rest of the grounds?"

"Maybe later," I answered, maintaining my steady glare at Maalik.

He gave me a tired smile and let go, fluttering his wings with false cheer. "Thank you, Holly. I think this will work perfectly. Allow me to venture downstairs with you. I must be on my way. Lots to move." He gave me a nod and closed the door behind them, leaving me alone in the alien place.

It was perfect. I couldn't argue that. Who doesn't dream of something better than the spoonful of crap life so often delivers? I just hated setting myself up for disappointment, and that's what this felt like.

Who's to say Maalik wouldn't get tired of me? Or that I wouldn't get tired of him? If I accepted this and became accustomed to this sort of lifestyle, would I be able to handle giving it all up? Well, I did have three hundred years of practice making it on my own. Maybe it was like riding a bike. I really didn't plan on staying long anyway. Right? It wouldn't hurt to live it up for a while.

I stood around in the sitting room for a good ten minutes thinking of all the ways my situation could be worse. And after all the hell I'd been through already, that wasn't hard. I finally scrapped together what was left of my pride and went to check out the rest of my new condo. I could throw that pride back in the blender later, while Holly showed me the pool and gym downstairs.

CHAPTER 9

"The more I see of the moneyed class,
the more I understand the guillotine."
-George Bernard Shaw

Josie tumbled through my front door, followed by my anxious hounds. They leapt over her in an effort to reach me. Saul jumped up on his hind legs and placed his coffee can sized paws on my shoulders, shoving me to the floor so he could lick my face, while Coreen sniffed my neck and arm pits until she was sure I wasn't in need of a healing spit-bath. I was still amazed that Holly was letting them stay with me in the condo. I guess she figured the extra security might be worth any curious stains they might leave behind.

"You lucky bitch." Josie dropped the bags and boxes she carried so she could place her hands on her hips. "It's just not fair. You so don't deserve this place. You're not even nice to Maalik anymore. You've really got him whipped, don't you?"

"I wish," I said as she began stalking from room to room to assess just how lucky I was.

I heard her gasp from the bathroom. "There's a freaking Jacuzzi tub in here! I hate you."

"You can take a bath in it anytime," I hollered back before pulling myself off the floor so I could figure out which box contained the dog food. I probably owed Josie a fridge full of groceries. The hounds just weren't satisfied without their special Cerberus Chow.

"This place has three bedrooms?" Josie rounded the corner as I set down a couple punch bowls of chow and stepped back before I became road kill. Saul almost slipped in a puddle of his own drool as he dove for his dish.

"Yeah," I answered, wiping my hands on my jeans. "Holly didn't have any studios available. I think she only has four. Most of the angels and nephilim who stay here have roommates. It helps balance out the expense, since most of them don't live here year-round."

"You need a roommate?" she asked.

"I said you could use the Jacuzzi anytime." I glared at her.

"Oh, come on," she huffed. "It's not *just* the Jacuzzi."

I smiled, thinking I was about to receive another safety lecture.

"I mean, look at this view." She turned away from my bewildered expression to gaze out the magnificent window in the sitting room. Okay, so it was a pretty kick-ass view of the city. Holly had taste. I'd give her that.

"You want some coffee?"

Josie turned around. "Yeah, better make a whole pot. Jenni and Kevin should be here in a few."

"Huh?" I dropped the can of grounds with a start. "Come again?"

"What?" Josie stepped into the dining room and gave me one of her looks. "Did you think getting attacked by a demon and having your apartment destroyed would overwhelm Grace with some newfound compassion and she would just pass you out of sympathy?"

"Well." I shrugged with a frown. I deserved a little slack, didn't I?

"Ha!" Josie howled and set both hands over her stomach, caressing her blue cashmere sweater. "Think again."

I scowled at her. "I think I've suffered plenty. I don't need you to help me with that one, thank you."

"Grief, Lana." Josie picked up a box of dishes and joined me in the kitchen to help put them away. "You're at Holly House now. Shut up and enjoy it for a second." Then she paused. "Tell Holly that if she has any more condos available for reapers to contact me."

"Really?" I squeezed a coffee cup in my hand and looked at her.

"Sure," she said. "Why not? I mean with me, Kevin, Jenni, and maybe one more, we could afford a place like this. Don't you think?"

"Maalik didn't put you up to this, did he?" I was going to scream if he rearranged one more aspect of my life without telling me about it first.

"Don't be silly," Josie snapped. "Besides, being friends with you seems to get more dangerous every day. A little extra security never hurt anyone."

"Gee, thanks," I said and grabbed another mug.

At least most of my dishes had survived the fire. I reminded myself to send a thank you note to Zibel, the local weather god who worked at Bank of Eternity. Maalik had informed me on the ride to Holly House that he had been a big help, drenching the Coexist Complex with rain to put out the fire.

The new kitchen came with quite a few accessories that weren't typically supplied, like a lightening-fast, stainless steel coffeemaker. You wouldn't catch me complaining about that one, but I did have my suspicions. I wondered if all Holly's condos came with thirty-speed blenders and antique china sets. There came a point when I just didn't want to know about anything else Maalik was doing for me without my permission. It just turned my pride into a hungry little worm that ate away at my stomach.

Josie filled a couple mugs of coffee and slid onto one of the barstools at the breakfast bar. She picked up a cloth napkin, folded in the shape of a dove, off one of the place settings and giggled.

"What's so damn funny?" I said, slumping into the stool next to her with my coffee.

"Oh, nothing. Just picturing you hosting a dinner party."

I picked up a fork and gouged her in the arm. "What makes you think I won't?"

"Oh, that would be rich. If you do, you better invite me and Kevin."

"You'd be the guests of honor," I said.

"Oh, yay." She clapped her hands together in mock delight.

The doorbell rang a singsong chime like church bells, and I hopped up to answer it. Coreen and Saul fixed themselves at my side, close enough to drip drool on my boots. The demon attack had surprised them pretty badly. They were going to be overbearingly protective for the next few weeks. I was sure that didn't bother Maalik any. That's why he had bought them for me in the first place.

I opened the front door and was greeted by Jenni and Kevin's gaping faces. Josie hopped to her feet to give them the tour, starting with the Jacuzzi tub. Kevin was already wagging his eyebrows at her. I made sure to pen in extra cleaning supplies on my grocery list.

"I brought my scythe," Kevin informed me as they came back into the dining room. "You know, just in case," he said with a goofy grin.

"You learn quickly, grasshopper." I handed him and Jenni each a mug of coffee.

"And I've brought you a supply of holy water," Jenni added, setting a gift-wrapped box on the table. "Think of it as a housewarming gift. Now, let's kick this studying business where it counts."

The four of us sat down and opened up our text books to the page we had left off on. There was an uncomfortable silence as we each looked up and at the front door. I hadn't noticed before, but a very long and complicated prayer had been engraved in Latin along the doorframe. I felt safer already.

"Let's get started," Josie said softly, dragging her eyes back to her book. "We've still got your mentor exam to study for after this."

"Yippee."

Kevin made a face at me. "You've got to be the only reaper not beating down Grim's door for the chance to train me in the art of harvesting. Do you realize that?"

"I don't think training you will be so bad. I just wish I could train you to take this test for me first."

"I'm helping you study for it, aren't I?" He flicked a sugar packet at me with a playful scowl.

"Let's not get distracted now," Josie snapped. "We only have two weeks left."

"Don't worry about me. I'm taking the next two weeks off work so I can study."

"Lana, are you sure?" Jenni looked up in amazement.

"I really want to make it on the Posy Unit," I lied. They didn't need to know about the demon training. It would just conjure up too many questions that I wasn't ready to answer. I wasn't sure I'd ever be ready for that conversation. And I would be using some of the time to study.

"That's very responsible of you, Lana." Jenni was beaming, like I had just slipped her the answer to the million dollar trivia question. Josie, on the other hand, looked like she was waiting for me to shout "Psych!" any minute. I really wished I could.

The hours crawled by, each one slower than the last, as we took turns reading aloud and quizzing each other on multiple harvesting techniques and how to select a soul for an apprentice to harvest. I was the only one taking the mentoring exam, so I felt like a lucky duck to have so many friends willing to waste their time just to see me pass. I developed a migraine somewhere in the midst of hour five and was about to beg Josie for mercy when a knock came at the door.

We all jumped in our seats. I stood to check the peephole. A nephilim waited out in the hall. He was a pleasant looking guy with a tumble of sandy blond curls and happy, green eyes. A basket of fruit and cheese dangled from his wrist, and I suddenly realized that I was starving.

"Can I help you?" I asked, opening the door.

"Uh, Lana?" The nephilim's eyes bulged and he dropped the basket so he could throw his arms around me.

"Whoa!" I gently pushed him away. "Do I know you?"

Kevin stood and Jenni reached into her pocket, searching for a vial of holy water.

"Warren?" Josie blinked at my guest with faint recognition. My jaw dropped.

CHAPTER 10

*"It's never too late
to be what you might have been."*
-George Eliot

The last time I had seen Warren, he was hiding out in a
filthy basement apartment, paranoid out of his mind. He
had rather reluctantly sold me a cherished battle axe, and at
a rather steep price. I had promised to take care of his father,
one of the fallen who had recently fallen for good. Of course,
I really couldn't take much credit for that feat. The demon
had perished with a good chunk of Caim's followers when
Winston sank a secret island out in the Sea of Eternity last
fall.

Warren beamed. "I live down the hall. I was just coming
to greet our newest tenant."

"That'd be me," I said, still ogling him.

Warren cleaned up nicely. I was glad Josie had
recognized him, because I never would have. Holly House
had been very good for him. He picked up the fruit basket
and handed it to me as I waved him inside. Jenni pulled her
hand out of her pocket. Relief flooded over her face. We
were all a little on edge.

"Warren, this is Jenni, a friend of ours. Jenni, meet Warren," I said.

Jenni nodded, a light smile tugging at the corners of her mouth. She had seemed surprised that I introduced her as a friend. We had never gone shopping or out drinking together, but she had just wasted five hours of her time helping me study with no promise of reward or even success. If that's not a friend, I'm not sure what is.

"How have you been?" I asked Warren, pulling out a chair for him, something I would have never thought to do for the old Warren, all skittish and grimy.

"I've been fantastic," he said and joined us at the table. He sat with perfect posture, gracefully holding his wings at a wider angle so they weren't pinched against the chair. He placed his hands on the table and grinned. "My business has exploded. When Holly found out what I did for a living, she was thrilled. She's sent me more clients in the past three months than I've dealt with in a century."

"Wow, that's great." Josie smiled and patted the top of his hand. He folded his free one over hers, drawing an unpleasant look from Kevin.

"I never got to thank you properly." His grin spread wider as he reached into the pocket of his robe. "Here are a few discount cards for thirty percent off everything. I'm running the business out of my condo, in the two spare rooms. That's how much inventory I have now."

"What exactly is your business?" Jenni asked, raising an eyebrow at the card he handed her.

"Oh, I sell things like weapons, protection charms, and holy water. And I even have a license to do so now." He gave Josie a playful grin. She had given him a pretty hard time during that first meeting.

"I see," Jenni said. "And this is for thirty percent off everything?"

"Yes, but I'm legit now, so I expect my clients to be too," he said sternly.

"Of course." Jenni looked perplexed and then cast Josie a surprised frown. "I keep all my licenses current."

Josie blushed. "I only bought one bottle of holy water, and I have a license now, thank you."

"When did you get a license for holy water?" I snorted. Guess I wasn't the only one keeping secrets.

"Last month." She looked a little embarrassed. "And I'm taking you to get yours next week."

"I've got one, too," Kevin added.

"Very good." Warren looked around the table with an excited twitch in his wings. "Would you like to see my latest inventory? I haven't even shown the guard yet?"

"The guard?" I asked.

Warren frowned. "Don't you watch the news?"

"We've been studying all morning, cramming for finals," I answered, not really wanting to admit I was afraid of the news lately.

I was just sure I'd find a picture of my charred apartment, or me lying unconscious on the floor with drool running down my face. And I was still waiting for the headline "Reaper Murders Deity, Execution Today" above a picture of a guillotine with the caption "Get your tickets now!" I'd even rerouted my walk to the office so I wouldn't have to pass so many *Limbo Weekly* and *Reaper Report* stands. Okay, so I was getting a touch pathetic. I'd phase out of it eventually. I hoped.

"The Nephilim Guard?" Warren tried again. "There was a group of nephilim protesters not too long ago, really coming down on Grim about deityship rights, and then they just stopped protesting. Don't you remember hearing about that?"

"Sure, but that was months ago," Kevin replied. At least someone was keeping up with the news.

"Well," Warren continued, "Grim introduced those same protesters this morning as his elite Nephilim Guard. He's paying them a pretty coin to be the city's new law enforcers."

"Do they get deityship with that pretty coin?" Jenni asked.

"No, but those serving on the guard do have permanent residency now, a place in this world." Warren sighed. "If my business wasn't doing so well, I think I'd join them myself."

"So the guard comes to you for their equipment?" Jenni was intrigued.

"Well, not *all* of their equipment. Their armor is being crafted by Artemis, and their robes by Athena," he answered modestly. "Let me show you what I'm contributing."

We followed Warren down the hall to his condo, which was as immaculately designed and decorated as my own. Holly was making a killing off her tenants, but at least she made the place worth it. Warren took a key from the pocket of his robe and unlocked one of his spare rooms. Inside was practically a different world. He really had gone legit. All the way to the bank.

The walls were covered from floor to ceiling with glass cabinets holding a wide array of knives, swords, maces, and even a flail, with a ball of shiny spikes dangling from its grizzly chain. The uppermost shelves held hundreds of worn volumes with spines labeled in Latin and Hebrew. Pressed against a far wall, I recognized the beat-up trunk that had once held my axe. The trunk had originally been Warren's whole store. His business had come a long way.

"See here?" He opened a glass cabinet and retrieved a golden spear. He ran a finger along the edge of the crystal tip. "This is a prototype of what the central guard will be carrying. As we speak, Holly is on her way to the holy city to ask for blood from the lamb to anoint them with."

"So Jesus is in on this, too?" Josie asked.

"Well, not yet, but he will be. Horus is consulting with the Sphinx Congress about a contribution to aid against the

Duat rebels as well." Warren placed the spear back in its cabinet and stood back to admire his collection.

"You know, I think I'm going to enjoy being neighbors with you." I folded my arms and smiled.

"And I, with you." Warren's wings fluttered, a happy movement that always gave me the urge to toss bread crumbs.

Holly House had more benefits than I could have ever hoped for. Things were looking up for a change. I decided that thanking Maalik wasn't entirely out the question anymore.

CHAPTER 11

*"God made Cabernet Sauvignon
whereas the Devil made Pinot Noir."
-Andre Tchelistcheff*

My first night in the new condo felt entirely wrong. I had
lived at the Coexist Complex for such a long time that it was
hard to sleep anywhere else. I woke Sunday morning,
tangled up in bed sheets from all my tossing and turning.
The bed was plenty comfortable. I just needed to relearn
how to relax. I didn't think it would take too long at Holly
House though.

The room I had chosen was at the end of the hall. It was
painted a soft gray. A large window, running along the same
side of the building as the living room windows, filled most
of the far wall. It was hung with green curtains, embroidered
with a fancy ivy design that matched the bedspread. A white
sofa rested in front of the window, and a matching chair was
placed on the opposite side of the bed, near the closet and
bathroom doors. A large, oak wardrobe dresser was pushed
up against the wall by the door leading into the hallway. It
was a majestic setup, and I was sure I would be sleeping
better eventually.

My ease at Holly House grew steadily as the day progressed. I decided it would be fun to prove Josie wrong, so I called her and Kevin and invited them to the first real dinner party I had ever hosted. The rest of the guest list included Jenni, Maalik, Gabriel, Amy, and as a special thank you for helping Maalik move my furniture, I even invited Ridwan.

I had to make a call down to the front desk to make sure inviting Amy, Gabriel's demon girlfriend, wouldn't be a problem. After an awkward pause, Charlie told me that would be fine and that he would put her down on my list of accepted guests for future reference.

After finishing my phone calls, I set to work preparing a feast fit for a crowd of angels, demons, and reapers, oh my. I wasn't big on cooking, but ordering pizza was out of the question. I did know how to do up a mean Cornish hen. I was thankful Kevin knew this as well. Josie had him do my grocery shopping while she packed my things at the old apartment.

After stuffing three hens and popping them in the oven, I fixed a giant bowl of salad and set it in the fridge. Apple pie was next on the list, a favorite of Saul's, my late mentor. The last time I had made an apple pie was the week before he had died. I just didn't feel right making his favorite without him being there to enjoy it with us.

I put the pie in with the hens and was about to peel some potatoes when the doorbell rang out its church bell tune. The party didn't start for another hour, but Maalik had promised to come by early to help.

"About time," I said, letting him in.

"Sorry, Ridwan needed a little help picking out a robe for dinner. I think he might actually be excited about coming over tonight. He hasn't gotten out much since we moved to Limbo," he said, taking the potato peeler from me. "The hens smell divine. Let me finish up in the kitchen while you get ready."

"Okay." I smiled and gave him a peck on the cheek.

I didn't have to worry about Maalik. In fact, it was probably better that he put the finishing touches on dinner. He was like Rachel Ray from Hell. And that had gotten him out of hot water with me more than once. He made a caramel cake that could even make an apocalypse seem bearable.

I slipped away into my new bedroom. I really liked that it was closed off from the rest of the condo. It gave me a sense of seclusion that I had never had in my very long stay at the Coexist Complex. The closet was smaller, but Josie had done me the favor of packing up the articles she deemed least stylish and had Maalik put them in storage with my furniture. She had enough sense to leave my favorites in the reduced wardrobe.

I rummaged around until I came across a snug, blood-red slip dress with a collar high enough to hide most of the black handprint on my neck. There was no telling how long I would be adjusting my style around the nasty reminder that I was a wanted woman. At least Josie had saved me a little trouble by moving all my turtlenecks and scarves to the front of the closet.

I took the dress into the master bath attached to the bedroom and hung it on the back of the door. It was time to try out the new shower. The glass and tile stall was three times the size of the one in my old apartment. It was just the right size for an angel to expand his wings to maximum capacity. I smiled, knowing this meant Maalik would be staying over more often.

I only had an hour until my guests would arrive, so I stripped down and turned the faucet on as hot as it would go. My muscles were still throbbing, and I would have made a deal with Lucifer himself just to be comfortable again.

The shower had an adjustable head in every corner, and a waterfall cascaded down the tiled back wall. It seemed a little overkill, but I supposed the angel and nephilim residents enjoyed the elegant birdbath effect. Maalik would too. Just imagining him in the shower sent a chill over me, despite the steaming water.

I toweled off, thanking Khadija that my aches and pains had subsided at least a little. Slipping into the little red dress, I turned to examine myself in a full length mirror that sat in the corner of the bathroom. There was only a dull throb in my shoulders now and an itchy sensation circling my neck. I wasn't sure if it was more from the silly scarf collar of my dress or the burn. I combed my curls out and ran a handful of gel through them before gently sliding on the crystal bands Saul had given me when my apprenticeship ended. They added a nice touch to the ensemble and drew some attention away from my neck. I dabbed on a little lipstick and slipped into a pair of black heels.

I headed back into the bedroom and stopped to give myself a pleased smile in the giant mirror anchored in the center of my new wardrobe dresser. Well, it was mine for the time being anyway. I was still getting used to all the new furnishings in the condo. They were nice, of course. Holly only worked with the best decorators in Eternity, but it felt strange to be surrounded by things I hadn't picked out myself.

Maalik turned to watch me walk out of the bedroom. He had an apron tied around his waist and a spoon in each hand. He nearly dropped them when he saw me.

"Wow." He blinked a few times. "You really look the part of a classy hostess."

"Well, that's what I was going for." I laughed and joined him behind the stove.

In the short time it had taken me to get ready, Maalik had whipped up a creamy potato soup, glazed carrots, and a batch of to-die-for stuffed mushrooms. The hens were cooling on a silver platter with bits of rosemary tucked under here and there.

"The pie should be done any second," he said, shooing me away as I snatched an unguarded mushroom. "Why don't you set the table and call downstairs to order some wine. I think maybe a vintage cabernet would go nicely. Perhaps a bottle from Jannah, the Khadija countryside. Eighteen forty-three sound good to you?"

"Holly has room service here?"

"Haven't you gone on the tour yet?" Maalik raised an eyebrow at me over his shoulder while grinding some more pepper over the potato soup.

"I'm saving it for tomorrow," I said, picking up the phone. I dialed zero and was greeted on the first ring.

"Front desk, how may I help you?" Charlie was in a perpetually good mood. I ordered three bottles of wine and tried not to cry when he gave me the price.

"The wine is my treat," Maalik said, noticing my horror-struck look that was quickly wiped away with resentment.

"Isn't everything these days?" I snapped.

The doorbell rang, squashing the potential argument. Josie, Kevin, Gabriel, and Amy spilled into the dining room, giggling in their formal wear. Well, except for Gabriel. He looked downright grim in his wrinkly white robe, like he would have rather been in drawstring pants, eating Cheetos on the couch.

"Have a seat. The wine is on its way," I told them.

"I hope you ordered enough," Gabriel grumbled.

"What's your beef?" I folded my arms.

Amy swatted her rude angel's arm. "He's just fussy because he had to dress up. But doesn't he look charming? And don't you," she said, turning her attentions away from Gabriel's scowl. "Well, give us the grand tour."

Amy was handling Holly House better than I had expected. I imagined Gabriel or Bub had already filled her in on the minor details of my demon dilemma. As soon as I finished showing off the new pad, the doorbell rang again. The tune seemed to change throughout the day, but it still retained its church-like quality. I wondered if that would bother Gabriel when he crashed over. He didn't like being reminded of his duties while he was recovering from a hangover. Of course, his drinking habit had diminished somewhat over the past few months. Amy had really done a number on him.

I answered the door for Jenni and Ridwan, the last of my guests, and just in time. Charlie followed them in with our wine.

"Enjoy, Ms. Harvey," he said with a small bow and placed the bucket of iced wine on the table before leaving.

"Ms. Harvey." Josie smirked and pulled a bottle from the ice bucket. Her eyes bulged. "You ordered a vintage from Jannah?"

"It was Maalik's choice." I handed her a glass to fill.

"Of course." she laughed and held her breath as she poured, like wasting a single drop would be a sin. With a price like that, drinking a single drop should have been a sin.

Soon enough, the table was set and we gathered around to begin our feasting. It was a pretty, if not snooty scene. Fine china and glitzy company generally had a nerve-wracking effect on me, but I found myself all too comfortable with it my new home. I would have given anything for Saul to see me now, sitting around the dinner table with council and committee members, dressed up like little democracy dolls. And in my own home, no less. I could just see him clutching his belt buckle and tucking his face into his hat so he could laugh himself silly.

"What's so funny?" Ridwan's eyes had followed me with a curious skepticism from the moment he had shown up. He wasn't a fan of mine and often complained of the times Maalik neglected his council duties to "entertain the reaper" as he put it. I was surprised he had accepted my dinner invitation at all, but maybe he was giving me a second chance. Then again, maybe he had a hidden agenda. I couldn't think of a politician who didn't these days.

"I was just thinking of my mentor, Saul." I smiled at Ridwan and spread a cloth napkin across my lap.

"Saul Avelo, yes?" Ridwan took a dish from Maalik and piled his plate with carrots.

"The one and only."

"Doesn't he have a memorial at the park, like Coreen?"

"He does." I passed him the potato soup, praying he wouldn't take the conversation south. Stabs at my dead mentor were grounds for decapitation in my book, and I had really been hoping for a peaceful, blood-free evening.

"And wasn't that Hare fellow who got himself terminated for stealing souls in your generation?" Ridwan asked next, throwing everything in a new and twisted direction.

"Yes, I believe he was," I answered sourly.

"So you knew all three of the deceased reapers intimately. Isn't that something?"

"I wouldn't say I knew them intimately. Coreen and Vince were barely acquaintances."

"Vince. Yes, that was his name." Ridwan gave me a vicious grin before turning his attentions back to his plate. His creep factor had just doubled. I wouldn't be inviting him to dinner again any time soon.

"Have you visited Saul's memorial lately?" Maalik picked up where Ridwan had left off.

I thought my eyeballs would fall out onto my plate. What he was really asking, and thank Khadija no one else knew, was if I had been to Coreen's memorial to see Winston. He had a lot of nerve, and I'd tell him that much and more once everyone was gone.

"At least once a year," I answered, silencing him with a Medusa glare. The tension was beginning to spoil my appetite, and I couldn't have that. There were stuffed mushrooms to massacre yet. A diversion was in order.

"Jenni, have you decided which unit you're going to apply for?" I asked.

Jenni froze, a forkful of hen held halfway to her polished pout, but she set it back on her plate, now that she was the new discussion target. "I don't know just yet. I'm eligible for every unit now, so I guess I'll see where I'm most needed at the placement ceremony."

"You're quite the role model for the younger reapers. Why didn't you take an apprentice this year?" Amy asked.

"Apprentices thrive best in a freelance environment." She blushed the instant the words escaped her. "No offense, Lana. Kevin is the best of his generation, and I think spending his apprenticeship in a unit could serve him well in the long run. He has certainly proved he can handle himself."

"Thank you." Kevin beamed and gave me a proud tilt of his chin.

"It was rather unexpected when Grim turned over Coreen's assignment and apprentice to you last fall." Ridwan jumped back in with the subtly ruthless remarks.

"Yes, it was," I agreed. "But he was in a pinch, and my team and I finished the assignment with great care."

"I'm surprised you went back to low-risk freelance work."

"I wanted to take a few classes first to brush up on my skills."

Josie's face lit up like a firecracker at that. She covered her mouth and pretended to choke to keep from laughing. I could have joined her. Brush up on my skills? Yeah, right. I was back in school because Grim was paying for the mentoring course I needed in order to train Kevin, and Horus was threatening to spill my beans if I didn't make it on the Posy Unit to do his dirty work. I just wanted to get through one year without anyone finding out I was a freak of nature, worthy of beheading.

Okay, it wasn't nature's fault. It was circumstance. I just happened to be in the wrong place at the wrong time when Khadija was handing out soul matter to the eighth generation of reapers. It wasn't my fault she decided to give me a little extra. I didn't even know what she had done until last fall.

"So what's this I've been hearing about a Nephilim Guard?" Gabriel asked, still sporting his scowl. He might have been in a pissy mood, but he still had my back. He gave Ridwan a sideways glance and crinkled his nose, like the angel's tasteless remarks were stinking up the room.

"The Nephilim Guard is a newer project of Grim's," Maalik answered Gabriel, mirroring his sour glance at Ridwan. "The offspring of the fallen have long hoped for permanent residency in Limbo City, and they may have very well found it."

"It's disgraceful." Ridwan stabbed a mushroom. "They deserve no place in this world. They're merely the product of betrayal and demonic lust."

"They didn't choose to be illegitimately born, you know." Jenni was heated now. Her fork clanged on her plate and she squeezed her fists together, pure poison spreading across her face. "Excuse me. I need to visit the ladies room." She stood and hastily made her way down the hall.

I had heard a rumor or two about Jenni's involvement with an underground association of reapers working towards deityship rights. We were already one step ahead of the nephilim. We at least had permanent residency in Limbo. But everybody wants more. I guess it's the human soul matter in us. Jenni supported the nephilim's cause, probably because she was hoping the nephilim would support hers. Now that they were becoming our equals, who knew where the balance would fall. Perhaps they would remain content with the bone Grim had thrown them. Then again, if you give a mouse a cookie...

Ridwan gave Jenni a cautious frown when she returned to the table. Luckily, he kept his prejudiced opinions to himself for the rest of the evening. We drank and ate and drank some more, until we were all fuzzy in the head, full in the middle, and giggling senselessly at every foul joke Gabriel could bring himself to recall.

Even with the mildly stinky company of Ridwan, I decided the evening was an overall success. If I didn't think too hard about the details of my situation, I could actually enjoy this lifestyle. Strange as it sounds, especially for being over three centuries old, it was the first time I really, truly felt important, like a valuable member of society. It was a good feeling, but at the same time, a little scary. Being noticed by those in power also made one a target for those opposing the ones in power. The charred remains of my old apartment could attest to that.

CHAPTER 12

*"One thing being in politics has taught me is that
men are not a reasoned or reasonable sex."*
-Margaret Thatcher

"Good luck tomorrow," Gabriel called from the elevator
as Maalik and I waved my guests goodbye. I gave him a
tight smile, quietly begging him for secrecy. I didn't need it
getting back to the enemy that I was preparing for them.
Gabriel winked at me, reading my thoughts with the "ah-
ha!" awareness normally reserved for crossword puzzles.

The elevator doors slid shut. I sighed and shut my own
door as I kicked my heels off. Maalik hummed a giddy tune
as he cleared the table and began washing dishes. He would
have made a nice little house-angel if he wasn't so tied up in
politics and micromanaging my life.

There was a tension between us lately, even though he
liked to ignore it. Sometimes, I wished I could ignore it too.
He meant well, even if he was becoming a tad controlling.
Maybe I could ignore that tonight. I just wanted some vision
of perfection, even if it was tangled through with deception.
I deserved some peace. And sex. Nothing like a near death
experience to hike up the libido. Apparently, Maalik thought

so too. I put the left over wine in the fridge and turned to find my angel waiting behind me, his eyes twinkling mischievously.

I smiled at him and tilted my head to one side. "So, first dinner party. How'd I do?"

"Perfect." He stared at me a moment longer and then smashed me against the fridge with a kiss, grating his teeth against my lips as I curled my legs around him. His wings fluttered, lifting high enough so that they wouldn't be crushed. I reached up and pulled at his curly mane, breaking the kiss with a desperate breath. Maalik dipped lower and nuzzled against my neck, moaning his frustrations into the thin fabric over my breasts. I gasped and tugged at his hair again while his hands worked their way down my back, hunting for a way to take the dress off without ripping it to shreds.

We just didn't do this enough anymore. Every time felt urgent, like I might explode with need. How had I gone so long without this, without him hurling me into oblivion, that dark place where nothing mattered, save for a blissful moment? Well, okay, a blissful hour.

Maalik found the workings of my dress and stripped me of it as I freed him of his robe. We migrated through the condo, stopping first at the dining table, then the couch. We lingered longer in the shower, where Maalik showed me just how useful the birdbath could be. We finished on the king-sized bed in my room, still half-wrapped in towels and glistening from the shower.

I sprawled myself across the pillows and waited for my heart to slow. Maalik lay on his stomach and stretched his wings out above us, drying them more completely now that we were good and spent. I smiled up at the feathered canopy and reached up to smooth my fingers along his minor coverts, the fluffy, uppermost feathers of his wing that could almost pass for fur. His had a dusty silver tint that sparkled as he shuddered at my touch.

Maalik's wings were far larger and stronger than the average bird, but they were still hollow like a bird, so we had to take a little precaution not to crush them when we tumbled around in our lusty fits. That precaution had gone out the door with our guests tonight. I strummed my fingers along the bony line of his wing and counted my lucky stars that it felt intact and he didn't flinch from any overlooked fractures. Gabriel had cracked his ulna a few years back, and he had spent a whole week laid over my coffee table with his bandaged wing tucked and quivering. Not a pretty sight.

"I was thinking," Maalik said softly, distracting me from the hypnosis of his wings. "Maybe you could wait until next year to finish your schooling and apply for the Posy Unit. Grim would surely understand, given your situation. I just can't imagine he would expect you to commute to school, at least not without protection of some kind, like the Nephilim Guard. Even then, you can't be expected to produce good test scores under this sort of stress—"

"Shut up." I closed my eyes.

"What?" Maalik jerked next to me.

"Shut up," I said louder. I was going to scream, just scream forever. This had to stop, right here. If I argued with him one more time, just to find out he had gone and altered yet another element of my life without my permission, I would crack *his* ulna.

"Don't you think you've forced enough changes in my life for one day?" I snapped.

"Is this place really so bad?" He pulled his wings back in with a hissing wind.

"Enough already. Leave my life to me. I'm a big girl, and I know what I'm doing. I will continue with school, I will do the demon training, and I will, I *will* be on the Posy Unit in two weeks."

"Are you so confident of my vote?" His jaw flexed, giving his glare a frightening angle.

"I don't need your vote. There are eight other council members." I sat up and reached for my robe, but Maalik caught my arm and jerked me back to him.

"Don't be stupid, Lana. I respect your decisions, when they are made wisely. Are you trying to get yourself killed?"

I looked down at his fingers, digging into my arm. "Let go, or so help me—"

Maalik flung my arm away and pulled his knees up to rest his arms on. "I won't force any more changes on you." He raked his hands through his tangled curls. "I trust you to make the right decisions on your own. I just hope you figure out what those decisions are before it's too late."

"I liked you better when you were cooking dinner." I smacked him with a pillow. He caught it and scooped me into him, squashing the pillow between us.

"And I liked you better when you weren't so ambitious."

"Look who's talking, Mr. Councilman."

Maalik laughed and tucked me in his arms as we snuggled back into the pillows. Sleep came, but not soon enough. I was still privately panicking. What if he had already gone and withdrawn me from my classes? Or told Bub I refused the training? Or just outright bought me from Grim, like some sort of pet or slave? Okay, so that last one was a little iffy. Should a girl really have to consider these things about her angel?

CHAPTER 13

*"God so loved the world that he made up his mind
to damn a large majority of the human race."*
-Robert G. Ingersoll

The gates of Hell were quiet Thursday morning. I spied Lucifer and Charon sharing a cup of coffee through the dusty windows of the Styx Stop, a little café along the coast of the Sea of Eternity. The River Styx mostly ran parallel to the Phlegethon, the boiling river of blood leading inland. But where the two came near the edge of the sea, they curled back and away from each other. While the Phlegethon twisted around towards the smoking lands of Jahannam, the Styx turned sharply eastward, leading the long way to Tartarus, the shrinking Greek underworld.

The Styx Stop was one of a zillion along the most famous river in all the underworlds. The franchise had been a business investment of Hades' after his territory had dwindled down from the size of a large country to that of a playground. It was his retirement plan, you could say. He and Persephone were real homebodies these days, only showing up at the Oracle Ball two or three times a century.

I tucked away the coin Bub had given me and stuffed my hands in the pockets of my jean jacket before making my way inside the Styx Stop.

Charon looked up from his coffee and waved a bony hand at me. "Lana, long time no see."

"Yes," Lucifer added with a smile. "What brings you to the mouth of Hell so early?"

"No deliveries for me today." I laughed, taking a seat next to Charon. "I was supposed to meet Bub here." I checked my watch. "Ten minutes ago."

"That boy would be late for the apocalypse, I swear." Lucifer shook his head before taking another sip from his mug. He was dressed more casually than I was used to, which was oddly comforting. His black hair was pulled back in a ponytail, and he wore khakis with a green polo shirt. Not exactly an ensemble most humans would have pictured him in.

A horned waitress scampered over to our table and asked for my order, casting flirty glances at both men. I ordered a cup of coffee to go, just in case Bub decided to show up and whisk me off.

"I hear they're still looking for that goddess that went missing last fall over on your side of the pond." Lucifer jumped in with the not-so-small talk.

"Yeah," I answered with a quick nod.

He waited for an uncomfortable moment, eyeing me with that expectant look people get when they want you to elaborate. The horny waitress set my coffee on the table as she zipped by, not even waiting for a thank you. I picked it up and nearly bit a chunk of Styrofoam off as I took a nervous drink.

"Grim has the Nephilim Guard and Anubis. He'll sort it all out," I said, hoping that would turn away Lucifer's questioning stare.

"Ah, the Nephilim Guard. So it's true? We hear so many stories over here. Never know which ones to believe."

Charon set his coffee down, grinning at Lucifer. "I think you owe me a coin, daddy-o."

"Yeah, yeah." Lucifer managed to grin and grimace at the same time as he dug around in his pocket. "Never make bets with public transporters. They hear too much," he warned, flipping a coin at the gloating ferryman.

The front door jingled, and Bub entered the café, drawing heated glances from every horned lady in sight. He wore faded blue jeans and an orange button-up with the sleeves rolled up, showing off the lean muscles of his forearms. Right then, I decided it didn't matter what he wore. He was edible. I wondered how many hours I was going to have to restrain myself from taking a bite.

"Morning, gentlemen." Bub took a seat next to Lucifer.

"About time." Lucifer elbowed him in the arm. "Keeping a pretty girl like her waiting. What's the matter with you boy?"

Bub only chuckled at the chiding. "Long night, Luce. Long night."

The horned waitress appeared at our table again, looking flustered as ever, eyes darting from Lucifer to Bub.

"Bring me a strong one, pet. Soup it up will all the sweets and creams, won't you?" Bub ordered before she managed to find her voice. She nodded and scampered away.

"So what have the two of you got planned for today?" Charon asked, sticking his nose right in our business by way of innocent small talk. I'd assumed Lucifer knew about the training since he was on the Hell Committee, but I was curious to see how Bub was covering it up for everyone else. I'd probably need a cover eventually, too.

"You didn't hear?" Bub gave him an astonished look. "Grim commissioned me to organize the placement ceremony this year. Lana's agreed to help me with the smaller details. Sort of an extra credit project."

It was all I could do not to look as confounded as Charon. It was so ridiculous, it was almost believable.

"Oh." The ferryman frowned and took a sip of his coffee. "I didn't know you were in the party planning business."

Bub shrugged. "I throw one hell of a party. Why not cash in on the skill?"

"I suppose."

"We better get going," Bub said just as the waitress delivered his coffee. We said our goodbyes and left the café, walking east along the Styx shore, towards Tartarus.

"Seriously? I could have come up with a better cover than that." I snorted.

"It's not just a cover. It's the truth," Bub said with a grin.

"What? Grim really put you in charge of the placement ceremony?"

"Is that so hard to believe?" His ears grew pink. "Haven't you ever been to one of my parties? They're to die for."

"Sorry, I've been trying too hard *not* to die lately."

"Let's see if we can't improve your technique." Bub placed a hand on my lower back, steering me towards a small dock where a tired, old houseboat waited. "I think it would be best if we train at my summer home in Tartarus. It's more secluded. We'll draw less suspicion than if we went to my flat in Pandemonium."

We climbed on board and Bub untied the ropes from the dock. The boat ran smooth, despite its antique appearance. Bub stationed himself at an oversized steering wheel anchored to a platform in the center of the front deck. The breeze tugged at the collar of his shirt and pushed back his dark hair that was free of gel today. He looked relaxed and comfortable. I imagined this was how he spent many of his weekends in Hell.

I expected the uncomfortable silence to be, well, more uncomfortable, but the soft hum of the boat, the sloshing river water, and the gentle whisper of the wind filled the void and set me at ease. I pressed my back against the railing and stretched my arms out to grip the weathered wood, tilting my head back to keep my curls out of my face. Bub gave me a strange smile.

"I've never been to Heaven, but I can't imagine it being any better than this, right here," he said.

I couldn't help but smile back. "You're not missing much. It smells like frosting and it's far too bright."

Bub laughed, showing his brilliant white smile and faint dimples to either side of his goatee.

We rode along in silence for another hour or so before the parched land of Tartarus came into view. The dock we pulled up to was a private one with only one other boat tied to it. It was a red speed boat with a demon pinup silhouette stenciled on the side. Curly letters sprawled beneath her spelling out *Solve Lora Infernis* Latin for "Unleash Hell".

Bub's summer home was a combination of a small stone castle and a log cabin. It rested on a sandy hillside about a quarter mile from the boat dock. There was a walking path, part stone and part wooden steps, which led the way.

The landscape of Tartarus was mostly desert, with red mountains lingering in the distance. A few gray trees and shrubs were scattered about, but nothing else for as far as I could see. It was eerie, but somehow reassuring. No one would be sneaking up on us here.

"Welcome back, sir." An old, demon butler greeted us at the front door. He nodded his horned head at me in a friendly gesture. "Would you like me to take your jacket, madam?"

"Thank you," I said, sliding out of my jacket and revealing my sleeveless black turtleneck that conveniently hid the blistered handprint on my neck. It was still too soon to tell if it would scar, but I wasn't holding my breath. I had a bad feeling that there were a lot of turtlenecks in my future.

"Why don't you start up some lunch, Jack? We might be here a while," Bub said.

"Yes, sir." Jack nodded and hurried away with my jacket.

Bub led me through the foyer and into a dark room that sank down a few steps. A couple leather sofas rested around a coffee table to the left, while a pool table filled the other side of the room. A big screen television was anchored to the wall behind a fully stocked bar in the corner. It was the ultimate bachelor pad. I could smell the testosterone.

"Have a seat. Would you like a drink?" Bub stepped behind the bar and pulled a bottle down from a shelf.

"Water's fine." I sat down on one of the leather sofas.

"Of course, you'd expect me to serve you ice water in Hell." He chuckled. He mixed a scotch and water in a short glass for himself and brought my ice water in a tall glass.

"So what exactly are we going to accomplish here? Are you planning on showing me how to beat a demon at a game of pool or what?"

"You'd be amazed at the things I've taught women in this room." He dropped down on the couch across from me and propped his boots up on the coffee table.

I could feel myself blush as I raised an eyebrow. I took a sip of my water and set it on the table before crossing my arms. Bub just grinned at me while he finished his drink, dipping his forked tongue to lick the bottom of the glass. I was suddenly uncomfortable.

"I have something for you," he said, opening a drawer under the coffee table. He pulled out a leather pouch and slid around the table to kneel in front of me.

Heat crawled up my face as my body went rigid. The effect he had on me was maddening, but I hadn't quite concluded that fear was the only culprit. He was certainly easy on the eyes, and his light English accent turned me to pudding, when I wasn't smirking about how horridly it went with his backwoods nickname. Come on, how many prim-and-propers do you know who go by Bub?

Bub grinned up at me. "Do you trust me?" he whispered, gently spreading my legs apart.

I frowned. Well, this was nice and awkward. "Sure." I tried to sound nonchalant, but I think squeaking murdered that affect.

He slid his fingers up one of my calves, drawing a shallow breath from my lips, before caressing my knee and venturing on up to my thigh. I refused to let him intimidate me. I was three hundred years old. These games were for amateurs. My pride swelled with each second I held his eyes with mine, purposely not pulling away to gawk down at what he was doing to my leg. The freak.

"There we go." He leaned back so I could comfortably examine what he had done. A leather strap was buckled around my upper thigh, holding half a dozen silver, star-shaped blades.

"What's this?" I pressed a finger to the edge of one, testing its sharpness.

"Throwing stars," Bub answered as he pulled himself back to his feet. "You need a little more long-range skill if you plan on playing with the demons."

"A little more?" I laughed. "Perhaps you haven't seen my resume. I don't have *any* long-range skill. That's always been Josie's arena."

"Well, you better start making it yours as well. Demons do not conform to suit your weaknesses. Quite the contrary, in fact. I guess you could say its part of our nature. Sort of like how I play on your fear of intimacy." He chuckled.

"I do not have a fear of intimacy." I frowned. "I have a fear of demons chopping my head off."

"Well, my pretty, let's get on with your training then." He walked around the sofas and opened a cabinet on the back wall to reveal a dartboard. "See," he said with a devilish grin. "You can learn all sorts of things in this room."

CHAPTER 14

*"I always say shopping is cheaper
than a psychiatrist."*
-Tammy Faye Bakker

The wooden dummy at Athena's Boutique folded her arms and began tapping her little oak toes along the rim of her platform. I had been assessing the black leather vest she modeled long enough to inflict impatience in an artificially animated object. Figures.

I scowled at the pushy dummy and glanced across the store, over to where Jenni sat with another model. She seemed to be getting along far better than I was. Her dummy held up two pairs of strappy heels in front of a cocktail dress she had persuaded it to try on and clapped with delight when Jenni made her selection.

I sighed and looked back up at my dummy. It had forgotten me altogether and began fingering through a rack of scarves within reach.

"Okay, hand over the vest," I grumbled.

The dummy wasted no time sliding out of the garment and flung it at me with annoyed disdain before selecting a flowery sundress to model next.

"Thanks," I huffed and made my way up the spiral staircase leading to the dressing rooms.

The vest covered the new demon scar on my neck perfectly, and it had enough charm that the purchase wouldn't feel entirely like a necessity. The oily leather ran smooth, right up to the bust and collar, where a web of swirly cutouts gave the leather a lace-like quality. Like most everything I tried on at Athena's, it felt just right, like it had been made for me. It hugged all the right places and displayed a healthy amount of cleavage through a diamond cutout below my throat. The collar wasn't too Dracula either. It would go perfect with my black pencil skirt and pumps. I was going for a more academic look at the placement ceremony. I was sure Grim could overlook the girly biker vest, considering it was the only thing I could find on such short notice to hide my pretty new scar.

I slipped back into my gray turtleneck, exited the dressing room, and spotted Artemis leaning over the checkout counter, whispering something dire to Athena. They both turned to watch as I came down the stairs. Jenni bumped into me on her way up.

"Oh, sorry." She blushed and stole a glance at the loot tucked in my arms. "That's a bold choice, but it suits you."

"Thanks. I'm going to checkout. If I browse around much longer, I might end up in a fistfight with a mannequin."

"Fair enough." She laughed. "I just need to try on a few things, and I'll be ready too."

I nodded and squeezed past her, down to the main floor.

"Did you find what you were looking for?" Athena greeted me with a suspicious grin while Artemis fiddled with a box of jeweled bracelets and pretended not to be listening.

"Always." I gave her a strained smile, hoping she wouldn't badger me with questions. I should have known better. Asking questions was her favorite pastime.

"I couldn't help but notice how much you're favoring your neck today. Do you mind if I ask what happened?" She took the vest from me and rang it up while I chewed on my bottom lip. Yeah, I minded, but I wasn't about to offend a goddess.

"Just a careless accident is all."

Athena's eyes narrowed. She folded the vest and nestled it down between some tissue paper in one of her fancy new bags. Silver outlines of dummies in dresses danced over the stiff, pink paper.

"I heard your apartment was attacked by a fire demon. Did everyone make it out safely?" Artemis asked, trying on a sapphire bracelet.

"Yes, thank goodness." I handed Athena my card, despite the hurt quickly creasing her beautiful face. Artemis wasn't looking too happy either. Normally, I didn't mind chatting with Zeus's girls, as long as the conversation didn't revolve around my personal life.

"All set?" Josie asked as she joined me at the counter, her arms loaded down with an assortment of blouses and a shoebox. I gave her a relieved smile.

"Yeah, Jenni's in the dressing room, but she said she's about ready too."

"Good." She glanced at her watch. "We'll have time to stop for coffee." Her smile faded as she looked up at the pouty goddesses eyeing us. "Who died?"

"We thought you might have, with what we heard about the attack on your apartment complex." Artemis sniffed.

"Oh!" Josie pressed a hand to her chest and giggled. "No, we're fine. That crazy demon picked the wrong apartment, that's for sure. She had no idea she was coming up against four trained reapers."

"My goodness. So it was just a random attack?" Athena asked.

"I suppose this is why we have the Nephilim Guard now." Josie sighed. "Terrorist attacks on the city have been getting worse ever since Seth fled the council."

"I heard there was a break-in at the records office last night too. It's just terrible." Artemis shook her head, but she and Athena both looked brighter. Nothing like a little gossip to perk a goddess up.

Jenni arrived at the counter just as Athena finished ringing Josie up. She smiled, handing her selection to Athena. This was the first time she had gone shopping with us, and she seemed a little nervous about the outing. I could tell she didn't do things like this often. She had even dressed up for the occasion, wearing a clingy summer dress and sandals. Her silky hair was pulled up with a pair of chopsticks, with a few strands slanted at an angle over one of her almond-shaped eyes. Josie and I looked grossly underdressed in our jeans and tee shirts.

It was nice having someone new along, but a little strange at the same time. I felt disoriented and old all of a sudden, being so set in my ways. Josie had been my only shopping accomplice for the past few hundred years.

"You ladies be careful out there," Artemis called after us as we left the boutique. We waved and hurried down the sidewalk with our pink bags.

"Was there an announcement in the paper, or do they just eavesdrop on everyone?" Josie asked when we were a safe distance away.

"Maybe they've been bugging all the clothes we buy." I opened my bag and glared accusingly down at the new ensemble.

Jenni looked at her watch. "I'd love to join you all for coffee, but I have a meeting before my class tonight. Let me know when the next study party is," she said.

"Of course." Josie gave her a quick hug and I waved goodbye as we stepped inside the Phantom Café.

It was still a little early for the late night coffee dates, so we mostly had the place to ourselves. Nick, a nephilim waiter, seated us at a small corner table and took our orders. Josie went with the same, simple black coffee she always had, and I ordered a chai latté.

"I'm kinda glad Jenni had to go," Josie said after Nick left our table. "I've been wanting to talk to you, but there always seems to be people around lately."

"What's up?" I folded my arms over the table and leaned in closer, still wondering if our clothes had been bugged.

"That's what I'd like to ask you," she said.

"What do you mean?"

"Lana." Josie gave me one of her annoyed sighs. "How long have we been friends now?"

"If you've got something to ask, just ask." I knew I was going to regret saying that last bit, but she was right. We had been friends a long time, and I owed her more than what I'd been giving her lately. I just wasn't sure how to get the words past my lips. My mouth went dry and my tongue seemed to swell up every time I even thought about all the things I wanted to tell her.

"Okay." She waited a moment while Nick delivered our drinks. We each took a sip and watched him disappear again.

"First of all, I'd like to know why you really want to be on the Posy Unit, and don't try to feed me any bullshit about some newly discovered ambitions. I know you better than that." She folded her arms and raised her brows at me.

I took another drink of my tea and a deep breath. I didn't have to lie entirely, but I really couldn't bring myself to tell her the whole truth. Not yet. Maybe not ever.

"You remember the soul we harvested last year?"

She nodded.

"He's not working out, and Horus wants me to find a replacement for him so he can take him home to Aaru. He thinks I'll come in contact with the most souls and find a

84

replacement sooner if I join the Posy Unit. And it will be less obvious than having the council vote on it and select a specialty team. The fewer people who know, the less likely we'll end up with a traitor in the mix who will sabotage the mission." I took another sip of my latté and waited for her reaction.

She tilted her head and frowned at me. "Why you?"

"I dunno. Maybe because I did okay the last time." I glared at her. I might be lazy, but I'm not incompetent.

"Why do I get the feeling you're not telling me everything?" she asked.

Because I wasn't. I'd left out the part about how I was the only one who could find the replacement soul since Khadija had gifted me, and the illegal bracelets Horus had given me, and that fact that Horus was blackmailing me because he knew I had killed Wosyet. And the part about how Grim didn't have a clue about this little mission.

"What else do you want to know?"

"Hmmm." She frowned at me. "How about, where the hell were you this morning, and why did Gabriel look so uncomfortable when I asked him about it?"

Shit. I tugged at my turtleneck and reached for my tea again. "You can't share this with anyone," I said.

"Well, obviously." She snorted.

"Not even Jenni."

"Deal."

I sipped at my tea and leaned in even closer. Our foreheads were almost touching. "Cindy Morningstar said she'll vote in my favor for the Posy Unit, but only if I take a demon training course."

"What?" Josie leaned back in her seat and ran a hand through her spiky hair. "I'm sorry. Where exactly does this make sense?"

"It's stupid. I realize this, but she seems to think Grim's going to choose me as his next second-in-command."

85

Josie's lips squeezed together and her face suddenly reddened. I frowned, not sure how to interpret her reaction, until she burst out laughing and slapped the table with both hands. Nick gave us a startled glance from behind the counter.

"Now I know you're lying." Josie gasped, trying to calm her laughter.

"I am not." I laughed with her. "I tried to tell her it would never happen, but she insisted this was the only way she'd give me her vote."

"Wow. That's good." Josie took a drink of her coffee and sighed. She smiled at me. "What would you do if Grim did make you second-in-command?"

"Die," I answered instantly. "I'd just die."

"Yeah?"

"It's a good thing he hates me too much to do something that stupid."

Josie shrugged. "You never know. He does have a strange sense of humor when it comes to these things. I mean, he gave you Kevin as an apprentice."

She had a point, but I just didn't see Grim taking things that far. An apprentice was one thing. If I were second-in-command, Grim would have to see me everyday. I knew he would hate that even more than I would. I'd just have to make sure he kept despising me.

"So you've been training with Cindy?" Josie asked.

"Uh, no." I blushed. "Beelzebub."

Her eyes bulged. "The Lord of the Flies? The lickable prince of darkness?"

I frowned at her. "You're such a tart."

"I don't think I'd be able to focus enough to learn a damn thing if I were in the same room as him."

"My goodness, what would Kevin say?" I chided her and swallowed down the last of my latté.

Josie shrugged. "I have eyeballs. I can't help it." She finished off her coffee and checked her watch. I never wore one, but she checked hers enough for the both of us. "We better get to class," she said.

I groaned and dropped a coin on the table to pay for both of our drinks. I was feeling guilty for all the secrets. And all the secrets I still hadn't told her. And also, slightly nauseous at the thought of class and having to see Craig again.

CHAPTER 15

*"There is a charm about the forbidden
that makes it unspeakably desirable."*
-Mark Twain

"Spread your legs wider." Bub kicked my knees apart with one of his and grabbed me under the arms before I had the chance to fall on my face.

I grunted. "Why are you always trying to get between my legs?"

He snickered over my shoulder. "Because that's where the ladies prefer me."

I snorted and took aim with another throwing star. I had managed to get three out of eight on the dartboard this time. The others lay abandoned on the carpet. All except for one that had lodged itself into the drywall about a foot above the board. Pathetic? Yes. But progress all the same, thank you.

The next star hit the board. Not a bull's-eye, mind you, but close enough that I jumped up and down for a second, all giddy and stupid like.

"See, isn't it better when I'm behind you?" Bub teased again.

I was finally easing into all his raunchy flirting. I'd concluded that it was just part of his evil nature, and since there was nothing I could do to fix it, I'd just go with it.

"You want a drink?" he asked, making his way behind the bar.

"Water."

"I know I've seen you out at Purgatory drinking before. Why do you always ask for water?"

"You really want to see how much damage I could do with these things while under the influence?" I asked, tossing the strap of stars on the coffee table.

"Hey, it might help. Lucifer knows you can't get any worse."

I glared at him and folded my arms. "Fine. You got tequila back there?"

"I got anything you want back here." He grinned and pulled a bottle of Patrón out of the cooler. "With juice or straight?"

"Throw in some lime."

He fixed my drink and his usual scotch and water. Normally, I didn't feel comfortable drinking around demons, but after four hours of practice, I really needed a drink. Long range was so not my specialty when it came to battle. Now give me an axe, and I'm in business.

"You're getting better," Bub said, softening my scowl as he handed me the tequila and sat on the sofa across from me.

I shrugged. "I think I'm more likely to gash open my femoral artery and bleed to death before I actually find these things useful in a battle." I took a long drink and shook my head.

"Don't give up just yet, pet." Bub downed his drink and clinked his ice around in the glass. "You'd be surprised at how much more accurate you can be in the heat of battle. You just need a little more focus. Isn't there anyone you detest enough to imagine as you're throwing?"

Craig Hogan came to mind.

"Ah, an old flame?" Bub grinned.

I blinked at him, utterly surprised.

"Please," he said, raising an eyebrow. "I've inflicted that look in enough women to recognize it."

"I imagine you have." I laughed and finished my drink.

Bub took my empty glass and stood, slowly making his way behind the bar. He was in blue jeans again today, and a snug blue tee shirt. I liked the way he dressed at home. He looked good in the sleek suits he wore to work too, but something about the jeans and tee shirt made him seem more approachable, more touchable, I thought as he turned around and caught me eyeing him. I blushed and looked away.

"Would you like another?" he asked in that voice of his that made everything sound far more suggestive than it had any right to be.

"I'll take a water, thanks." Getting tanked was not on the list. I still had to study for finals at some point in the evening, and I really needed to take Saul and Coreen out for a run. Most days, they came to work with me. They didn't enjoy being cooped up at Holly House during my time off.

"Let's try again," Bub said, setting our drinks on the table. "This time, focus on that heartbreaking bastard of yours."

I snatched up the throwing stars and assumed the position. Bub slid up behind me again. I had a moment to wonder if my lousy aim didn't have something to do with his muscled chest pressed up against my back. It was distracting as hell the way my pulse raced whenever he was this close. I tried to forget he was behind me and let my mind rewind back to class the night before.

Craig was impossible. Not only was he thrilled that Grace had thrown us together, but he was also trying to play it off like he somehow needed to pass this class, insisting that we get together as soon as possible to layout our presentation. And then when I insisted that we meet at my place, he had the audacity to act concerned about the demon attack he'd overheard Artemis gossiping about.

I cringed and looked up at the oval clock on Bub's wall. Craig would be meeting me at Holly House in two hours.

"Anytime now, love." Bub sighed over my shoulder, dropping one hand from my waist down to my hip. My pulse leapt again, reminding me where I was and who I was with.

I scowled at the board, trying to picture Craig. The star felt heavier in my hand. With Bub at my back and Craig in mind, my stomach was doing somersaults with an overwhelming mix of anger and desire swirling around in there. I took aim and flung the star with enough force that half of it sank into the dartboard when it struck. It wasn't perfect, but it was touching the bull's eye. I let out a little yelp when Bub scooped me up from behind and spun me in a circle.

"Thank the abyss." He laughed, tickling the back of my neck with his goatee as he set me down. "One more day of this, and we're moving on to something new."

"Really?" I rotated in his grasp to face him. "It's not another long range weapon, is it?"

Bub smirked, flashy one of his dirty grins. "There's a joke in there, but I think I've made you uncomfortable enough for one day."

"What? I never said I was uncomfortable," I protested.

Bub released me and sauntered behind the bar. "I've been standing all of three inches away from you most of the day, and you think I can't tell?" He chuckled softly as he mixed us another round, pouring me another tequila without even asking.

I put my hands on my hips. "You're a demon. How exactly do you expect me to feel with you standing directly behind me?"

"Well, I could tell you how most women feel when I'm directly behind them." He winked.

"Oh, grief." I sighed. "You really just can't help yourself, can you?"

He came around from the bar and handed me the drink. I took it from him and tilted my head back to down it in one swallow. I'd show him uncomfortable.

Bub's perpetual smile faltered as he swept his fingers under my chin and tilted my head back once more to examine my neck. My pulse quickened again. "You're healing up nicely."

The scarf I had worn to hide the nasty burn on my neck laid abandoned on the sofa with my jacket. The blistering had gone down, but I still had a pinkish gray handprint wrapped around my throat. I was feeling less self-conscious lately, since all of Eternity seemed to know about it anyway.

"I'm really hoping it's gone before the placement ceremony." I said, gently pulling away from him.

His smile returned, and he took my empty glass, letting his fingers linger over mine. "Another?"

I looked at the clock again. "I can't."

"Afraid I'll take advantage of you?" he asked.

"Don't you have enough ladies to tend to without having to harass me?"

"But none of them blush quite as brilliantly as you do."

My thoughts dove off the deep end and somehow circled back to the memory of the Oracle Ball and the late night coffee with a blushing Maalik. My stomach knotted. "Are we finished?"

Bub frowned. "For today."

"Good. I have a study date tonight." I snatched my jacket off the sofa and tugged it on.

Bub beat me to the scarf. I folded my arms as he slowly looped it around my neck and tied a knot over the side with the scar. "See you in the morning, pet."

"Yeah," I said, tucking the strap of throwing stars in my jacket pocket.

I made my way back to the foyer and out the front door. Like most homes in Eternity, currency travel was inactive while inside. I took a few steps away from the patio and found my coin. Rolling it three times, I said the coordinates for the courtyard outside Holly House and left Tartarus behind.

CHAPTER 16

"My grandmother was a very tough woman.
She buried three husbands and two of them were just napping."
-Rita Rudner

Living at Holly House still seemed strange. I felt like a vandal every time I stepped foot in the courtyard, like any minute snipers would pop out of the bushes, demanding to know what I was doing there. I could have sworn that I was the only one in the entire building who even owned a pair of blue jeans.

"Evening, Ms. Harvey," Charlie called from the front desk as I hurried towards the elevators.

"Oh, hi," I said back.

He always caught me off guard. At the Coexist Complex there was no front desk and no chipper, friendly face to greet residents or guests. I considered myself lucky if the landlord even answered the phone when I called to register a complaint about a leaky faucet.

I rode an elevator up to the tenth floor and entered my condo to find Saul and Coreen fighting over a dainty, white couch cushion. "Drop it!" I snapped.

Saul let go first, sending Coreen tumbling into the coffee table. He wagged his tail and innocently pranced over to me to lick my hand. I glared at him for a minute and then sighed, reaching down to scratch his ears. Coreen slipped up beside him with her tail between her legs. I scratched her chin and her tail looped in time with Saul's.

"I'm sorry, you guys. I've just been so busy. Go fetch your leads," I told them.

They raced for my bedroom and dug their leashes out of a basket on the floor. I still had an hour before Craig would make an appearance, and the hounds desperately needed to get out of the condo for a while, before they destroyed it and each other.

The park didn't get much action as far as I could tell. I'd only seen two or three souls wandering through the gardens in all the times I'd gone to visit Winston. So it came as quite a surprise when I ran into Anubis and his jackals sniffing around the rose hedges.

"Lana!" Anubis gave me a nod with a cheerful smile. He had a lead in each hand, same as me. His simple black robe would have made most mistake him for a reaper, if it wasn't for the jeweled belt at his waist.

I smiled and nodded back, ignoring my heart as it leapt in my throat. I secretly prayed to Khadija that I had scrubbed vigorously enough to rid myself of any trace of Wosyet.

The jackals and hounds took turns sniffing each others butts and then resumed panting and wagging their tails.

"Any luck with your search?" I asked.

"Not a lick." Anubis sighed and tilted his head to one side. "Is it safe to assume Horus filled you in on all the extra details of my visit to Limbo?"

"You mean about how you're trying to locate where the rebels are slipping in?"

"Yeah." He frowned and glanced around the park before taking a step closer. "My boys are catching scents here and there of known traitors, but there's too much coin activity. The trails go dead in so many random places, it's impossible to tell which ones are relevant and which ones are decoys."

"I see." I nodded, relaxing a little. He hadn't mentioned Wosyet at all. Horus had been right. The primary objective of Anubis's search was to figure out how the rebels were entering the city.

"I heard you were attacked. How are you doing?" he asked.

"Fine. I'm fine." I smiled.

It was strange having a god genuinely ask after me. Athena and Artemis only seemed to care if they thought it would give them a good subject to gossip about with customers and each other. Anubis had a gentle kindness and humor about him that seemed displaced in a death god. I should have been more on guard around him with his association with Horus, but I couldn't help it. A comfortable ease settled around me when he was near, like we had been friends for ages. Like I didn't have to sweat when my back was turned to him.

"I better get back to work. You take care, Lana. I'll see you at the placement ceremony." He gave me another nod and disappeared around the hedges.

Saul and Coreen tugged me around the park, circling the main fountain several times while sniffing the ground. They had gotten used to aiding me on the job, and I knew they were itching to get back to work, but that would have to wait until after my new placement. I had a feeling they'd come in handy on the Posy Unit.

We made it back to the condo just in time to run into Craig as he entered the front gate. He looked like a traveling salesman in his gray slacks and blue button-up, complete with a matching gray tie. He sported the same military, buzz cut he had for the past three hundred years. It gave his head a grayish tint, drawing out the splash of gray freckles across his nose and cheeks. He flashed me one of his sparkling, fake smiles, and it was all I could do not to snarl.

The hounds sensed my disappointment and took the opportunity to stare down my unwanted guest and sniff him over. My mood perked at his bulging eyes.

"Doesn't Holly have some sort of pet restriction?" he asked, taking a shaky breath. Coreen huffed and tilted her nose in the air.

"She made an exception for me," I said, entering my personal clearance code on the cross-shaped security box.

"Why's that?" he snapped.

"Because I'm special, jackass." Grace was forcing me to work with him, but that didn't mean I had to play nice.

I led the hounds through the lobby and stopped at the front desk to visit with Charlie and let Craig sign in.

"Did you have a nice walk, Ms. Harvey?" Charlie asked.

"It was lovely. Say, would you mind bringing me up a bottle of Merlot later, around ten? Maalik should be stopping by if the council lets out early." Maalik wouldn't be stopping by again until Sunday, but I wanted to have an excuse to throw Craig out as soon as possible.

"Certainly, Ms. Harvey." Charlie smiled and took the visitors log from Craig, carefully inscribing his initials next to Craig's sloppy signature.

"Shall we, Ms. Harvey?" Craig grinned.

I rolled my eyes and turned for the elevators. Coreen and Saul made sure to take up as much space as possible in the little golden box, forcing Craig to press himself into a corner. I smiled at his mangled expression. "Why, Craig, I was sure you were a dog person." I snickered.

"And I was sure you weren't."

"I dated you, didn't I?" I said as the elevator doors slid open.

"Hey, Lana!" Warren waited in the hall, cradling a wooden box in his arms. He gave Craig a curious look as he traded us places in the elevator.

"Keeping busy?" I asked.

"Oh, yes. I'm going to need an assistant if I keep going at this rate." He laughed as the doors pinged shut.

"I don't remember you being so social," Craig said as I opened the door to my condo.

"A lot changes in two hundred years."

"So I see." He took a deep breath as we walked into the dining room and I flipped on the lights. The city was gently fading through the enormous window in the sitting room, and our ghostly reflections stared back at us. Mine looked irritated and bored, while Craig's appeared surprised and a little uncomfortable.

I took Saul and Coreen's leads off and gave their ears a ruffle before they scurried around the table to wait at their food dishes. I sighed and went to fetch their Cerberus Chow out of the pantry.

Craig opened his messenger bag and carefully stacked his text books and folders on the table. I was sure he already had our final complete. This was just his way of trying to weasel back into my life. To get in on all the action and information he was so sure I had, and then use it to somehow take a step up in life. That's all I had been to him while we were dating. But I had learned a lot over three hundred years, and my secrets were just that, mine. He was going to have to find someone else to be his stepping stone this time.

I flipped on the coffee maker and found a mug, hesitating before I grabbed a second one. Assholes like coffee too, I suppose.

"You still take yours black?" I asked.

"I'm touched that you remember." Craig grinned as he arranged his pencils and calculator out on the table like the OCD freak that he was.

I resisted the urge to spit in his mug and instead filled mine with all the sugar and cream I could stand. While I waited for the coffee to finish, I slipped out of my jacket and laid it over the counter. Craig knew about my demon encounter, but I left the scarf on. The last thing I needed tonight was his insincere coddling. I filled our mugs and took the seat across from him.

He eyed my throat a moment and then met my glare. "Wouldn't this be easier if you sat over here, so you can see what I've got drawn up so far?"

"Is it so difficult to slide it across the table? I mean, I'd hate to spill my coffee on you," I said.

"Fine. Have it your way." Craig pushed a notebook towards me.

Grace's final assignment sounded simple enough. There were three scenarios for us to pick from, and then we had to map out a strategy solution and present it to the class. Since the Wandering Souls course covered the Posy Unit and Lost Souls Unit, we were expected to identify which unit was best suited for each catch. Three souls were in question in each scenario.

Craig had already picked a scenario for us, of course.

"Axe murderer," I read aloud. "John Smith has recently murdered three women and buried them in his backyard in New Mexico. The traumatic circumstances of their deaths have caused their souls to leave their bodies before their scheduled harvests. Jane Doe A was abducted from a gas station fifty miles south of Mr. Smith's home. She was a single mother of two and a ballet instructor for twenty plus years. Jane Doe B had a flat tire and was picked up by Mr. Smith thirty miles south of his home. She was a senior in college, majoring in child psychology, and she worked at a daycare not five miles from where she was abducted. Jane Doe C was a waitress, abducted from the parking lot of the café she worked at forty miles east of Mr. Smith's home. She had recently moved to the area from Mexico, after the death of her parents."

"Does that one work for you, or would you prefer the plane crash or suicide bomber?"

"This one's fine." I folded my arms. "I'm sure it's easier for you to relate to, having to harass and abduct women before they'll give you the time of day."

His grin tightened, but he cleared his throat and took the notebook back, maintaining his poise. "Obviously, Doe C is most suited for the Lost Souls Unit. I think Does A and B would be covered by the Posy Unit, especially considering their closer proximity and local histories."

I don't know why, but I was a little surprised that Craig wasn't drilling me for more personal information. He was actually focusing on our assignment. Maybe he did need to pass the course. Then again, maybe this was just a new tactic of his, I thought with a frown.

"So I'll take A and B," I said. "If we're working on separate parts of this, we don't really have to work together, right?"

Craig looked panicked for a moment. "Well," he stammered. "We'll still need to present the assignment together, and we'll want to prepare and practice."

I wrinkled my brow at him. "I think we each have plenty of other people we can practice on."

Craig's frustrations were beginning to peek through his scholarly façade. "Am I so awful to be around? Don't you have a single good memory from all the time we spent together?"

"Those memories grew a little pale, once I found out how meaningless it had all been to you."

Craig's grin suddenly warped into something that might have been considered sincere, if I hadn't known better. He unfolded his hands and reached across the table towards mine. I almost fell out of my chair as I jerked away before he could touch me.

"God, Lana." He sighed. "I know we have a sordid past, but I had no idea how hard you took the breakup."

"Please," I scoffed, feeling myself redden. "That was centuries ago. Why can't you just let me be?"

"I'm trying to apologize, and you're not making it very easy," he said.

"It's a little late for apologies, Craig. And that's not what I invited you over here for. We have a final due next week. If you're not interested in passing this class, I can do it on my own."

"Right," he shot back. "I'm sure your new friend Jenni would be thrilled to help you."

"Yes, I imagine she would be. So I really don't need you hanging around after two centuries, sticking your nose in my business and trying to turn my life upside down all over again."

"Hey, you invited me over." Craig folded his arms.

"Yeah, well, now I'm uninviting you. I think we've coved enough to get us through this final."

"You're impossible." He sighed and began stuffing books back in his messenger bag. "I can't believe I was actually going to ask you out to dinner."

I threw a hand to my chest. "Oh, no! Looks like I blew my big chance. Whatever shall I do? Oh, I know. I'll celebrate. With my *boyfriend*. Tonight." I opened the door for him.

Craig's jaw tightened as he reached up to loosen his tie. He gave me one last look, like he might have just one more stupid comment left in him. I lifted my chin, daring him to try me. Instead, he drew his lips together in a tight line and shook his head before storming out. What an asshat.

I don't consider myself an unreasonable person or hard to get along with. I was still friendly, or at least civil, with most of my exes. Craig just rubbed me the wrong way. It was true that he was my first and longest relationship, but that wasn't what grated my cheese. Craig had used me. Really, truly, used me. He cheated on me at least twice that I knew of and dumped me numerous times for random, half-ass reasons. And every single time he came back around to kiss and make up, it was coincidentally right before a big exam. We had naked study parties rather than actual dates. The only reason the bastard scored higher than me on the exit exam was because I had spent the night before crying my eyes out after he had dumped me, yet again.

I was sure he was at least subconsciously responsible for my complete disdain for school. It was also possible that he was partially responsible for my lack of ambition. By staying at the bottom of the totem pole, he was less likely to try to use me as a stepping stone again. I should have expected him to come sniffing around once I started moving up in the world. Fortunately, I was beyond over him. The only thing I felt when I saw him now was the sting of embarrassment. No one likes to be reminded of how stupid they were once upon a time.

CHAPTER 17

*"The rules of fair play do not apply
in love and war."*
-John Lyly

By Wednesday evening, I was actually beginning to look forward to going back to work. Between the nerve-wracking training session with Bub and Josie's little study party obsession, my body and mind were suffering from extreme overload. Bub had gone mild with the flirting today, but only because the new lesson involved more concentration than I could muster with him breathing down my neck.

After another vigorous session with the throwing stars, he had busted out the text books. I was expected to identify all seventy-two demons who worked for Solomon, and the difference between an Incubus and a familiar. Bub even had a collection of bespelled jars containing the essence of various demons that he demanded I learn how to recognize by scent alone.

I almost cried when I got home and found the study gang waiting for me at the dining table. I seriously considered asking Josie to give back the spare key I'd given her. That was for emergencies only. Study parties did not register as an emergency in my book.

We barreled through three hours of studying, and just about the time that I decided throwing myself out a window might be a reasonable solution, they left.

I glanced around the condo and sighed. The hounds' bellies were full, and they were already napping on the rug in the sitting room. I was actually too tired to sleep, and my brain hurt something awful. Purgatory sounded pretty good about now. I grabbed my jacket and slammed the front door behind me.

It was a cooler night than usual, but I didn't mind. The breeze felt nice. I had only made it a couple blocks away from Holly House when an overwhelming sense of doom set in. The streetlight above me flickered and went out. I stopped and took a look around. The sidewalks were empty, an alarming situation in any big city. The hairs on the back of my neck stood at attention while every muscle in my body tightened, subconsciously preparing for whatever lurked in the dark. A hiss rolled through the air behind me, snapping furiously in my ear as something sliced through my jacket and up my back. I screamed and dropped to my knees.

I struggled to catch my breath. The sound came again, fiercer and quicker, biting into my flesh and sending me squirming against the pavement like a worm sizzling in the sun, certainly not the most elegant blow I've taken. The disappointment was almost worse than the pain. All that damned training, going to waste.

I wedged my elbows underneath me so I could roll onto my side and glare up at my attacker. She was bad news all the way, and I was raw hamburger on a demonic cooking show.

She couldn't have stood any taller than I, but her leathery black wings stretched out, extending the height of her horror to monstrous proportions. From my defeated position, I had a perfect view of her glossy black pedicure. It matched her black dress and the sandals laced up her taunt calves. Her skin glowed a pallid shade, just a hint grayer than my own pinkish tones, and it seemed to peek out like twilight from underneath her cursed Tinker Bell getup. Black curls hung down to the bend of her knees. She was easily breathtaking, though my breath was tortured by her less admirable characteristics, like the glinting barbs of the whip clenched in her dainty hand.

Slowly, she tilted her head and admired the short work she had made of me with a lucid grin. A single drop of blood oozed from one of her black eyes and slid down the apple of her cheek.

"Hello, little reaper," she whispered. Her voice vibrated with a pleasurable purr. The best I could do was grunt.

I highly considered playing dead, but the deities are not so easily fooled. And though I didn't recognize her, from her glow of power I could tell she was some form of lesser deity. I was fucked.

Worse than that, and despite the agony I was in, I felt a pinch of guilt for Bub. Granted, I wouldn't be around to see how creatively the committee would punish him, but I knew they would. And it would be all my fault. I should have begun my training sooner. I was an imp, and I was about to pay for it.

In my last moment of despair, a sharp pain bit into my leg and I remembered the strap of throwing stars Bub had buckled to my upper thigh before I left his place. The memory would have made me blush, but there would be time for that later I told myself, feeling a bit less like road kill. I rolled onto my back and seized a star. The lovely demon's smile wavered as she lifted her chin, eyeing me with amused curiosity. I smiled back this time and hurled the star at her. It made a juicy thud as it sank into the pearly flesh of her bosom.

"Ingrate!" she hissed. "Yours will be a bloody fate." She dug the star from her chest, hardly wincing, as she cracked her whip again.

I fumbled to my feet and shakily fetched another star. A little damage was the least I could do. Bub wouldn't be entirely disappointed in me. Who knew, I might even end up with a memorial statue in the park. My back ached, and I could feel the sting of sweat trickling down into my wounds. A light mist rose up from the street, growing thicker with each crack of bat-lady's whip. She lashed out at me again, but I dove away from her, throwing another star in her direction. The second one nicked her calf, hardly shifting her focus as she struck her whip again like a python with a twenty foot range.

I reached for another star just as the goddess's whip coiled around my wrist. I had a moment of pure terror as I gasped and jerked my gaze up to meet hers. Her cruel smile returned as she wrenched me up into the chilled night air.

Everything froze. For one peaceful second, I was suspended above the city and the fog below. The streetlights flickered, shrugging off the spell I hadn't noticed until too late. I sucked in a breath of air, feeling the dread and doom leaking from every pore and escaping back into the night. The bitch was mine.

I took advantage of the few seconds I spent plummeting back to the street below and sliced the star in my free hand across the whip. It spiraled away with a hiss, miraculously giving me enough time to roll over like a cat and land on all fours.

Bat-lady's disgruntled rage shook the streets of Limbo, rattling store windows and sending me scurrying to my feet. I tucked my last two stars into the palm of one hand with a quivering breath, trying not to notice the swelling in my limbs. I had the hopeless feeling that I should just give up. If Seth was so bent on destroying me, was there really any point in fighting? I mean, he had the power to take down

Osiris at one time. Of course, Osiris had a devoted goddess of a wife who had the power to resurrect him. Me? No such luck.

The dark goddess reeled her whip back, ready to slash me to ribbons, when a sickly buzz filled the air. She looked up just in time to spot a swarm of insects before they descended on her. Ripe howling swallowed up the night. I spun around, a tsunami of relief spilling over me.

"Miss me, love?" Bub perched on a roof across the street. The black lapels of his jacket flapped around him as he leapt down to join me.

"You... you were," I gasped, gripping the stars tighter.

"Watching?" he offered. "Supervising?"

"Spying!" I choked out, but the grin threatening to rip my face in half killed the accusation in midair. I was going to live after all.

Bat-lady's shrieking stopped suddenly and was replaced by a sharp pop accompanied by green smoke, like someone had just uncorked a bottle of vaporous poison. Bub waved his hand, fading his winged warriors back into nonexistence.

The fog had died down and so had my nerves. Now I was just shaking uncontrollably as the adrenaline fizzled out of my system. The city turned gray and spotty. Streetlights glared harsh reflections from every puddle, dully animating the lingering steam of battle. I wrapped my arms around myself and squeezed, trying to maintain a sliver of focus.

"Lana, are you all right?" Bub took a step towards me. His grin drooped and concern flicked through his dark eyes. I gave him a whisper of a laugh as the world faded and I tumbled into his open arms. Either my eyes were still open, or tarantulas were mating on my eyelids. I could hardly bring myself to care. Bub was saying my name, over and over, and somewhere inside, I was smiling.

CHAPTER 18

*"If you don' take care of yourself,
the undertaker will overtake that responsibility for you."*
-Carrie Latet

Meng's little temple was becoming a familiar sight. Unfortunately, that meant the nasty tea was becoming a familiar taste, and worried bitching was becoming a familiar sound.

"Stupid girl," Meng mumbled to herself as she arranged her tea tray on the bedside table. "Always in trouble, wasting my precious tea."

"Precious?" I croaked.

"She awake!" Meng hollered over her shoulder, ignoring me. She scooped up her tray and left just as Bub walked in.

"Hey." I sighed.

Bub frowned and sat on the edge of my bed. "Never a dull moment with you, eh?"

"I'm just tons of fun." I gave him a cheerless smile.

He took my hand in his, sending my heart racing. "That was Tisiphone," Bub said quietly. "She's the fiercest of the furies, the angry daughters of the night. Until very recently, she was employed in Tartarus, torturing the souls of murderers. Unless she's shrugged her morals along with her employer, you've got some explaining to do."

"What do you mean?" I said, fearing I already knew his answer.

Bub met my pleading gaze. "Tisiphone might have joined Seth and Caim's army willingly, but she will not attack another unless they fit her profile. She only torments those who have committed an unforgivable murder."

He leaned in closer, leaving only an inch between us so we wouldn't be overheard. "Who was it, Lana?"

I opened my mouth, but I couldn't make anything come out. It was answer enough. Bub let out a slow sigh and rested his forehead on the headboard. "Lana. What am I going to do with you?"

"Who else saw Tisiphone last night?" I asked.

Bub lifted his head to frown at me. "Not a soul. I told Meng and Cindy it was just a rogue demon, but you've got a serious problem on your hands."

"No kidding." I laughed and held up my bandaged arm. "I've got tests to take and papers to write."

"If Tisiphone is after you, she won't stop until the job is done. Especially after tonight. If she shows up again, I don't know how you're going to explain her presence to Grim." He looked genuinely worried about me.

I had to smile. "Let me worry about Grim."

"Am I interrupting?" Maalik crossed his arms and leaned against the doorframe. His eyes flicked down just as Bub released my hand and stood.

"No, not at all," Bub answered. "I was just making sure my pupil would be well enough for class tomorrow."

"Are you so concerned about all your pupils?" Maalik was steaming. I could almost smell the hellfire brewing in him. I shuddered.

"Someone needs to be concerned about her." Bub turned to face Maalik. The teasing mood he normally portrayed in these uncomfortable situations was gone, and so was Maalik's patience.

"Why do you think I put her up at Holly House?" he hissed.

"Well, we see how much good that did."

Maalik snarled at him, balling up his fists as his eyes began to swirl with flames, a dangerous warning I had never witnessed before.

"Please, you guys, I think I have enough turmoil in my life right now." For once, I was actually looking forward to Meng's tea.

"Of course." Bub's jaw clenched. He reached back to pat the top of my hand, never taking his eyes from Maalik. "You rest now, dear. I'll see you tomorrow."

Maalik's eyes didn't lose their fury until Bub stepped around him and disappeared down the hall. Then he turned to me and sighed. The fire swirling around his pupils faded to a smoky gray and then shifted back to their more soothing brown. Part of me was relieved I had never induced that much anger in him, but that didn't mean I was going to bow down and let him have free reign over my world. A line had to be drawn somewhere, but I was beginning to get the impression that Maalik was blind when it came to those lines.

"He saved my life tonight." I shoved myself back further into the pillows, relishing in the comfort more to ease my mind than my aching body. "You'd think you would have shown him a little gratitude."

"Lana." Maalik managed to look hurt a split second before he looked embarrassed. "I'm sorry, I just don't trust Beelzebub, or any demon for that matter. I know you're doing this for Cindy's vote. I guess I just wish she had found another way to help you without involving the Lord of the Flies."

"Why? Bub is the best Cindy has. Who could do a better job than him? And in case you haven't noticed, I need all the help I can get." I closed my eyes and clenched the bedspread in my fists, trying not to let the burning lashes on my back distract me. Maalik was getting too good at manipulating me when I was weakest. I needed to put a stop to it, but that was going to be tough to do all banged up in Meng's guest room.

Maalik pulled up a chair next to the bed and slid his hand under mine. "Lana, you should really wait until next year to apply for the Posy Unit. Limbo City just isn't safe right now —"

"Maalik." I gritted my teeth and glared at him. "I'm kind of in a lot of pain right now. So if it's all the same to you, I'd prefer to be rested and healed before you go trying to arrange yet another aspect of my life without my consent."

He pressed his lips together and looked down as I pulled my hand away from his. The line had been drawn. Now it was time to see if he respected me enough not to cross it.

"Well, I guess you should at least know that Grim has two nephilim escorts waiting outside for you. That first attack was obviously not as random as we had thought, and he doesn't want to risk losing you and what you know to the rebels."

I arched a brow. "Great."

"So it would probably not be such a good idea to visit Coreen's memorial any time soon."

I narrowed my eyes at him. He stood and bent over the bed to kiss me softly on the cheek. "Rest well, Lana. I'll see you later."

After he left, I let out a long breath. Things shouldn't have been this difficult between us, but then again, I had never dated a council member before. Maybe all men with power were this controlling. Hell, maybe the women were too. Maybe that's why most angels and deities only mingled with their own kind. It was nearly impossible to find a balance. Whoever had more power always felt the need to use it, even with the ones they loved.

A rattling at the door jerked my attention around with a gasp. Meng hobbled in, carrying a cup of tea. My shot nerves gave her a small smile of delight. She actually smiled back, which was a little eerie to behold with her stained teeth peeking out from under all her wrinkles.

"You safe here," she cackled. "Jai Ling learn very fast. She make special oil for lanterns in garden. It make nasty demons forget why they come."

I took the tea from her without hesitation and downed it in one swallow, much to Meng's surprise.

"Slow down!" she grumbled. "This not Mao-tai you can throw back like in bar." She disappeared around the corner to refill my cup, returning with a bowl of rice and vegetables as well. "Slower now. Give drink time to work," she instructed me before handing the tea over.

I nodded in agreement as I rolled my tongue around my cheek and crinkled my nose at the awful aftertaste. The rice would help a little, but what I wouldn't do for a basket of meat and cheese. I could already feel the tea doing its magic on my back. My skin tightened, and I actually felt the wounds begin to draw in on themselves and close. I sighed in amazement, feeling stronger and more at ease than I had in a very long time. The tea hadn't worked this fast before.

"You do something different this time?" I gave Meng a skeptical smile.

She gave a short nod and moved closer, taking the chair by my bed. "And you have my vote, reaper, if you do one thing for me."

"Not again," I groaned.

Was there a single council member who ever did anything unless it could somehow benefit them? I wasn't even sure about Maalik anymore, and now Meng too. I should have guessed. It wasn't like she was a good buddy of mine, going out of her way to ease my suffering, but come on. Enough was enough.

"Listen here," she snapped. "Meng help you. You help Meng. Why so hard to do? All I want is you to ask Grim to give me meeting with Fates, like he promise. Ask him, that's all."

"Really?" I raised an eyebrow.

"No worse than demons." She stood with a huff and set the bowl of rice down hard on the bedside table before stomping out of the room.

I sipped at my tea and picked the carrots and peppers out of the rice while enjoying the tingling sensation of my healing skin. It felt like feathers and silk handkerchiefs roaming up and down my spine, giving me some fresh bedroom ideas I decided to stow away for future reference. I'd stomach the abominable tea for that any day. I had almost drifted off in a blissful, mindless sleep when a sharp knock came at the door. I didn't bother opening my eyes. I could smell the sniveling swine as he entered my room.

"You're building quite a fan club among the demons," Horus said and clicked his tongue.

I opened my eyes long enough to glare at him, but ended up chuckling instead. He had brought me another basket of meat and cheese with daisies. As much as I hated him for blackmailing me, I couldn't help but appreciate his efforts to win my favor. It was almost as if he were apologizing in a subtle, god-like way for being the shit that he was.

"Hand over the basket and I won't have Meng chase you outta here with her broom," I said, trying to suppress my smile.

"With pleasure." Horus smiled and set the basket down next to me. He waited until I had devoured a few sticks of sausage before taking the chair by my bed. "I would like to know if there are any measures that can be taken, on my part, to ensure your safety," he said.

"Ha," I mumbled through a mouthful of Swiss cheese. "You just want to make sure I don't die before getting a chance to break the law for you."

"Well." He grinned. "That, too."

I swallowed and wiped a hand across my face before pushing my tangled black curls behind my ear. "Apparently, I'm being babysat by the Nephilim Guard until further notice."

"Hmmm. I was wondering what they were doing outside. Probably for the best."

"Maalik thinks I should wait and apply for the Posy Unit next year."

"Does he now?" Horus sighed. His brows dropped into a more thoughtful line. "And what do you think?" Well, he certainly knew where my pride button was. But that didn't mean I was suicidal.

"I think I'd like to get this over with sooner rather than later." Horus grinned again, but I waved him off. "That doesn't mean I don't see why he's so concerned," I said, setting the basket on the bedside table. "And I don't think all this extra attention will be very good for the little assignment you'll be sending me on soon. How am I supposed to secretly tag souls with demons breathing down my neck and guards following me around?"

"That does present a problem." Horus propped his elbow on the edge of the bed and cupped his chin. "Anubis will hopefully have some good news for us soon."

"He better." I snatched the pillows from behind my head and dropped them into my lap so I could graze my back against the headboard. Meng's tingle-tea was wearing off, and my aches and pains were returning with the addition of a horrid itch, prancing along my mostly healed back.

Horus gave me a funny look and stood.

"Hey," I called as he turned around. "Think you could scratch my back before you go?"

"Uh." He held his hands up, clenching and unclenching his fingers with a nervous air about him. "Sure," he answered reluctantly.

I leaned forward and peeled my shirt up over my shoulders.

"Here?" he asked, gently scratching along my spine.

"Oh yeah," I groaned. At least I didn't have to worry about him cutting my throat while I wasn't looking, and it sure was fun watching him squirm. A god, afraid of me. Well, at least someone was.

"Thanks," I said, pulling my shirt back down and replacing the pillows.

Horus nodded, looking relieved to have some distance between us again. He cleared his throat and made a beeline for the door, keeping a wary eye on me over his shoulder.

"Feel better soon," he said and then disappeared down the hall.

CHAPTER 19

"What sculpture is to a block of marble,
education is to the soul."
-Joseph Addison

I would have loved to skip my mentoring class Thursday night, and it's not like I didn't have a good excuse, but I really needed to pull off a passing grade. It wouldn't do any good bickering with Maalik about staying in school if I flunked out. Besides that, I really doubted Grim wanted to pay for my tuition twice. I imagine that's why he sent the nephilim escorts instead of a note to excuse me from class. He was bound and determined to keep Kevin under my wing and in my hair. I guess he figured I'd be less inclined to break any rules with a witness around.

The nephilim escorts Grim had assigned to me were quite the duo. Abe, the taller of the two, did all the speaking. His partner, Frank, just nodded and grunted occasionally when addressed. They each carried one of the golden spears crafted by Warren and wore golden armor with a royal blue cape. Their helmets were fashioned like the ancient Romans, with a matching blue crest. They managed not to crack a single smile in my presence, though I was hardly surprised.

I was demon bait, and if they failed to protect me, it would look bad for their fragile new status in Limbo City.

Abe insisted that we travel by coin from Meng's to Holly House, where he took it upon himself to search my condo for intruders before allowing me to enter. I quickly fed the hounds and changed into a fresh pair of jeans and a green turtleneck. The nephilim seemed to relax a bit at Holly House. It was highly unlikely that a demon would breach the front gate, let alone the tenth floor. I gathered my school books and grudgingly followed Abe and Frank back downstairs and outside, where our coins would be active once again.

I stopped Abe before we ventured on. "I don't want to interfere with your assignment, but do you think you could keep a little more distance between us when we get to the Academy? I don't want to draw any more attention than we have to."

Abe frowned at me and looked over at Frank who gave a soft grunt. "We'll do what we can," he answered.

We made it to my mentoring class twenty minutes early, which meant there weren't too many reapers around to notice the guards showing up with me. Abe had a quick word with the professor and positioned himself in a back corner of the classroom, while Frank stood watch just outside the door.

My mentoring class was as boring as Grace's Wandering Souls class was annoying. Edgar Dorian, an entirely bland fourth generation reaper, instructed the class in a joyless monotone, mostly reading aloud from a grossly outdated textbook. The only thing I could appreciate about the guy was the fact that he didn't make us do group work, which was surprising, since the class was supposed to teach us how to mentor another reaper.

I couldn't imagine being paired up with anyone in the class for an assignment. While it was true that no one was as unappealing as Craig Hogan, the other students weren't exactly warming up to me either. I'm sure part of it had to do with the fact that I was the only reaper taking the class who already had an apprentice. Apparently, I was the only one who thought that wasn't something to be envious of.

As the other students arrived, it became painfully obvious that my private life was not so private after all. I couldn't count the number of glances that began on Abe and ended on me. I cringed, thinking how impossible my next shopping trip to Athena's was going to be.

Edgar looked up at the clock on the wall behind his desk and cleared his throat. "Please turn to page four hundred and twelve and follow along," he said in his Ben Stein voice. "The last chapter we will be reviewing covers how to command respect and obedience from your apprentice over their century term with you. Independence will be a natural struggle for your pupils, but it is a lesson you are expected to teach them, as it will also prepare them for a lifelong citizenship in Limbo City. We will first examine the benefits of training apprentices with the punishment and reward system..."

When I actually paid attention to the class lectures, I found myself disgusted with the content more often than not. I couldn't remember Saul ever using any of the techniques I was expected to learn and use. Of course, Saul was a first generation reaper who was taking on apprentices a few hundred years before the academy even opened. The fact that I had already broken more than half the rules with Kevin so far was a bit discouraging as well. I really couldn't see myself commanding respect and obedience from him. Once again, I thought about how much better off he'd be if Josie had been selected as his mentor. The thought of her commanding his obedience made me picture her as a dominatrix and I had to put a hand over my mouth and cough to hide my laughter.

Class couldn't go by quickly enough. My skin crawled from all the eyes lingering on me. I was plotting how to make a mad dash out of there without upsetting the guards too badly, when Abe approached the professor. Edgar nodded and peered at me over his tiny spectacles.

"Ms. Harvey?" He crooked a finger at me. I gathered my books and hurried to the front of the class.

"Didn't want to lose you in the crowd after class," Abe explained once we were in the hall. Frank fell in step next to us and handed me a coin. I wanted to argue that it wasn't necessary, but I knew it wouldn't do any good.

When we arrived back at Holly House, Gabriel was waiting in the lobby. From the look on his face, I could tell he had heard about my second trip to Meng's. He took my arm without a word and walked with us to the elevators. We rode up to the tenth floor in silence. He stopped the guards at my front door.

"She's perfectly safe with me," he all but growled. "You can stand watch out here."

Abe nodded to Frank, and they turned to press their backs to either side of the threshold.

Once inside, Gabriel pulled me into the living room, out of range of any eavesdropping. My elbow was beginning to ache from his grasp, but I was too afraid to speak. He seized my other arm and pulled me around to face him.

"What the hell is going on, Lana?" he said.

I opened my mouth, but nothing would come out.

His brow dipped and he leaned in closer. "We've been friends far too long for you to not trust me, and while I'm waiting patiently for you to come to your senses and talk to me, you're out nearly getting yourself killed every other night. So spill. Right now."

My breath caught in my chest, and I felt a sob rising in my throat. Tears stung my eyes. I was trembling, terrified of what I was about to confess, even though Gabriel was right. I knew I could trust him more than anyone else in all of Eternity. Including Maalik.

"I killed Wosyet," I whispered, squeezing my eyes shut.

119

"Impossible." He gave me a gentle shake.

"No. I did, and now the rebels want me dead and Horus is blackmailing me into joining the Posy Unit to find another soul for him." I sighed, knowing the momentary relief wouldn't last, but still somehow hoping Gabriel would know what to do. I opened my eyes to see his horrified expression.

He swallowed hard. "Holy shit."

"And I'm deep in it."

"How the hell did you get yourself into this big of a mess and not tell me until now? Wait, does Josie know all this?"

I froze. "Not exactly. She knows I'm gunning for the Posy Unit to get a soul for Horus, but I didn't tell her about Wosyet or how Horus's job isn't exactly sanctioned by the council."

"Does anyone else know?"

"No, and we really need to keep it that way."

"Really?" he scoffed and dropped my arms to pace around the coffee table. "I don't know how you killed a deity. Even a lesser one should have been immune to your efforts. If this gets out, you're dead." He paused and touched my arm again, more gently this time. "Lana, this is really bad. God, I don't even know what I can do to help you at this point."

"Well, I feel so much better now," I said dryly.

"You need to lie low and keep those guards close. If you absolutely must travel, do so by coin. Let's not risk anything."

"Well, that sounds like a nice paranoid existence."

Gabriel's grip on my arm tightened again. "This is serious, Lana. Be cautious. At least until we eliminate the rebel base in Limbo."

"I'm just sick about all this. I've never felt so helpless, and I can't stand it." I rested my forehead on his shoulder.

"It's going to be all right, Lana. I promise."

"I really hate promises."

Gabriel put a hand on the back of my neck and kissed the top of my head. "Yeah, but you know I actually keep mine."

CHAPTER 20

"Love is like war:
easy to begin but very hard to stop."
-Henry Mencken

A warm breeze drifted up from the River Styx and tugged at my curls as Bub's little houseboat sputtered along its way to Tartarus. We hadn't said much since he picked me up from the gates of Hell. The nephilim escorts were relieved that their duties were only required in Limbo, but not nearly as relieved as I was. I hadn't realized just how valuable my personal space was until Abe tried to follow me into a public restroom. I was almost positive Grim would assign a female nephilim to me upon my return to the city.

Saul and Coreen scampered from one end of the boat to the next, taking in all the sights and scents. They hadn't been to Hell since our short vacation last year, and they had only been out of the condo for short walks through the park since the apartment incident. The Nephilim Guard welcomed the extra protection when I suggested they accompany us. They needed more exercise, and I really loathed the idea of the guards following us around the park for everyone to see.

Bub abandoned the steering wheel and joined me on the deck of the boat. He was in jeans again and a gray dress shirt with the sleeves rolled up. I was really growing fond of his casual look. He leaned his back against the railing and folded his arms, frowning at me.

"So how'd you do it?" he asked.

"Excuse me?" I blinked at him.

His gaze narrowed. "Let's not play games, pet."

"How did I do what?" I stammered.

"Wosyet?"

"Oh. That." I pressed my lips together and stuffed my hands in the pockets of my jean jacket. Of course he was going to want an explanation, and I owed him one. He kept my secret, after all. If he wanted, he could have had my head on a pike by now. That was a sobering thought. Which led to a disturbing question. Either he really liked me, well enough to preserve my life anyway, or he was afraid of what else I could do. Or maybe he was like everyone else and was still wondering how I might be able to help him with his own personal agenda.

"I'm waiting." Bub clicked his tongue nervously.

"Decapitation. With my axe," I said matter-of-factly.

Bub's eyes widened at my crassness. He unfolded his arms and turned to rest them on the railing with a sigh. "Where did you get this axe?"

"A vender in Limbo." I didn't want to incriminate Warren for something that wasn't his fault, but if I could pass off the incident as a mishap caused by my weapon of choice instead of exposing my secret, maybe, just maybe, I could get out of this alive. "It was in self-defense. Wosyet ambushed my team while we were collecting a soul on that special assignment last fall."

"Self-defense or not, your ability to slay a deity, even a lesser one, is enough to charge Grim with breaching the peace treaty." Bub looked less than thrilled. "If this gets out, the rebels will use it to gain a larger following. It could mean war for Eternity. Again."

I swallowed. "Well, I guess we just won't let it get out."

"Easier said than done. Especially now that Tisiphone is onto you." He sighed heavily.

"What do you suggest we do?"

"I don't know. Maybe we can convince the council somehow that Tisiphone's morals have gone askew since she abandoned her post. You obviously slayed some lesser demons last fall as well, so perhaps we can credit her vengeance to that?"

"You would know better than I how the council would receive that." I ran a hand through my curls and looked out over the river.

I had to admit, I was a bit surprised at how eager Bub was to help devise a cover story for me, and even more surprised that he didn't poke and prod at me to discover what he might have to gain in return. I was still holding my breath, waiting for the catch to reveal itself.

Bub furrowed his brow a moment and then relaxed. "I think it just might work." He gave me a quick grin and went to kill the engine as we neared his summer home. Jack, his demon butler, waited on the dock, readying the ropes to secure the boat.

My stomach was doing flip-flops, and it wasn't from the ride down the river. The number of people who knew the truth about Wosyet's demise was growing far too fast. I had a feeling the rebels were just targeting me from vague assumptions based on the assignment details they received from Seth. They hadn't gone after Josie or Kevin, but then again, I was the one put in charge after Coreen. I shuddered, thinking about how much more attention they'd be giving me if they actually had any substantial proof.

We walked Saul and Coreen around the property once to give them some boundaries to work with, and they began vigorously patrolling Bub's estate. It wasn't really necessary, but they were thrilled to have something useful to do.

Bub led me back to the den where we held our awkward little sessions. "I took the liberty of gathering your throwing stars, and Jack has cleaned them. Are you feeling up to physical work or should we stick to the books today?"

"No books, please," I begged. Josie's study parties were really starting to wear on me. Lately I was spending the majority of my waking hours with my nose in a book. I had nightmares about reading a textbook that never ended. I just keep turning page after page, and the words just kept getting longer and harder to pronounce.

I tugged off my jacket and threw it over one of the couches, revealing my blue, sleeveless turtleneck. It was a favorite and perfectly covered the scar on my neck. The material was a soft cotton, so it stayed cool on my skin, even though Bub kept his thermostat a good ten degrees higher than most. I had the sneaking suspicion that he did that just to encourage women to remove more clothing. My jeans were worn and had holes in the knees, so they stayed nice and cool as well.

Bub's eyes glanced over my bare arms before they reached my face. "Aside from the throwing stars, which you're obviously comfortable using now, there are some defensive maneuvers we could go over."

"Super."

He grinned and wandered over behind the corner bar. He fixed us both a drink and rummaged around in a cabinet below, tucking something small in the breast pocket of his shirt before joining me around the coffee table. He set our drinks down and motioned for me to sit with him on the sofa.

"Most demons give off a certain heat signature, and with enough practice and focus, even a reaper should be able to sense one approaching and their exact position. This goes even beyond the scent trial, and will enable you to fight a demon should you find yourself in total darkness, which is considered an ideal ambush setting for most demons." He pulled a small wooden box from his pocket and set it on the table before us.

"What's that?"

Bub gave me one of his devilish grins. "It's a shortcut." He opened the box and sat back to watch my reaction.

I frowned and folded my arms. It looked like a box of Cuban cigars, except it was small enough to belong on a desk in a dollhouse.

"A shortcut?" I raised an eyebrow. "Are you telling me I have to get high in order to sense a demon approaching."

Bub laughed and picked up one of the tiny smokes, running it under his nose with a savory sigh. "Just the first time or two. That should give you enough direction to get you there on your own afterwards."

"I don't think I care for this plan."

"This is the purest blend of raskov. A clan of Slavic crones harvest it in Summerland. The effects last no more than an hour or two, so you have nothing to fear."

My skeptical glare stayed in place. Bub rolled his eyes. "It seems a demonstration is in order." He held a hand out to me. I cautiously took it and let him lead me around the sofa to the open area in the middle of the room. Bub's hand slid up my back. My breath hissed out before I could contain myself. While the slashes Tisiphone had left me with were nearly healed, they were still sensitive.

"Sorry." I blushed. "I'm—"

Bub took my arm and pulled me around, lifting my blouse up to examine my scarred back. He pressed a gentle finger against one of the marks. I was surprised at the coolness of his touch.

"I sometimes forget how fragile you are. You're not quite human and not quite deity. It's perplexing to say the least." His fingers trailed up my spine, lingering softly on each mark until they found my shoulder.

I stiffened. "We have work to do."

"We do? We do." He stepped away in a daze, and blushed a deeper shade than I had.

126

I might have been flattered if I hadn't thought his affections had something to do with his illicit nature and the fact that he was spending too much time training with me to get it out of his system properly. It did seem odd that his comfort level had shifted. I'd seen far crasser advances from him in the past, and none that ever made him blush.

"Where were we?" He shook his head. "Okay, close your eyes."

I let my arms fall to my sides and did what he said.

"Now, concentrate and tell me when you can feel my heat against you."

I felt myself flush as I grinned. Sometimes I wondered if he just couldn't help sounding perverse. Perhaps it came as naturally as breathing to him. In a few moments I felt a slight warmth to my right. I opened my eyes and found Bub standing six feet away from me.

"Well, that was better than I expected from you, but it's still not good enough to do you any good in battle. We can do better." He put the raskov roll between his lips and lit it with a small zippo, taking a deep pull.

The thick smoke drifted over to me and soon fogged over the entire room. The scent was soothing, like ancient spices being burned over a woodstove. I was momentarily lightheaded and hesitated when Bub offered the smoke to me.

"The dizziness will pass," he assured me.

I took the smoke and lifted it to my lips, taking a slow drag. The sensation Bub had been trying to describe hit me at full force. His body was suddenly a pulsing, red light burned into my consciousness. I was shocked to sense a fainter red pulse coming from further away in the house. My eyes widened. "There's another—"

"Jack. My butler," he answered, reading my mind.

I relaxed. The haze in the room seemed to thicken and the red pulses of Bub and Jack intensified until they were mere outlines containing webbed, neon lights. I turned away

127

Angela Roquet

from Jack's glow and focused on Bub's, stepping closer to the demon. I lifted a hand and reached out for him, watching as the pulse of his glow quickened. My own pulse seemed to slow. It was a dull, heavy sound that vibrated through my chest and down to my fingertips, hovering over Bub's chest. The heat coming from him was almost too much. I started to pull my hand back, but Bub caught it and pressed it to his chest, drawing a gasp from me. The pulsing red light shot through my fingers, up my arm, and into my chest, sparking my dull heartbeat to life once again. I felt dizzy. Laughing, I pressed my remaining hand to the other side of his chest and drew a gasp from him this time. Like an electrical current, the red light flowed through my other arm, back into him. Even through the haze, I saw the whites of his eyes expand in surprise.

Bub's hands slid over mine, up to my shoulders, and then down my sides to rest on my hips. The red pulse quickened again as he pulled me against him. Some little nagging voice in my head kept insisting that this was all wrong, but for the life of me, I couldn't say why. My consciousness was floating around somewhere in the smoke, and I was enthralled with the pulsing red light. Absolutely hypnotized. Which is why I couldn't even fathom pulling away when Bub crushed his mouth against mine.

His forked tongue slipped out and caressed the inside of my mouth, deeper than anyone had ever explored before. He tasted like hot chocolate. I felt the length of his lust press into my stomach and I moaned into his mouth. The nagging voice was getting louder. Something stabbed at my heart, and guilt began to settle in my gut. I ripped myself away from him.

"No," I rasped.

"No?" he echoed, as though the very word was foreign to him. I imagined it usually was when it came to women.

"No," I said, firmer this time and pried our bodies apart. I was taken, and as mad as I was at Maalik, I couldn't do this

128

to him. I'm not perfect, and I've screwed up my fair share of relationships, but I've got my limits.

"Maalik," he said, reading my mind again. He looked angry for a moment, but it slowly fizzled into a distant sadness. "Right." He let go of me and backed away, shaking his head as though he were clearing his mind.

I couldn't find my voice. I couldn't even look at him. My hands felt awkward. Now that they weren't on him, I hardly knew what to do with them. I laid one across my stomach and crossed the other over my chest.

"We'll pick this up tomorrow. I don't think there's much more we can do today with the state we're in," he said, the innuendo holding more bitterness rather than its typical cheer. He rounded the couch and picked up the wooden box of smokes, closing it sharply.

I didn't say goodbye. I just left, slipping quietly out of the den. I found Coreen and Saul outside and waited for them to brush against my legs before rolling my coin to take us back to the front gates of Holly House. Abe and a new female guard were waiting for me. I gritted my teeth, fiercely hoping she wouldn't try to follow me into my own bathroom. I had the miserable desire to cry my eyes out in the privacy of my shower. I really didn't need an audience.

CHAPTER 21

"Sorrow is the mere rust of the soul.
Activity will cleanse and brighten it."
-Samuel Johnson

I was apprehensive about seeing Bub again the next day.
I thought I might go into cardiac arrest when he called to tell
me to wear running shoes and light workout clothes. This
was a new turn in my training. That much exposed flesh
couldn't be a good idea around him.

I was so damned nervous that I tried on six different
outfits, twice each, finally settling on an orange sports bra
and gray spandex shorts that cut off just above the knee. I
dug through the antique wardrobe until I found a loose gray
tank top to pull over the revealing ensemble. I didn't bother
covering my neck. It wasn't like it was a big secret anymore
and the scar had faded quite a bit. I slipped on matching
orange and gray sneakers and pulled my curls back with an
elastic band.

Saul and Coreen waited anxiously by the front door with
their leads. The hounds were smart and knew that when I
wore workout clothes, it usually meant a good, long run for
them. They had polished off their breakfast in record time. I

had skipped breakfast altogether, and I'd only drank one cup of my beloved coffee. I was jittery enough as it was.

Abe and Linda, the new female guard assigned to me, waited just outside my door. They both managed to look tired, yet still fiercely alert. After my pity party in the shower, I had found my manners and offered the guest bed to them if they wanted to stand watch in shifts. They had politely refused, stating they would sleep while I was training with Bub.

I had to hand it to the nephilim. They were top notch guards. Not a one of them had said a cross word to me or questioned what I was doing at the academy or why I was training with the Lord of the Flies. Their demeanor was entirely professional and focused. They were really proud of their new station in Limbo and seemed desperate not to screw things up for their kind.

Abe and Linda silently walked me just outside the front gates of Holly House where coin travel was accessible. They scanned the sidewalks and stood firm as I bid them farewell and rolled my coin.

Bub had asked that I come directly to his house and forgo the gates of Hell. It was a hell of a lot more expensive to travel that far by coin, but he was picking up the tab, so I did as he asked. I was more than a little bummed to be missing out on the boat ride down the Styx.

I found Bub waiting outside for me. He was in a pair of black spandex shorts that hugged his muscled thighs. A white cutoff tee shirt showed off his arms. I hadn't realized just how nicely built he was before. Of course, he had felt nice beneath my hands. I blushed at the memory and shook my head to clear it before approaching him.

He stretched one arm across his chest and stepped forward into a lunge. "We're working on endurance and speed today. Your hounds will love this. We're taking a run through the mountain trails."

"A run? I do that all the time with the hounds in the park."

"Trust me. You've never taken a run like the one we're taking today. You're going to want to stretch first."

I rolled my eyes and mirrored his lunge, pulling an arm across my chest. We stretched together in silence for another twenty minutes. Each second felt more awkward than the last, but I knew anything I tried to say would sound like forced filler to distract us from the incident of the day before, which would in turn make us think about the incident even more.

Bub finally gave me a strained smile. "Okay, try to keep up." And then he was off. Saul and Coreen dashed ahead of him, occasionally glancing back to make sure they were going the right direction. I started off slower, bringing up the rear.

The red-orange mountains behind Bub's house were closer than they had originally appeared. It took all of ten minutes to run across the flat, dusty desert and reach their base. I was good and warmed up by then, but I was used to mild terrains. The steep, uphill climb was going to be a challenge. Saul and Coreen looked more excited about the challenge than I.

Bub stopped at the foot of the mountain trail and stretched a moment as he waited for me to catch up. "Doing all right?"

"Yeah." I had hardly broken sweat.

"Good." He took off at a steady pace uphill. The hounds sprang ahead once again.

My body began to protest about thirty minutes later. Although, the scenery on the mountain trail was a blissful distraction. Small, tangled shrubs dotted the parched earth, with a splash of green cacti here and there. The trail weaved through mountain tunnels that provided occasional shade, but little relief from the heat. The view of the Styx from so high up was inspiring. I could see all the way to Hades' smoking manor at the heart of Tartarus. The sky was a deep pink, tinted with tangy shades of orange. It contrasted beautifully with the parched red and gray landscape.

I caught up to Bub at a level interval in the trail that held an observation deck with a massive telescope. He was stretching again and looked entirely unfazed by the run so far. I bent over and placed my hands on my knees, panting to catch my breath. My tank top was soaked.

"That was a nice warm-up," he said, grinning.

I glared up at him and then over to the telescope. He followed my gaze and blushed. "My estate is bespelled to show the stars from the living realm. That little charm cost almost as much as the house."

I had seen the stars on the human side a few times while working late. Normally, I was on a nine-to-five type of schedule, but Grim liked to punish me with an extra heavy workload when I bent his rules. The stars were almost worth the late night harvests. They were breathtaking. Apparently, Bub thought so too. His eyes lit up at my interest.

"You could come out one evening and view them, if you like," he offered, uncharacteristically blushing again.

"Yeah, maybe," I said.

He shuffled his feet around a moment and then seemed to remember what we were doing. "Let's get back on track. We've got a ways to go." He took off back up the trail.

The hounds lingered behind him this time, glancing back at me. I groaned and sprinted after them.

Three hours later, I decided that I hated Bub. Every muscle in my body screamed. I was drenched. My curls were dripping with sweat and my skin felt gritty with salt. I had the dreaded feeling that he was trying to break me for some reason, but I refused to complain.

We finally reached the top of the mountain and the end of the trail. Bub turned around to face me. His cheeks were red and his hair artfully mused. He was breathing hard, but not like we had just ran our asses off for nearly four hours.

He smiled at me and then gazed out at Tartarus, fanned out below us.

It was a painfully beautiful view. The River Styx lazily floated past Bub's manor and disappeared beyond the sunbaked horizon. Little smoke tails lifted from three tiny Styx Stops that could only be noticed from this high up. The sky had faded to a dusty orange, and it seemed to swallow us whole. The intensity of it took away what little breath I had left. I stood in awe for a long while, and when I turned around, Bub was watching me. In all my life I had never met someone who could break a heart with a single look, the way he was doing now.

He closed the distance between us in a few short steps and reached up to gently skim his fingers along my arm. I closed my eyes as my pulse quickened. There was no denying what his touch did to my body, but he didn't need to know what it was doing to the rest of me.

"Look at me," he whispered.

I pressed my lips together and closed my eyes even tighter, shaking my head. He snatched my arms, forcing me to meet his stare with a gasp. His dark eyes were wilder than usual. Flecks of gold and red swirled in them like the stirrings of a cyclone. Then his lips were on mine. It could hardly be called a kiss. It was too harsh and forced. I struggled against him, knowing he was far stronger than I and it would do no good. He finally released me with a growl of frustration.

I pressed my fingers to my bruised mouth and gaped at him a second before my shock was replaced with anger. Before I could think twice about it, my hand sprang out in a wide arc and slapped him hard across the face.

"I'm sorry. I'm sorry." He stepped back and ran a hand through his hair, haphazardly spiking it into a crazy mess. "I thought the exercise would help blow off some of this crazy energy I've got building up, but it seems to have grown worse."

"Oh." That was all I could muster as my heart twisted itself into a tangled knot inside my chest.

Bub paced the ridge of the mountaintop a few times, frustration and confusion seeping from. "I think we're good for today. Let's take a break tomorrow and start over on Monday. You can travel back by coin from here." And poof, just like that, he was gone, leaving a blast of sulfuric smoke in his place.

I stood alone in the silence for a moment, shifting through a plethora of emotions with alarming speed. I was so angry and confused, I wanted to cry or scream. I was supposed to be in love with Maalik. This awkward situation with Bub shouldn't have had this sort of effect on me. I shouldn't have been wondering if I was falling for a demon. My life was complicated enough. Trusting the prince of darkness with my heart was so not a good idea. Of course, I had done dumber things in the past.

I had hardly made it through my front door with the hounds when the doorbell rang. I had a moment of panic. What if it was Maalik? Would he smell Bub on me? What if it was another demon trying to assassinate me? Of course, then I remembered I was at Holly House. I groaned and opened the door, still in my sweaty workout clothes.

Jenni Fang waited in the hall. I suddenly remembered there was a study party planned for the evening.

"You're early." I let her in and closed the door behind her.

"I wanted to talk to you before everyone else arrived." She followed me into the kitchen. Maybe it was just me, but Jenni seemed different lately. She was lighter and more social. She smiled more and dressed in brighter colors. It seemed awkward and misplaced at times, but it was still a nice change. Today she wore a pair of jean capris with a ruffled, purple blouse. Her long, black hair was fastened in a knot and held up by a pair of glittery chopsticks. She smiled, noticing me admiring her.

I smiled back. "Coffee?"

"Sure."

I filled us each a mug and we ventured into the sitting room, taking opposite couches from each other. I tried to put Bub out of my mind so I could give her my full attention.

"Lana, I know we're not very close, but I trust Josie's judgment, and I've grown fond of you these past few months. I admire your newfound career ambitions. I'm not exactly sure what your motives are." She paused, giving me a moment to consider filling in the blanks for her.

"Ah, that's the million dollar question lately, isn't it?" I laughed.

She chewed her bottom lip and frowned. "I have my theories."

"Everyone does." I hated it when people beat around the bush. Was it really so hard to come right out and ask a direct question? Not that I would answer it, but still.

Jenni sighed. "Your current motives are really none of my business. However, I would like to offer another motive for you to consider, if you're interested."

Wow. I really hadn't expected to ever draw this much attention from Jenni. This was the most I had ever heard her talk. She was normally more reserved and mysterious.

Jenni Fang, a sixth generation reaper who intimidated most second generation reapers, was rumored to be the head of an underground association of reapers working towards deityship rights. I had a feeling I knew what she was offering. A year ago, I would have refused her because I was in enough hot water with Grim. Now I would refuse her because the events of the previous year had redefined the term hot water for me.

I really should have known more about Jenni, considering how one of my best friends was her roommate. I imagined Josie stayed quiet because she either knew I wouldn't be interested or because she was sworn to secrecy. Josie was a stickler for rules. She pointed out the ones I broke every chance she got. Not that I let that stop me. At least I had her beat in the stubborn department.

Jenni patiently stared me down. She crossed her legs and folded her hands on top of her knees.

"I'm sorry, Jenni. I think I know where you're going with this, and I'm flattered. Really. But I just can't fit anything else on my plate right now." I gave her an apologetic smile.

Jenni blinked a few times and tilted her head to one side. "I'm sorry. I thought with all your new future goals that you would be interested in some better reward for your efforts."

"I think *better* would be a matter of opinion at this point." If a group of reapers did rebel and demand deityship, Grim would have no problem waving a hand and wiping them out of existence, and gosh, I really liked existing, even with all the current drama.

Jenni blushed. "Our profit yields are at least double that of any savings or investment plan available to reapers in Limbo City. Where exactly have you found a better deal?"

"Excuse me? What are we talking about again?" Now it was my turn to blush.

"Retirement plans."

"Retirement?" I laughed.

"Of course. What else would we be talking about?" To her credit, she looked even more confused, and maybe a bit annoyed.

"Never mind." It occurred to me that perhaps I had taken some rotten gossip to heart. "Tell me more about the plans you offer."

Jenni's smile returned and her eyes twinkled. "It's really quite genius." She rattled on for nearly an hour, and when she was done, I was compelled to agree. It really was genius. The basic plans required a reaper to turn over between three and eight percent of their income for a term of five to eight hundred years. This collection was then invested in reasonably stable stocks in various afterlives. As expected, the longer a reaper invested and the higher the percentage of income they invested, the larger their retirement payments would be. Some plans were set up like an extended vacation, with a reaper returning to the field after a hundred years or so. But some of the plans were set up with continued investment, so a reaper could, in theory, enjoy eternal retirement.

"Sounds pretty fool-proof," I said when she finished.

"It is." She beamed. "And I'm going to present this plan to Grim soon to request he start offering it as a withholding option on his payroll. I'm hoping he will invest as well. It would be profitable for him, and it would mean more retirement funds for the rest of us."

"Sign me up." The more reapers on her list, the better. Grim was a numbers kind of guy, and he was fully aware of the need for incentives and goals among the reapers. He'd be a fool for passing up her offer.

"Great!" Jenni clapped her hands together, a little joyous gesture I had never seen her do before. "I'll drop off a contract Monday before you head to class for your final."

I groaned and closed my eyes. I was so not looking forward to standing at the front of the class with Craig. This was going to be a nightmare.

Jenni read my pained expression all too well. "It will be over before you know it. Then we can celebrate."

"Honestly? I'd take the class all over again if I didn't have to be in the same room with Craig Hogan."

Jenni nodded. "Ah, yes. Mr. Hogan. He's a rather good reaper. It's a shame that he's turned out to be such an egotistical slug. I don't think I know a single female reaper who doesn't either hate him or adore him."

I snorted. "I better get a shower before the others show up. Help yourself to more coffee."

"Thanks."

I left Jenni in the sitting room and went to freshen up with a nice hot shower. I could still feel Bub's kiss on my mouth and his scent lingered on my skin. I wouldn't be remembering a damn thing we studied if I couldn't manage to wash the memory of him away.

CHAPTER 22

"Three may keep a secret,
if two of them are dead."
-Benjamin Franklin

Grim sat with his back to me, reclining on one of the wide benches that lined the sidewalk circling the bronze statues of Saul and Coreen in the park. He wore brown slacks and a white polo shirt, which was more dressed down than I had ever seen him before. A dusty fedora rested on his head, and a dark leather briefcase lay under the bench.

This certainly wasn't what I had anticipated when Abe rang my doorbell extra early Sunday morning, insisting that we leave right away for a private meeting with the boss man. I dressed myself while half awake and luckily managed to match a blue blouse with a blue and gray plaid skirt. I chose black ballet flats over my favorite boots, hoping to avoid tripping as I sleepwalked my way out of Holly House so Abe could coin us off to the meeting. I hadn't expected the meeting to be in the park. I pinched myself to be sure I was awake and not having a nightmare. If Grim had discovered Winston's stash and found out about our visits, it was highly probable that I wouldn't survive the meeting. I held my breath as I walked over to him.

"Take a seat, Ms. Harvey," he said, never taking his eyes from Coreen's statue.

I quietly obeyed.

The small clearing that the memorials stood in was surrounded by clusters of young tulip trees. The sticky, sweet perfume of rotting petals stung my eyes. I hadn't really noticed them before as I rushed in and out for my visits to Winston, but they really were quite lovely. We sat there for a few silent moments, watching petals catch in the wind and fall like snow.

Grim turned to look at me with a sigh. "I had really hoped assigning you an apprentice would keep you busy enough to stay out of trouble for a while."

I tried to look surprised. "I haven't broken any rules, so I'm not exactly sure what this trouble is you're speaking of."

"Oh?" He folded his arms. "It's no secret that everyone thinks you're in line to be my new second-in-command. Applying for the Posy Unit is quite an ambitious move, and it only gives the rumor more credit."

"So that's why you think they're targeting me?"

"Why else would—" The color drained from his face. "No. They can't possibly know."

"I heard the records office was broken into…"

Grim grew even grimmer. "There was a fire. We lost a large selection of hard copy reaper logs, but they were backed up on a private network."

"Is there a possibility that some of those logs were stolen instead of burned?" My hands were suddenly clammy. The reaper logs didn't exactly spell out that I killed Wosyet, but they did list me as being in the wrong place at the wrong time. It wouldn't be too hard to make the connection.

Grim blew out a slow breath.

"Well, if you're right, and I'm only being targeted because of a false rumor, then the attacks should stop after you announce your new second at the placement ceremony." I was momentarily relieved. "And then they'll have someone else to target."

"I'm hoping Anubis and the Nephilim Guard have the situation under control before then, which brings us to the next reason I called you here." He dropped a hefty coin in my lap.

"What's this for?"

"I need my guards back. You're a big girl, and Cindy tells me you've almost finished with the training she requested. Besides, isn't your best friend an archangel? If you need an escort, call him. In the meantime, be smart and travel by coin. You're not particularly useful, but I really don't want another dead reaper on my hands. And I may need you in another thousand years to take on another special assignment."

"A thousand years? You're going to keep him that long?"

Grim tensed. "That subject is not up for discussion."

"I don't know. I might be retired by then."

He laughed. "So you've finally worked your way up high enough to warrant Ms. Fang soliciting you for her retirement program, have you?"

"I have." I was feeling like quite the grownup for making such a conscious investment in my future.

"Well, good for you." His look grew serious all of a sudden. "You've really become quite popular lately, among quite a few crowds. The council's attention isn't always a good thing though, Lana."

I snorted. "You don't say."

"Be careful who you trust. It only takes telling one wrong person your secrets, and then you *and* I are both screwed."

"Trust me, I'm not in any big hurry to tell anyone my secrets. I haven't even told Maalik about Wosyet."

His eyes widened at that revelation. "Even though he already knows about Khadija's error?"

"Error?" I grinned. Grim had not been pleased about Khadija imbuing me with an extra special dose of soul matter. He didn't like that I could see the potency of souls the way he could. I'm sure it had less to do with the fact that he wanted to maintain superiority, and more to do with the fact that what she had done breached the peace treaty the gods had agreed to in order to stabilize Eternity's chaotically shifting territories. The peace treaty had ended the War of Eternity, and it turned over a large chunk of control to Grim who used his secret power source, Khadija at the time, to steady the boundaries of the afterlives.

The peace treaty also allowed him to monopolize the soul harvesting business for the most part, granting him the ability to create a few additional reapers every hundred years for his lucrative soul-harvesting corporation, Reapers Inc. The condition was that the reapers were not to be granted deityship. Eternity most certainly did not need any more gods. I didn't really think Khadija had installed that much power in me, but if the council found out, they would still view me as a threat and insist that I be executed. I was sure of that much.

Grim gave me a sour look. "I suppose it's one less secret for Maalik to hold over your head after your relationship has run its course."

"I suppose so." I sighed.

"Well, good luck on your exams." Grim stood and waved a hand at the nephilim. They circled him, my two guards included, and all coined off simultaneously.

I looked around, stunned to be alone so suddenly. The silver coin Grim had dropped in my lap was heavy. There were enough marks on it to get me through a month, easy. I really hoped I didn't need it that long.

The park felt darker, even though it was early in the day. A breeze swished around the tulip tress and skimmed my

143

bare legs, sending a shiver through me. It was crazy how a couple near-death experiences could make something as simple as sitting on a quiet park bench such a nerve-wracking experience. I hated being paranoid and unable to enjoy simple things the way I used to. I swallowed my bitterness and rolled the coin to take me back to Holly House.

CHAPTER 23

"Education is simply the soul of a society
as it passes from one generation to the next."
-Gilbert K. Chesterton

I spent the rest of my Sunday morning sitting on the floor of my king-sized shower, letting the hot water rain down on me, while I shuffled through all the ways my life sucked lately.

The rebels were trying to kill me, and I still wasn't exactly sure if it was because they thought I was Grim's new second or if it was because they knew I had offed Wosyet. Something said by the demon bitch who had set my apartment ablaze was still eating at me, too. She had asked where *he* was. Maybe they were still looking for Winston, another sucktacular highlight of my life.

I had to find a better way to make Grim's secret weapon stay put. The weekly life support trinkets I brought him were only going to entertain him for so long. Grim really needed to think about replacing him a lot sooner than a thousand years from now. A retirement plan wouldn't do me much good if I still had to babysit him all the damned time. Of course, I was pretty sure Horus wouldn't allow for that, especially since he planned on taking Winston back to Duat with him after his hundred year term on the council was up. That's why he was blackmailing me into joining the Posy Unit and finding a replacement.

I was shocked and somewhat disgusted to realize that I was actually missing work. I had only been away for a little over a week, but I guess I was longing for the sense of accomplishment it gave me. So much for that retirement plan. Maybe I'd feel better after I passed the upcoming exams and finished my training with Bub.

Bub. The thought of him made my chest ache, and the thought of Maalik made my head ache. My love life was a complete wreck. The two men that consumed my thoughts were complete opposites. One seemed to only want one thing, and the other wanted far more than I was willing to give.

It's not that I didn't appreciate what Maalik was trying to do, but I was not some helpless damsel in distress, and I didn't appreciate him trying to mandate my life without giving my input the slightest consideration. Holly House was great, but I resented the fact that Maalik was paying my rent. If I was going to stay there, that was going to have to change. I really didn't like the idea of having a roommate, but I knew it might be my only option. Josie's inquiry came to mind.

The shower was growing thick with steam, and my fingers were good and pruney. I sighed and pushed my thoughts away to marinate in my subconscious some more. I hated dwelling, but there wasn't much else I could do, considering I was confined to my condo until further notice. I finally decided to suck it up and get out of the shower. Josie and the gang would be over soon for our last study party before the dreaded final project with Craig. I was just glad she hadn't insisted that I invite Craig over to join us.

I had just finished pulling on a pair of jeans and black tank top when the doorbell rang. I groaned, hoping Josie wasn't early. I needed at least three cups of coffee in my system before she started in on me with the studying again.

I opened the door to find my apprentice waiting alone in the hall. "Kevin?"

"Hey, Lana. We need to talk."

"Okay." I let him in and went into the kitchen to fix my coffee and went ahead and fixed Kevin a cup too. It was getting eerie how many people were trying to get me alone for serious discussions lately. Why couldn't I catch a good, mindless conversation anymore?

Kevin seated himself on one of the barstools, putting the long counter between us. He took the coffee I offered him and set it down with a sigh. I hadn't really had many one on one talks with him, which seemed odd since he was my apprentice. I guess I thought there would be plenty of time for that after I was actually qualified to train him.

Kevin chewed his bottom lip and looked up at me with his innocent, concerned eyes. He laced his fingers together and then pulled them into his lap, struggling with whatever it was that he couldn't bring himself to say just yet.

Reapers didn't age, as it goes with most immortals, but some take on the common air of age over time. Some emphasized their age and superiority by donning certain items, like Grace Adaline's horn-rimmed glasses or Paul Brom's bowler hat. On the other hand, sometimes a new reaper can really emanate an air of youth and naivety in their first century or two. I had a feeling that this was Kevin Kraus's fate.

Kevin's look hadn't changed since he graduated from the academy. Shaggy black curls framed his face. His full mouth looked almost feminine above his slender jawline. He had the air of a lost puppy, even though he had been at the top of his class. I was fortunate that Josie was around to help him along. She had taken him shopping recently, and it was nice seeing him in blue jeans instead of the standard black robe.

He took a deep breath and straightened his posture before starting in on what was obviously a practiced speech. "Lana, I'm sure there's a perfectly good reason why you want to be on the Posy Unit. And honestly, I don't hold it against Josie for not telling me what that reason is. I hold it against you."

I raised an eyebrow. Kevin frowned at me and gripped the edge of the counter. "I know you're supposed to be my mentor, and I'm supposed to be the humble, obedient apprentice, but I'm going to be working under you for the next century. It would be nice if you clued me in on why you're making certain decisions, since these decisions will be affecting my future too."

I'm sure I looked like a deer in headlights. How had I been so thoughtless? I was even taking a class that was supposed to teach me how to be better at this mentoring gig. Fat lot of good that was doing me.

Kevin sensed my remorse and lightened his tone. "Don't you know that the first century of my resume is in your hands? The path you put me on will be the one I'm expected to stay on, unless I want to start over from scratch a hundred years from now."

I swallowed and found my voice. "I'm sorry, Kevin." My mind scrambled around for a quick solution. I needed to tell him enough so that he would feel better about my decisions, but not so much that he had the ability to screw me over. Enough people had that power, thank you very much. "The thing is, I've been asked to take on a special project that requires my presence on the Posy Unit. Don't be mad at Josie for not telling you anything. I haven't shared the details with her either. It's really nothing for you to be concerned about, and it won't interfere with your apprenticeship. In fact, I think the Posy Unit will be good for you. Jenni said she thought so too at the dinner party last week. You'll be the only apprentice on a specialty unit."

Kevin nodded. "I'd like to believe it will be good for my career. It's just hard to trust you right now. You don't seem to even consider me when making decisions, and while I know everything is ultimately up to you, I really didn't count on feeling so insignificant. I'm not one to brag, but I was at the top of my class. I guess I just expected more."

Now I was embarrassed. Of course, he expected more. He had originally been assigned to Coreen Bendura, Grim's late second-in-command. There was no higher honor. Grim had turned Kevin over to me as a punishment, but Kevin was the one suffering the most from the new arrangement. God, I was feeling just about tall enough to play handball with the curb.

"I know everything sucks right now, but I promise, it will get better. I'm going to pass this class tomorrow, and then you and I are going to go harvest a boatload of souls. You'll have more harvests on your resume than you could ever imagine, and if you don't care for the Posy Unit, maybe after a couple decades or so, we can switch over to freelancing medium-risk souls or something else. How's that sound?"

Kevin gave me a timid smile. "That sounds nice." Then he frowned again and blushed. "Would you mind if I stayed with you for a couple weeks? Just until I get another paycheck? I lost my apartment after my bonus from last fall ran out. I've been crashing at Josie's, but I think it's starting to become a problem for Jenni. She expects me to split the rent, and I just can't right now, not until I go back to work."

Wow. I had to be the shittiest mentor ever. While I was going to school to get qualified, Kevin had been out of work and waiting around for me while his savings dwindled. I was a total jerk.

A distant memory hit me suddenly. Saul Avelo, my late mentor, had brought me home with him the evening of the Oracle Ball after I had been announced as his apprentice. He wasn't very happy about the arrangement, and it had been hard for him not to take it out on me. Even through all his resentment, he had still made up a room for me, and I lived with him for nearly a decade before finding my own place.

I looked across the counter at Kevin's hopeful expression and smiled. "I've got plenty of room. You stay as long as you like."

"Thanks." Kevin let out a breath he had been holding. "I'll pack up my things and bring them over Tuesday."

A little nagging thought tried to remind me that Maalik was paying for the condo, but Kevin was my apprentice, and I was supposed to be considering this my home. Maalik was hardly ever around anyway. If he had a problem with Kevin moving in, he could kiss my ass.

CHAPTER 24

*"My luck is so bad that if I bought a cemetery,
people would stop dying."*
-Ed Furgol

"Don't say it's a fine morning, or I'll shootcha!" John Wayne sounded even grouchier in surround sound. Or maybe it was just the mood I was in. It was nearing ten, and Maalik still hadn't shown. The council meeting was probably running over again. Sometimes I wondered if Grim didn't work them so much lately just to spite me.

Sunday was really the only day of the week I got to see Maalik, and even then, it wasn't a guarantee. Lately, he had missed more dates than he kept.

I had a moment of hope when the doorbell rang out its church bell tune. Maybe he was just running late. Maybe he would show as promised, after all. But it was just Gabriel, looking about as miserable as I felt. His wings twitched, shaking loose a few feathers in the hallway.

"Interrupting?" he asked, looking past me.

I shook my head and let him in. "McLintock?"

"McLintock," he grumbled, making his way to the refrigerator to stash away the case of Ambrosia Ale he'd brought with him. He was wearing a pair of his ragged drawstring pants, and the red in his eyes told me he had started drinking a little earlier in the evening than usual.

I grabbed a bag of Cheetos out of the pantry and joined him on the sofa. I had already changed out of my date clothes and into a tank top and yoga pants, ready for my pity party. At least I wouldn't be sulking alone now. Gabriel handed me a beer and I passed him the Cheetos.

"Amy?" I asked.

He nodded. "Maalik?"

I rolled my eyes. You know you've been friends with someone a long time when you can hold an entire conversation with the exchange of single words.

I unpaused the movie and skipped it back to the beginning before stretching out and kicking my legs up in Gabriel's lap. We quietly sipped our beers as John Wayne and Maureen O'Hara bickered on screen.

I couldn't remember the last time we'd watched a movie together, and I suddenly felt guilty. I guess our new relationships and job ventures had something to do with that, but I missed our quality time. We hadn't had a poker night in some time either.

"You up for a game of poker next week?"

Gabriel nodded. "Yeah. Maybe that'll give Amy something else to bitch about."

"Is she still carrying on about occupational responsibility?"

"You know it." He snorted. "Maalik's trying to get you to be less ambitious and Amy thinks I should be more ambitious. Maybe we should just swap partners."

"Ha. I've already got one demon after me." I bit my tongue immediately after I said it. I could feel Gabriel tense.

"Excuse me?"

"It's nothing." I shifted my legs around in his lap. "You know Bub. He flirts with everyone."

"You'd think he'd show a little respect for Maalik. They're both Hell-dwellers, after all." His mouth twisted into an involuntary snarl, much like the one he wore when he had first found out about Maalik's interest in me.

Gabriel wasn't jealous, but he was protective. Sure, I had my moment of swooning, girly crush on him when we had first met, but that had passed quickly enough. Gabriel had shifted into something of a big brother. I loved him unconditionally, even when he crashed at my place after hitting Purgatory Lounge and puking on my couch. Hey, what were friends for? I was relieved that he wasn't harassing me about the dangers of my efforts to join the Posy Unit, like nearly everyone else. But like a big brother, he probably knew chewing me out wouldn't accomplish anything. Instead, he was inconspicuously hanging around to keep an eye on me. I smiled, loving him even more for protecting me without smothering me, something Maalik needed to take notes on.

Gabriel let out a huff as Wayne took the coal shovel to O'Hara's ass. "If only all relationship problems were that easy to solve."

"Yeah." I sighed.

"Look at us." Gabriel laughed. "Your lover's never around, and mine won't leave me the hell alone."

"They got good reasons. Sometimes." It was funny how I could gripe about Maalik all day, but the second someone else did, I felt the need to defend him.

Gabriel yawned and scratched his head, tumbling his blond curls around. "Mind if I crash here?"

"Not at all. I've even got a guest room set up."

"Moving on up in the world." He snorted and tickled my feet.

"Hey!" I kicked at him and pulled my legs up. "I'm just looking out for you. I don't think a set of apocalypse mugs will suffice Holly if you puke on one of her white sofas."

"You're never going to let me live that down, are you?"

"I forgave you. I think that's good enough." I grinned.

Gabriel stood, and only stumbled once before catching his balance. He stretched his arms and wings out with a yawn. "Lead the way, pilgrim."

I hadn't really given much notice to the other two rooms in the condo, but they were really quite nice. Each one had a private bathroom, though not as fancy as the one in the master suite. The bedroom I led Gabriel into was decorated in shades of gold and green. Gauzy curtains were layered over the window, and an engraved armoire rested in one corner.

Gabriel looked around the room with a frown. "Maybe I should leave myself a note. So I know where I am in the morning."

I laughed. "I'll wake you up with breakfast."

"In bed?"

"You wish."

He shrugged. "Worth a shot."

"You good?" I asked.

He pulled me if for a hug. "Yeah, thanks." I hugged him back, breathing in the smell of beer and frosting. I hadn't spent much time in Heaven, but I was sure there had to be some killer bakeries there. Everything and everyone from there smelled like cake.

"Goodnight, Gabe."

"Night." He plopped on the bed and was snoring before I had even flipped the light off.

CHAPTER 25

*"We always long for the forbidden things,
and desire what is denied us."*
-Francois Rabelais

"Lana? Lana, wake up."

I opened my eyes to find Maalik sitting on the edge of my bed and sat up with a start. Usually he let me sleep in after he stood me up, waking me with the delightful smells of his impressive cooking skills to cool my anger. Not this morning.

"Maalik." I relaxed back against the headboard with a yawn, and rubbed at my eyes with the palms of my hands.

I wanted to give him hell, first for standing me up, and then for not making it up to me with breakfast, but I changed my mind in a hurry. He looked like he hadn't slept in days. His chocolate curls were frizzed, and his formal robe was wrinkled and spotted with coffee stains, and he- I sniffed him- yup, he actually smelled.

"Good lord, when's the last time you showered?"

He blinked a few times. "I'm not certain." Then he frowned. "That's not important. We need to talk."

"Okay."

"Lana, I need you to tell me something." Maalik looked at me with his sincere brown eyes. He reached out to squeeze my shoulders, holding me in place before him.

"What?" I frowned, not liking the direction this was headed.

"Why is Horus cultivating favor for you among the council?"

"The assignment I completed last fall was very important to him, I guess." I looked down at his chest, knowing full-well I was as bad at lying as I was at intimidating demons.

"No, Lana." Maalik shook me, startling me enough to look up at him again. His eyes had lost their sincerity. Now they were desperate. "What does he have you doing for him? What is he planning?"

"Nothing!" I shrieked, jerking my arms from his icy grasp. I threw the covers back and stormed off to my closet, suddenly feeling entirely underdressed. Having an argument in pajamas just didn't demand the proper authority.

Maalik followed me. "Lana—"

"Is it so impossible that someone thinks I'm capable of more than low-risk harvesting?" I said over my shoulder as I pulled on a gray sweater and a pair of jeans. "Do you think I'm not good enough for the Posy Unit? Is that it?"

"You know it isn't. Damn it, Lana, you're going to get yourself killed." Maalik stepped inside the closet and grabbed me, turning me around to face him again. "Is that what you want?"

Now I was fuming. "I'm taking all the proper precautions. I've hardly left the condo, except for school and my training—"

"With Beelzebub. In Hell. Where half the rebel army is from," he growled.

"Yes, with Beelzebub, who is just as equipped to protect me as anyone else."

"And you really think he would, don't you?" Maalik scoffed.

I paused a moment, and then looked back up at Maalik with a soft smile. "I know he would."

The hurt in his eyes was almost too much. He released me so suddenly that I stumbled and caught myself on the closet doorframe. He ran a hand through his unkempt hair and swallowed as his eyes glazed over. It was frightening seeing him this way. He was always so cool and collected, even when we were bickering. Today, he just looked lost and somewhat frantic. I was afraid to touch him.

I inched towards the bedroom door, never turning my back on him. "Why don't you take a shower and get some sleep. I have to go."

He glared at me a moment and then buried his face in his hands with a sigh and slumping down on the bed. "I'm losing you to him."

I could feel the heat crawl up my face. "I don't know what you're talking about." Part of me wanted to go to him, to wrap his body in mine and crawl back beneath the covers and make his misery vanish. But another, stronger part of me wanted to run from the room, as far and as fast as I could.

"I have to go," I repeated.

"Then go," he said, his face still in his hands.

I turned and left him there, sitting alone on my bed. I felt like a traitor as my heart leapt at the thought of seeing Bub.

I poked my head in the guest bedroom I had set up for Gabriel, but he had already left. The bed was sloppily made up, but I smiled that he had even bothered. He never had to worry about making a bed when he crashed on my couch.

Saul and Coreen were finishing up their breakfast. I decided it must have been Gabriel who fed them, considering Maalik's frazzled condition. I snatched up their leads and rushed out the front door, waving them to hurry along before Maalik changed his mind and decided to try and stop me again.

I felt mildly guilty for not telling Maalik the whole truth, but he was a by-the-book kind of guy. He could overlook the fact that I was different from the other reapers since it was his prophet's wife Khadija who had made me different. He could even respect her reasons and appreciate the fact that the replacement soul I had found made it possible for Khadija to go home to Firdaws in Jannah, the Islamic heaven.

What Maalik didn't know was that I had killed Wosyet. I wasn't even sure he knew that Khadija had gifted me so greatly. Horus knew, and he was using it to blackmail me into hunting down another soul for him, something not sanctioned by the council. I couldn't tell Maalik one secret without exposing the other, and that would be too much for him. His took pride in his loyalties, and those loyalties would force him to take my secrets to the council. The ultimate decision would be my execution, whether that was his intention or not. So I pretended that Horus was still patting me on the back. In a way, I guess he was. After all, he was paying me.

I took the quick route to Bub's Tartarus home, skipping the gates of Hell as he had instructed. The hounds took up guard duty without any prompting from me. They were doing a lot better now that they were getting out more often. I think being in their homeland was helping improve their moods as well.

An intoxicating blend of nerves was swirling in my stomach. I wasn't sure if it was the uncertainty of how Bub was going to act around me today, or if Maalik was right about me falling for the demon. Maybe it was a combination of both. My hands were sweating as I climbed the front steps of Bub's summer home, and I missed the first few times I reached for the doorbell. Jack answered the door.

"Ms. Harvey." He gave me a short bow and welcomed me inside with a wave of his hand. "This way, please."

He escorted me through a different section of the house that I hadn't seen before, into an elaborate office with wall-to-wall bookcases. The room was long with a round table on one side and a heavily engraved desk on the other. The matching chair behind the desk backed up to a tall, picture window, displaying red mountains in the distance against an amber sky.

Jack cleared his throat. "Master Beelzebub requested that I express his deepest apologies. He is unable to join us today, but he has fully instructed me on what lessons he desires you to cover, and he has laid them all out on the study table. I am quite versed in demonology myself, so I will be at your disposal for any questions, and I will be commencing your review at the end of the day."

I frowned. "Okay." This was awkward.

"I'll fetch some tea while you get started." He left the room, leaving me standing there, unsure if I should be pouting or relieved.

Was Bub really unable to be here, or was he intentionally avoiding me? I was ashamed at how disappointed I was.

I opened one of the books, but I found myself constantly distracted by my thoughts. Bub had laid out quite a bit for me to study. I frowned, wondering if this was somehow punishment for dodging his advances. Or maybe he was really that concerned about the possibility of me encountering six hundred different kinds of demons. Right.

The morning dragged on into the afternoon. I spent the majority of my time reading and rereading, and then reading aloud different incantations for Jack so he could correct my pronunciation with an annoyed scowl. Incantations and spells wouldn't do much good if they weren't spoken correctly, and Latin was hard. Wowzers. There were a few lines Jack finally gave up on teaching me altogether. When I felt like my brains would start leaking out my ears, he finally relented and brought in a small gift bag.

"I took the liberty of hunting down a few additional items for your protection." He set the bag on the table.

I smiled at him and reached into the bag, shuffling through a heap of tissue paper before retrieving a small bottle of... hairspray. I frowned. "You have a problem with my hair?"

Jack sighed. "It's angelica mace. The holy root is ground into a powder and diluted with holy water. It's quite potent against evil spirits."

"Oh. Neato." The bag still felt heavy so I reached back in it and found a small, flat box at the bottom. It was white with a creamy peach ribbon tied neatly around it and into a bow on top. It looked like something jewelry might come in. I raised an eyebrow at Jack.

"That one was at Master Beelzebub's suggestion."

I grinned and tried to keep my hands from shaking as I untied the bow and opened the box. A black, silk pouch was nestled inside. I loosened the drawstring on the pouch and emptied its contents into the palm of my hand. Dozens of triangular crystals glittered up at me.

"What are they?"

"Crystal tips for your throwing stars. I told him I thought it was overkill. These are peasant rebels you're dealing with, but he insisted that they have worthy players. Those crystals were mined from caves in the Jerusalem Mountains of Heaven before they passed legislation forbidding it, so use them sparingly, my dear."

"Of course. Thank you." I shifted my fingers, admiring their twinkle before replacing them in the pouch. It wasn't exactly jewelry, but it was pretty damn close, if you asked me.

"Master seems quite fond of you," Jack said. I couldn't tell whether or not he was happy about that. Hell, I couldn't really tell whether or not I was happy about that.

Jack looked at me as though he was expecting a reply.

"Well, he was hired to train me. I don't suppose my death would look good for him," I said with a shrug.

Jack chuckled, making his short horns quiver. "I suppose not, but I suspect his interest in you runs deeper than that. He has never invited a reaper into his home before. Not even Grim."

I gave him a strained smile. "Well, aren't I a lucky girl?"

It felt an awful lot like he was prying, and call me crazy, but I really didn't feel like spilling my guts to a demon, even one as harmless seeming as Jack. A clock somewhere in the house chimed five bells, and he jumped in surprise.

"Time to prepare dinner already. Well, my dear, it seems we are finished for the day. Would you like me to walk you out?"

"I can find my way, thank you." I gave him a smile and put my gifts back in the bag as I stood.

"Very well. Good evening, Ms. Harvey." Jack left in a hurry, presumably to prepare dinner, and I had a moment to wonder if Bub would be dining alone or if he had guests coming over. Which also made me wonder if he had come home yet. I really didn't have time to snoop around and find out.

I wanted to go over my final project one last time before presenting it with Craig. I didn't really *need* to go over it again, but I was paranoid. I couldn't fathom the idea of letting that bastard show me up in front of an audience. Josie and the study gang had drilled me on the last assignment enough times that I could have recited it in my sleep. Not even Jack's extensive demon review could scour that from my mind. Jack might not have been impressed with my Latin, but I had a hopeful feeling that Grace Adaline would find my harvesting expertise more satisfactory.

CHAPTER 26

*"Education is a progressive discovery
of our own ignorance."
-Will Durant*

I had entirely forgotten to mention to Gabriel that I didn't have the nephilim escorts for class anymore, but I wasn't surprised to find him waiting for me when I got home.

"Need a date for class?" He wagged his eyebrows at me.

I grinned. "You bet, handsome."

In the past, I might have been mildly perturbed at the notion of needing a babysitter, but with all the unwanted demon attention I'd been receiving, I actually welcomed the supervision, especially since it was Gabriel. Also, there was Josie to consider. I really didn't think I could live with myself if she got caught in the crossfire because of my stubborn pride, and she would be on her way to collect me for class soon. I dropped some Cerberus Chow in the hounds' dishes and went to fix a pot of coffee.

Gabriel shook out his wings and perched himself on one of the barstools. He was wearing one of his nicer white robes, which made me wonder if he had just come from an assignment or if Amy had threatened to crucify him if she spotted him wearing his drawstring pants in public again. It was still bizarre to me that Gabriel was dating a demon, and odder yet that she was the positive influence on him.

"What happened to our breakfast date this morning?" I asked, dumping some sugar into a couple coffee mugs.

Gabriel blushed and looked away. "I, ah, I heard Maalik come in. Thought you two could use some privacy."

"Yeah." I sighed and filled the mugs with coffee. "Any news on the rebel situation or my demon admirers?"

"Not yet." Gabriel frowned. "Amy's been extra busy lately with Cindy's camarilla. She's helping them compile a missing list of the bigger players in Hell. The civilian demons are harder to track, but there are a few notable absences, and I think they suspect them of joining the rebel forces."

"Super." I frowned and took the barstool next to him, passing him a mug of coffee.

"Amy's hosting a Hell Committee summit at her chateau in a few weeks to discuss a plan of action. I don't know what the Sphinx Congress is doing to minimize the damage coming from their side, but at least Hell has got it together."

I laughed. "That's got to be near the top of the list of things least likely to be said by an angel."

Gabriel nodded in agreement. We finished our coffee in silence, both lost in our own thoughts. I was growing restless about the demon situation. I was starting to wonder just how long the babysitting detail was going to last, and what Winston would do if I didn't show up when he expected me. I also wondered how I was supposed to go back to work and focus on harvesting souls while simultaneously watching my back.

Before I could dwell too long on how impossible my life was, Josie arrived and we all headed off to the academy by coin. Gabriel followed us down the scholarly passages hung with inspirational posters and class schedules for the following semester. He made himself comfortable across the hall from our classroom on a cushioned bench, looking like he might try to squeeze in a nap. It was highly unlikely that a demon would make an attempt on me in such a crowded setting.

The classroom was noisier and more frantic than usual. No one looked like they had slept well, but everyone was dressed a little nicer for their presentations. A handful of students were last minute speed-reading their papers, mouthing the words to themselves with furrowed brows. A group of ladies from the Mother Goose Unit, dedicated to harvesting child souls, huddled around a table, rearranging their notecards and touching up their lip gloss.

I took a seat at an empty table while Josie went to join Miranda Giles, Craig Hogan's girl toy from the Lost Soul's Unit. Josie wasn't especially happy about being paired up with her, but the pickings were slim, especially since she was friends with me. The notion that I, a low-risk harvesting peon, might be Grim's new second-in-command, didn't exactly make me popular among the reapers. Miranda just happened to be available because Craig was paired up with me.

I opened my messenger bag and pulled out a bundle of folders and neatly stacked them in front of me, along with a thumb drive containing my visual presentation. I was actually pretty pleased with myself. I had done every last bit of work for the project, and that was saying a lot, considering I went ahead and did Craig's part too, just in case he flaked out on me. Of course, Josie had done a fair amount of editing. I really owed her a big one for keeping me afloat academically. I really didn't know how I would have fared without her guidance.

Craig was the last to arrive, which was uncharacteristic of him. He stood inside the classroom door and scanned the crowd until he caught sight of me. He donned one of his cocky grins and strutted his way to my table. I couldn't help but scowl as he took the seat next to me. He reeked of sulfur. He had probably gambled away his afternoon with shady demons in Purgatory. Shooting craps was one of his vices back in the day, one I thought he had kicked. Apparently not.

"New cologne?"

"What?" He froze.

"You stink of demons. You couldn't have saved Purgatory for after class?"

Craig blinked a few times and shook his head, mirroring my scowl. "What do you care?" Then his nasty grin returned. "Are you telling me you're concerned about my well-being now?"

I huffed. "I'm concerned about your hygiene, and only for the next two hours. Then you can stink all you like around someone else."

"Sure." He set a similar messenger bag on the table next to mine and pulled out a binder, clearing his throat. "I figured you would be stubborn and resist working with me, so I prepared your half of the project as well. You can thank me later," he said, handing the binder to me.

I slapped it away. "You wish. I'll be presenting what I've prepared. If that's not to your liking, too fucking bad. I'm more than capable of presenting the entire project on my own."

Craig smiled and leaned in closer, dropping his voice down to a whisper. "Is that so?"

"It is," I hissed back.

"So you won't mind if I call your bluff?"

"Excuse me?" I sat back and blinked at him.

"If I drop this class, right this moment, do you suppose you'll be able to pull it off on your own and make it on the Posy Unit?"

"What's your game, Hogan?"

"Dinner."

"What?"

"Agree to meet me for dinner after class, and I'll stay and make sure you pass this final. Refuse, and you're on your own. I know you, Lana. You've been away from the academy too long, and Josie can't save you this time."

Heat crawled over me like Hell had just blown me a kiss. I leaned in as close as I could stand to be to him and gritted my teeth. "I would rather eat entrails than have dinner with you. Do your worst, asshole."

Craig went pale a moment, and then I realized he really hadn't considered me refusing him. Dropping this class at the last minute was going to look bad for him, but would he consider it worthwhile if it meant potentially seeing me fail and lose my chance at the Posy Unit? He couldn't possibly know how well prepared I was, and I didn't see any reason to tell him again. He hadn't believed me the first time.

He swallowed and struggled to regain his composure. "This is your last chance, Lana."

"Eat shit, Craig," I said with a smile.

"Suit yourself." He stood, knocking his chair over as he shoved the binder back in his bag and stormed off to Grace Adaline's desk. She had just taken her seat and looked up at Craig with mild disdain.

"You're team is fourth down on the list, Mr. Hogan, not first," she said.

"I'm not up here to present the final. In fact, I won't be presenting the final at all. Lana refused to work with me, so I guess I'll be dropping this class, unless you would allow me to show the presentation I prepared on my own?"

Grace sighed and looked over the top of her spectacles at me as she laced her fingers together on top of her desk. "Is this true, Ms. Harvey."

I wanted to break Craig's face. I wanted to call him every name in the book. Twice. Instead, I smiled sweetly at Grace and folded my hands in my lap. "Of course not. Craig even came to my condo at Holly House to consult with me on the final. We decided on a scenario and which sections we would each be doing. If you don't believe me, feel free to call the deskman and ask him to review the guest log. Craig signed it himself."

Craig's jaw dropped.

Grace rolled her eyes and stood up from her desk. She took her glasses off and glared at Craig. "I do not have the patience or the time for this juvenile BS. Get out of my classroom, Mr. Hogan."

"But—"

"Out. Now."

Craig shrank away from her and made his way to the door in disbelief. He cast me one last poisonous look before slamming the door behind him.

Grace cleared her throat and put her glasses back on. "Is this going to present a problem for you Ms. Harvey?"

I smiled again. "Not at all, Professor."

"Good. Let's get started then. Galla. Giles. You're up."

Josie gave me a wink as she walked by, letting me know she had enjoyed my small victory as well.

The presentations were as boring as expected, but everyone seemed to do okay, including me, all by myself. I didn't need the notecards for my half or Craig's. Grace actually complimented me when I handed her the typed report that went along with my presentation. I never knew how satisfying academic progress could be. I guess I was always too busy pining over Craig during the classes of my apprenticeship to care about the pride of achievement.

The multiple choice exam that followed the presentations was a breeze after all the studying I had done. I was one of the first to hand it in.

Grace stopped me before I left her classroom and pulled me aside. "Lana, I just wanted to express how impressed I am at your growth in my class. I was concerned about you for a while there, but you've really turned things around. Saul would have been proud of you," she said.

My chest tightened at the mention of my mentor. I knew as well as Grace did that Saul was more of a field guy and never cared much for the academy, but it was the thought that counted, right?

"Thanks. That means a lot." I gave her a soft smile and left to join Josie and Gabriel in the hallway. Gabriel gave us both a high-five.

"One down, one to go," Josie said with a sigh.

I wasn't quite as concerned about my final in Edgar Dorian's mentoring class. It was a basic, multiple choice exam. I would still be glad when it was over and I had my new certifications in hand.

We left the academy with pretty high spirits. Things seemed to be going well, until we ran into Craig, sitting on the steps outside. He sneered when he caught sight of us and stood, running a hand over his buzzed head.

"I bet you're real pleased with yourself," he said, balling his hands into fists.

I folded my arms with a grin. "Yeah, I suppose I am."

He took a step towards us, but then glanced cautiously at Gabriel and decided to glare at me from a distance instead. By now, our entire class had made it outside.

"I'd love to stay and chat, Craig, but I've got somewhere better to be," I said, taking a coin from my pocket.

Josie and Gabriel found their coins too, and the three of us zipped on out of there before Craig could blink. It was glorious.

CHAPTER 27

"We cannot banish dangers, but we can banish fears.
We must not demean life by standing in awe of death."
-David Sarnoff

I was downright depressed to find out that Bub had left my lessons in Jack's hands again on Tuesday. It wasn't that Jack wasn't a nice enough guy. He even kept his disappointed grimaces to a minimum as he reviewed me at the end of our session. I just needed to see Bub. I was feeling pathetic about it too. Especially when my heart leapt at the sound of his voice as Jack led me back through the house to the foyer.

"Is Bub here?" I asked, trying to hide my excitement as I glanced down the hall leading to the den.

"I believe he's currently in a meeting," Jack said, just as Bub stepped out into the hall.

"Jack, could you bring us a bite to eat?" he asked, and then noticed me. "Lana. How was your lesson today?"

"Fine." I could hardly find my voice. I had been so anxious to see him, and now I didn't even know what to say.

He nodded slowly. "Good."

Then a sultry, female voice called from the den. "Bub, you devil, where's that bottle of Summerland vino I left in the chiller?"

My breath caught in my chest.

"Check the wine rack," Bub answered, not taking his eyes from me.

I hadn't really thought I meant anything to him, had I? All the same, I felt ridiculous, standing in his foyer, jealousy coursing through me like a poison. And he could see it, which made it ten times worse.

He took a step towards me. "Lana, I—"

"I have to go." I backed away from him, reaching blindly for the door. I found the handle and nearly jerked it off its heavy hinges in my attempt to get out the house.

Coreen and Saul were waiting for me, having given up their futile patrolling to lazily sunbathe on the dock. They bound up the hill and met me halfway down. I heard Bub's front door open behind me, but I didn't bother turning around as I rolled my coin and got the hell out of there.

I couldn't get back to the condo fast enough. After I let the hounds in and dumped some food in their dishes, I retreated to my shower. I found the elaborately tiled stall comforting for some reason. I rested my head against the cool tiles and let the multiple shower heads massage the tension in my back and shoulders while I breathed in the soothing steam.

Everything was all wrong. I had no right to be mad at Bub, but I was mad all the same. He had made move after move, and I had turned him down. What did I really expect him to do? I had Maalik. I wasn't supposed to want him. So why did I? I couldn't put my finger on it.

Maybe it was because he was a bad boy. Girls always wanted bad boys. Or maybe it was because he didn't try to micromanage my life the way Maalik did. Maybe it was simply because I was spending so much time with him, and I could hardly catch Maalik's attention for more than five minutes. Whatever it was, my libido was ready to follow him off a cliff. I couldn't get a handle on it, so I was just going to have to avoid the hell out of him and stew and grumble over my misplaced lust. And what better place to do that than Purgatory Lounge?

It had been almost a week since my run-in with Tisiphone. Grim didn't think I needed the guards anymore. Bub wasn't too concerned with my training. I had passed my first final with flying colors and had even managed to put Craig in his place with an audience. That last one alone warranted a celebratory drink or twelve.

I hopped out the shower with a new attitude. I squeezed the water out of my ebony curls and ran a towel over them as I browsed through my closet for something festive. A shimmery, silver halter top caught my eye. The back was nothing more than a strip of material that ran along my waist and the tie that went around my neck. Tisiphone's gashes were hardly visible anymore. They had healed up a lot faster than the burn on my neck, which was still pink and raised around the edges. I added a pair of dark skinny jeans and went back to the bathroom mirror to run some gel through my damp curls. A soft, pink lip gloss completed the look just as the doorbell rang out a hymnal tune.

"Just me!" Josie called out, more for the hounds than me. She was really getting comfortable with that spare key. I didn't mind though, as long as she wasn't using it to throw surprise study parties.

I went to greet her in the kitchen, putting in some peacock feather earrings on the way, and caught her digging through the refrigerator. Her short, spikey hair was mused and she was still wearing her black work cowl.

"I see Gabriel's been over." She snorted as she cracked open one of his Ambrosia Ales and took a drink.

"Long day?"

"You have no idea." She started to laugh, but stopped suddenly when her eyes fell on me. "Where do you think you're going?"

"Purgatory. You're welcome to join me. I'd stay and drink with you here, but I've got to get out of this place. I'm getting cabin fever in a bad way."

Josie set her beer down on the counter and went to stand near the front door. "You really don't want to be down there tonight. In fact, Maalik asked me to come keep you company so you wouldn't be out and about. The Nephilim Guard is out in full force with Anubis tonight. They're crawling the city. Something big is going down. I'm sure of it."

I sighed. "Something big has been going down for weeks now. I'm tired of waiting."

"Seriously, Lana. You're not going out in that. I gave Maalik my word." Josie could be a bossy twit sometimes, but she usually softened her ranting with skewed humor and playful smirks. Not tonight.

"That's your problem." I laughed, pulling on my jacket.

Her face scrunched up with a peculiar mixture of worry and anger as she watched me step into my boots, not even giving her warning half a thought. She folded her arms and held her ground, conveniently blocking the front door.

"Lana, I don't think you're hearing what I'm saying. The city isn't safe right now, not for you."

"Is it ever?" I groaned and leaned against one of the white sofas. "Josie, I know I'm not safe. Hell, I've woke up at Meng's twice in the past two weeks. But I can't live under a rock for the rest of my life. I've been studying hard and training even harder. I need a break. Some relief. A stiff drink."

"You're going to find a whole lot more than a stiff drink if you go out tonight." She wasn't going to budge. The last thing I needed was another Maalik telling me what to do.

Until that moment, I had never actually thought about the best way to take Josie down. I guess if I really had to, I could always have Saul and Coreen corner her. Of course, she'd never forgive me for that. Maybe I could use the angelica mace Jack had given me. But that would be wasteful, and it wouldn't detour her for long since she wasn't a demon.

Josie watched my brow furrow and widened her stance, foreseeing the plot of my frustrations like a good friend usually does. She bit down on her bottom lip and frowned. "You could make this a lot easier on both of us and just pop in a movie. I'll even sit through one of your John Waynes," she offered.

I crossed the dining room and stood directly in front of her, daring her to challenge me. The condo had grown unbearably quiet the past few days, and I just didn't think I was ready to submit to its lonely demure for yet another night.

"Josie, you can get the hell out of my way on your own or you can get the hell out of my way with assistance. Your choice."

"Don't threaten me, Lana. I'll tie you to the coffee table if I have to, but you're not going anywhere," she snapped, lifting her chin with a dignified air that brought the late Coreen to mind.

I tilted my head back to cast her an admiring gaze. She knew I wouldn't stand for this, but she was doing it anyway and probably because she truly thought it was in my best interest. It didn't mean that I wasn't going to kick her ass over it, but I could admire her while I did, right?

I waited for her intimidating posture to go stale. If you stare absently at a person long enough, you can see the confusion dawn on them with such clarity that it's nearly impossible not to strike. And strike I did. I slugged Josie in the stomach hard enough to double her over. I grabbed the back of her robe and flung her over and onto the dining room table.

"Don't wait up," I said, pulling the front door closed behind me. I felt a twinge of guilt, but Josie should have known better. I took heavy strides towards the elevators, wanting to make it downstairs before she made it out of the condo and caught up to me. I was sure she would, but she didn't have to. Warren met me at the elevators.

"Hi." I tried to smile, but I feared the scowl I'd been carrying around all week was becoming a permanent fixture.

"Where are you going?" Warren looked horrified.

"Uh, out." I frowned at him.

"That's probably not the best idea tonight."

"You too?" I clenched my teeth, debating just how nasty I wanted to get with him for not minding his own business.

"Forgive me," he said. I felt a pinch in my arm and staggered back, groping my shoulder. Warren dropped whatever he had stabbed me with and reached out to catch my fall. "I'm so sorry, Lana. I didn't want to, but—"

"Is she down?" Josie stormed down the hallway, her face red and distorted. She carried a coil of rope around her wrist. If she hadn't been serious before about tying me to the coffee table, she was now. I was just glad I wouldn't be awake for it.

The golden walls of Holly House rose above me as I slid to the floor. Warren was still babbling his apologies, and if my mouth had been working, I would have told him it was okay. I'd kick his ass tomorrow.

CHAPTER 28

"Alcohol may be man's worst enemy,
but the bible says love your enemy."
-Frank Sinatra

My head felt like it was no longer attached to my body. I lay awake in my bed for a good hour before the feeling in my limbs returned. It took entirely too much energy to roll over. I waited for the room to stop spinning and focused long enough to glance over at my alarm clock. I was sure it was broken. There was no way it was four in the afternoon.

Hushed voices drifted in from down the hall. I sat up with a groan, and the voices suddenly stopped. I wondered if maybe they were only in my head, and then Maalik appeared in my doorway, wearing his formal black robe and carrying a tea tray.

"Hey," he said softly, though my head throbbed anyway.

I didn't care for tea, even before being exposed to Meng's nasty concoctions. I was sure he knew this already, but if not, the snarl I met him with probably set him straight.

"It will help soothe your headache," he said, apologetically setting the tea on my nightstand before sitting down on the edge of the bed. He reached for my hand, but I pulled it away. Maalik sighed and dropped his hand on my lap instead. "It was for your own good, Lana."

"Wow. We're skipping the apology altogether this time, are we? Color me impressed."

Maalik closed his eyes and pressed his lips together. "Do you have any idea what happened last night?"

"Sorry, I was tranquilized since I wouldn't stay in my cage like a good little pet reaper," I said through gritted teeth as I rubbed my temples.

He grabbed a copy of the *Daily Reaper Report* off the tea tray and thrust it at me. I snatched it away from him with equal zeal.

The front page was one huge picture of the street in front of Purgatory Lounge. At least a dozen demons were being led out the front door by the Nephilim Guard, including the skanky fire harlot that destroyed my apartment. She sneered, like she could see me on the other side of the thin newsprint. The headline read "NEPHILIM GUARD ELIMINATE REBEL THREAT IN LIMBO CITY" in big red letters. A small caption in the bottom corner of the picture requested that readers turn to page two for the full story. I did so with shaking hands.

Apparently, Anubis had found a hot spot in the city and set several spies around the location to notify him when there was a substantial amount of activity. The spies followed a group of ten rebels to Purgatory Lounge Tuesday night, where they were meeting up with some of their comrades to discuss new attack plans. Anubis stated that he was confident the rebel base in Limbo had been eliminated, and he intended to return to Duat the following week, after Grim's formal announcement was given at the placement ceremony.

I tossed the paper down with a huff. "The Nephilim Guard was out in full force, and yet the city still wasn't safe enough for me to be out and about?"

"There was too much risk for an ambush attack. Rebels have been spotted outside Holly House. They know you live here. What if some of them had been waiting for you while the guards were all distracted?"

"What if?" I was belligerent now, and I didn't care. "What if?" I said louder, refusing to let my throbbing skull dull my outrage. "What if I don't want to live my life walking on eggshells and looking over my fucking shoulder every goddamned day? What if *that*? What, do you think you can just tranquilize me until I start seeing things your way?"

"I don't know what I think anymore." Maalik stood and nervously paced around the bed. "Apparently, you have a death wish, and I really don't know what I'm supposed to do about it. I love you, but you're driving me insane." He glanced down at his watch. "I have a council meeting. We'll talk about this more later." His tone was foreboding. I imagined he used that same voice to condemn plenty a deserving soul, but I wasn't one of them. And I'd be damned if he was going to talk to me that way.

"No, we really won't." I threw the covers back and pulled myself out of the bed, only wobbling for a second as the room whirled around me again.

Maalik moved to help me. I stepped around him and found my jean jacket resting across the back of a chair. I pulled it on over my day old outfit, not caring that it was wrinkled or that my hair was probably a mess.

"You should really be resting," Maalik said.

I glared at him. "You should really be minding your own business."

"Lana." He growled and balled his hands into fists. "I don't have time for this."

"You know what?" I said, pulling on my boots that had been discarded next to the chair. "I don't really have time for this anymore either."

Maalik blew out a breath like I had struck him. "What are you saying?"

I righted myself and ran a hand through my tangled curls. "This isn't working anymore. You and me. Things haven't been right for a while now, and I'm finally realizing that they aren't going to get any better. I'm tired of constantly having to fight with you just to live my life the way I see fit."

"Then stop fighting me," he said, and like it was actually a legitimate solution.

I looked at him a moment, in complete and utter disbelief.

"I'm sorry." He sighed and reached for me again.

I put my hands up and took a step back. "This isn't a debate anymore. Do you understand? I'm done. We're over. Goodbye, Maalik." I stormed through the condo and slammed the front door behind me. I hated to admit it, but it kind of felt good leaving him standing there with his mouth hanging open. He had done it to me enough times. He could handle a little of his own medicine for a change. Tears were stinging my eyes, threatening to spill, but I knew I had made the right decision, and I was ready to stick by it.

I wasn't sure where I was going yet. I just had to get out of Holly House, my prison, cleverly disguised as home. Sure, it was one of the nicest places to live in Limbo, but the whole stigma surrounding it left a bad taste in my mouth. I was tired of being a damsel with a demon problem, hiding out at Holly House. Today, I was going to be a damsel with a drinking problem, hiding out at Purgatory. Maalik could just try and stop me. I wasn't beneath screaming obscenities at him in a bar. Not today, anyway.

I took an elevator downstairs and spared Charlie a quick wave at the front desk before bolting out into the courtyard and through the front gate, where I stopped to breathe in the bittersweet smell of freedom. It smelled suspiciously like the pizza joint across the street, but I didn't care. I closed my eyes and let a soft breeze tug at my curls, just for a moment. Maalik would be out soon, either to follow me or to head off to his council meeting. I took off down the sidewalk, rounded the corner, and ran right into Bub.

I gasped and nearly fell over backwards, but Bub caught my arm. His black hair was slicked back and he was in leather pants and a shiny, green dress shirt. It was more intimidating, not at all like the casual look I had grown so fond of, but I suppose he had a public image to maintain.

"Lana, what are you doing out here? You should be at home, where you're safe." The words sounded strange coming from Bub. God, he was just as paranoid as rest of them breathing down my neck.

I really didn't have a death wish. I just couldn't stand the thought of always having to look over my shoulder. It brought to mind Warren before he found his way to Holly House. I did not want to end up cowering behind a door with a dozen deadbolts, painfully aware of my surroundings but somehow oblivious to personal hygiene.

I frowned at Bub, remembering his female guest the day before. Though it pained me, I pulled away from him and straightened my jacket. "The city's safe now. Haven't you read the paper? I'm going to Purgatory for a drink."

Bub gave me a lopsided smile. "Oh?"

"Yeah." I glared, daring him to try me.

"I'll join you."

"I don't need a babysitter."

He cleared his throat. "You didn't show up this morning for your training, and I was worried about you. The least you could do is buy me a drink after putting me through that sort of distress."

I huffed and walked around him. He fell in step beside me.

"I'm sure Jack was really disappointed. Send him my apologies, won't you?"

179

"Lana, I'm really sorry. These past couple days, I had something come up, and I wasn't available to work with you."

"Oh, I heard your guest yesterday. I have a pretty good idea what came up," I said, glancing briefly at his crotch.

He actually blushed. "My goodness. What's gotten into you today?"

"Nothing yet, but a whole lot of tequila is on its way."

We pushed through the front door of Purgatory and froze. The place was nearly deserted. It was still early, but even at this hour, I'd never seen the place so dead. A few nephilim were playing pool and a couple of lesser pagan deities were seated at a corner booth. One of the front windows was boarded up. Xaphen was busy sweeping stray bits of glass off the floor. He paused to look up at us.

"Lana. B." He nodded his head in greeting.

"Hey, Xaph. What's cooking?"

"Nothing, now that there's a rumor flying around that I've been harboring rebels," he grumbled.

"That's ridiculous. People should know better. They'll come round." I took my jacket off and laid it over a barstool before sitting down. Bub took the stool next to me. I frowned at his smug grin.

"What'll it be, kiddo?" Xaphen asked, stepping behind the bar and pulling a lowball glass down from the overhead rack.

"Triple shot of Patrón, on ice, with lime."

"And a godfather. Her treat," Bub added.

Xaphen whistled. "If you two plan on drinking like that all night, you just might keep me in business." He pulled a second lowball glass down and fixed my tequila and lime first before digging the good scotch and amaretto out from under the cabinet to fix Bub's drink. He garnished mine with a slice of lime and dropped a couple cherries in Bub's.

Bub turned to me with a familiar and mischievous grin. "What shall we drink to?"

I should have been tickled to be sitting next to him, leisurely enjoying a drink, but I was still reeling from the tranquilizers and the fight with Maalik. And I was still sour over the fact that I was jealous of Bub's female visitor. He knew it too, and he was enjoying it entirely too much.

"To your new girlfriend," I said, not caring how snippy I sounded, and tossed my drink back with wild abandon. I called out to Xaphen as I slammed my glass down, bouncing a few ice cubes out onto the bar. "Same."

He gave me a frown, but refilled my glass.

Bub sipped at his drink as he tried not to smile. "Lucky me. I wasn't aware I had a new girlfriend."

"What do you call her then? Your playmate? Booty call? Demon delight?"

He laughed. "Demon delight? I like that."

"I bet you do."

"That was Lili. She works for me. She just got back from a long stint in the human realm, since she prefers the company of naughty Jewish men."

"Succubus?"

"Yes, and a rather good one. But she's needed here right now to help aid us against the rebels."

"Oh." I was feeling a little better.

"So, tell me." Bub rested his arms on the bar and reached into his drink to retrieve a cherry. "Why are you so torn up over seeing another woman in my home, when you obviously don't want me for yourself?"

"Torn up?" I snorted. "Right."

"Then what's with the sorrow drowning?" He nodded at my glass.

I looked down at my hands and sighed.

Bub shifted uncomfortably beside me. "Ah, Maalik."

"He had my neighbor tranquilize me to keep me at Holly House last night."

"What?" Bub laughed. "You're kidding?"

181

"No." I frowned at him. "I understand things got pretty eventful last night, but I'm not fucking helpless, and I'm tired of hiding out, waiting for the world to be safe again."

He nodded. "So he let you out tonight?"

"Well, he didn't try to tranquilize me when I left him."

"By left, you mean…"

"Yeah." I sighed and finished my second drink before holding it up to motion to Xaphen for another.

Bub downed his and tilted his glass in the air as well. When Xaphen came around the bar, Bub slipped him a Pandemonium Bank card.

"I thought this was my treat," I said.

"Well, being tranquilized is a fair enough excuse for skipping out on your training, and what kind of gentleman would I be if I let you pay for our date?"

"Date?" I nearly choked on my drink. Xaphen gave us a funny look, but quickly glanced away.

"A man and a woman. Sharing drinks and conversation. What would you call it?"

"Not a date, that's for sure."

"What if I asked you to dinner tomorrow evening? Would that be a date?"

"You don't waste any time, do you?" I blushed.

"No, I don't. So will you have dinner with me tomorrow?"

"I can't," I answered. "I have class."

"Then the night after?"

"Oh, good lord." I set down my drink and turned to face him. "Fine. I'll have dinner with you."

"Good." He smiled at me and tossed his drink back, running his forked tongue around the ice cubes at the bottom of the glass. I looked away. His husky, musical laugh sent a chill through me.

"I should probably get home," I said.

The alcohol, nearly nine shots of tequila to be exact, was starting to hit me and hard. It was also possible that the tranquilizer hadn't quite made it out of my system yet either.

"Let me walk you." Bub stood and reached for my jacket, but I beat him to it.

"That's all right." I gave him a forced smile as I slid off the barstool. "I'll see you in the morning."

"Lana." He caught my arm. "Anubis may have made some arrests, but I somehow doubt Tisiphone was among them."

My jaw tightened. "Fine."

Xaphen noticed me pulling on my jacket and came back around behind the bar. He ran Bub's card and handed it back to him.

"You two be careful tonight," he said.

"Of course." Bub gave him a polite nod and held the front door open for me.

The streets were growing darker. There were a few souls and reapers wandering about, but with the recent scare, it looked like most were staying in for the night. I stuffed my hands in the pockets of my jean jacket and glanced sideways at Bub. I was trying to be excited about him walking me home, but the notion that he was only doing it for my protection kind of ruined the fun of it. It also made me wonder if the dinner date was a setup for him to babysit me too, now that Maalik was relieved of that duty.

Bub glanced around, trying not to look too obvious as he scanned the people around us for signs of danger. When he noticed me watching him, he gave me a quick smile. "Are you excited about the placement ceremony this Saturday?"

"Sure. It will mean I'm finished with school and can forget about it for another few centuries."

"You think you'll have enough votes to make it on the Posy Unit?"

"Yeah, I think so."

"You don't sound as excited as I thought you would be."

I shrugged. He already knew about Wosyet, but I really didn't want to tell him about Horus's illegal side job. Josie and Gabriel were the only ones I had told about that. Neither of them had ties to the council the way Bub did. He would feel obligated to tell Cindy Morningstar about it. I really needed to guard my secrets more diligently.

If I passed the training and my classes and I still didn't get enough votes to make it on the Posy Unit, that was Horus's problem. I already knew I had the votes of Horus, Meng, and Cindy. I had a feeling that I wouldn't be receiving favorable votes from Maalik or Ridwan. How Holly Spirit, the Green Man, Kwan Yin, and Parvati would vote was anyone's guess. Maybe Horus had been working on them. The only one I could even hope to gain an audience with would be Holly, since I was living at Holly House. I wondered if Charlie could set up an appointment with her for me.

Bub and I arrived at the front gate of Holly House. He gave the fountain in the courtyard a questionable look.

"Can you tell by looking at it that it's holy water?"

"Yes, but not all demons could," he answered with a frown.

"I think I can make it from here."

"You're not going to invite me up?" he asked.

I raised an eyebrow. "You're not concerned about being in Holly House?"

"I've been in Holly House before."

"Oh?"

Bub grinned. "We may not be able to vote as the Abrahamic Elite, but we still gather and discuss business on occasion, and Holly has hosted a summit or two here before."

The Afterlife Council thought that allowing the Abrahamic heavens and hells to work together would allow them to overrule the council's checks and balances system. So they broke up the original group of delegates into the

Board of Heavenly Hosts and the Hell Committee. It was really just for show. The Abrahamic Elite still gathered, but on the council they were recognized as two separate entities.

Holly House didn't necessarily pose a threat to demons. As long as they stayed clear of the relics and had good intentions, the protective Latin prayers carved all over the building wouldn't do them any harm.

Bub followed me to the front door, and I nervously punched in the code.

Charlie gave us a double take when we entered the foyer. "Evening Ms. Harvey. Beelzebub," he said, pushing the guest log across the counter.

Bub smiled and signed his name. I panicked briefly, wondering if Maalik was allowed to review my guests. That would have to go on the list of things I needed to discuss with Holly.

Bub pushed the log book back to Charlie. "It's been a while, Charlie. How's life treating you?"

"Can't complain," the nephilim answered. "Enjoy your stay."

We took an elevator up to the tenth floor. My heart was racing. By the time we made it to my door, I was a nervous wreck.

"Do you drink coffee?" I asked, struggling to put my key in the door lock. I stepped inside the condo and listened for the soft sound of Coreen sniffing the air to validate that it was me.

"Don't you think we've drank enough tonight?" Bub asked.

"What?" I raised an eyebrow as he reached up and fingered one of my curls.

I might have been drunk, but I wasn't that drunk. I was still fully aware of what was happening. I had a moment's hesitation to wonder about Maalik, and then remembered I had pretty much dumped him, just a few short hours before. Still, guilt flooded in, along with a hefty dose of exhilaration.

I knew in that moment that if Bub made another move, I was done for. He knew it, too.

He took a step closer, and his body heat engulfed me. I ran a hand down his chest, caressing the shiny material of his shirt. It was such a small gesture, but it was all the invitation he needed.

Bub stepped inside the condo. He reached out and touched the side of my neck softly before racking his fingers through my curls and pulling me into a crushing kiss. My heart skipped, excited by the rush of raw need. I was frozen with disbelief for a moment, letting him handle me without reciprocating much. He noticed my hesitation and started to pull away.

I opened my eyes slowly and looked up at him.

"This is probably a bad idea," he rasped, looking torn between wanting to stay and wanting to run.

"The worst," I said, grabbing the sides of his collar and pulling him back to my mouth.

He leaned into me, pushing us further into the condo and pushed the door closed behind us. We stumbled across the dining room, somehow removing my jacket and kicking off our boots without ever taking our lips from one another. When we made it to the living room, Bub lifted me to sit on the back of one of the sofas. He untied my halter top and let it fall in my lap as he pulled his mouth away from mine and worked it down my neck and chest, stopping to flick his forked tongue over one nipple and then the next. I gasped and arched back to give him better access.

When he finished teasing my breasts, they glistened in the city lights filtering in from the living room windows. He grinned up at me, the gold flecks in his eyes glowing in the dark room, and then he moved lower, tickling his fingers along my hips before digging them under the waistband of my jeans. He gathered the halter top and jeans together and pulled them down my legs in one motion, leaving them in a pile on the floor.

I suddenly felt very naked, especially since he was still wearing his shirt and pants. All I had on was a pair of black, lacey panties and my peacock earrings. Bub moaned his approval as he dropped to his knees and pulled my legs over his shoulders. When I felt his slender tongue work its way around the lace, I was done for.

I screamed out my pleasure, and would have fallen off the sofa if he hadn't had ahold of me. He tore the lace away and devoured me entirely, until my legs were trembling and my throat was raw from breathing so hard.

When Bub finally stood, he lifted me in his arms and walked around to the front side of the sofa to lay me down. His eyes danced over me as he removed his clothing.

I was still breathing hard when he came to me, gently nestling between my thighs and nipping at my breasts again. When the head of him pressed into me, I cried out. I was still moist and throbbing, and unsure if I could take more just yet. He pressed in anyway, slowly, until he filled me. I dug my fingers into his back and bit down on my bottom lip. He stayed there a moment, pressed firmly inside me, carefully watching my expression.

"Do you want me to stop?"

"Don't you dare."

He laughed and then eased back to thrust inside me again. I closed my eyes and tightened my legs around him. He trailed kisses up and down my neck, nipping at the edges of my scar as he rocked over me, each thrust harder and faster than the last, until we were both panting like wild animals. When we came, our voices echoed one another in a blissful crescendo.

Bub collapsed on top of me and rolled onto his side, wedging himself between the couch and me, before looping an arm under mine and cupping my breast. I lay there, my legs tangled in his, listening to our breathing slow with a smile on my face, and wondered if he could see how ridiculously satisfied I was despite the darkness.

CHAPTER 29

"Sex alleviates tension.
Love causes it."
-Woody Allen

Waking up alone should not have bothered me as much as it did. I was actually embarrassed, and the feeling only got worse when Kevin emerged from one of the guest bedrooms. He caught sight of me and threw a hand over his eyes.

"Wow! Sorry! You didn't mention that you slept nude in the living room when you told me I could move in."

I snatched one of the oversized pillows off the couch and covered myself, wishing the damn thing was big enough to hide my face with it too.

"Were you here all night?" I asked, trying to keep my eyes from falling out of my head.

I had entirely forgotten that Kevin was moving in on Tuesday. I was probably taking my tranquilizer nap while he was unpacking boxes. I guess that was one way to get out of helping. Josie must have given him her spare key. Boy, did I feel stupid.

Kevin turned his back to me and faced the dining room. "I thought I heard you come in last night. The dogs didn't bark, and I heard, well, it sounded like you and Maalik were busy, so I didn't want to bother you."

Well. This was awkward.

"Sorry, I don't usually sleep out here. I just forgot you were moving in. I'll get dressed. Would you mind starting some coffee?"

"You bet." Kevin hurried off to the kitchen.

I made a run for my bedroom and closed the door behind me, pressing my back against it and squeezing my eyes shut.

I had a lump in my throat and the urge to burst into tears, but I pushed it away. I didn't have time to feel sorry for myself this morning, and I didn't really feel like I had a good reason to be upset anyway. Bub hadn't made any promises. At least he wasn't poking and prodding me for information or trying to tell me what I could and couldn't do.

I took a quick shower and threw on a pair of jeans and a black turtleneck, but still managed to feel naked when I met back up with Kevin in the kitchen. He gave me a tight smile and handed me a mug of coffee.

"Sorry, again," he said, blushing.

"Forget about it. Literally. Forget it happened."

"No problem." He sighed. "So, how about those rebels?"

It was a pathetic attempt to change the subject, but I'd have a discussion about knitting socks if it meant never having to talk about our little surprise encounter ever again.

"I think those rebels have been given the boot, and I'd like to give your girlfriend a boot upside the head for the shenanigans she pulled with Warren Tuesday night."

"Yeah, I heard about that." Kevin winced.

"When's she planning on showing her face around here again? I've got a piece of my mind I'd like to give her."

"She said something about stopping by after work, before you head off to your last class."

"You may want to be scarce for that conversation."

"You want I should take the dogs for a walk, boss lady?"

"Yeah, that'd be great. They're going to need it. I'm not taking them with me to train with Bub today."

Kevin perked up at the mention of my demon training. Josie had probably said something to him about it. "You really think Grim might make you his second?"

I about choked on my coffee. "Not a chance in hell, and I have no idea why everyone else seems to think that. I guess they just think he's trying to be secretive when he says he loathes me."

"Oh." Kevin frowned. "Well, it would have been cool if you could have taken me with you to train against demon attacks."

"Trust me, cool is not the word for it, but I'll teach you a few of the more useful things I've learned once I'm all finished."

"Sounds good."

I looked up at the clock on the kitchen wall. "Gotta run."

"I'll be here, unpacking. Just so you know. Don't want to risk another—"

"I thought we were forgetting that happened," I said through gritted teeth.

"Right."

I put my coffee mug in the sink and left in a hurry, hoping Kevin was smart enough not to mention my morning condition to Josie or anyone else. Otherwise, I would have to gouge his eyeballs out.

Once I made it past the front gate, I took the quick coin route to Bub's house. I could hardly bring myself to climb the steps leading to his front door. My hands were shaking and a wave of nausea made the coffee in my stomach feel more like acid. Jack greeted me before I found the nerve to ring the bell.

"Ms. Harvey!" He sounded awful chipper. I felt myself blush as I wondered if Bub shared his sexual conquests with the old demon. "Master Beelzebub was called away early this morning to Pandemonium for an urgent matter, but he did instruct me to give you this." He handed me a small, leather-bound folder. "It's your certification stating that you've completed your training. Congratulations!"

I took the folder and swallowed, trying to keep my face blank. "Thanks, Jeeves. Been nice knowing you."

Jack looked stunned. "I'm sure we'll be seeing each other again. Soon."

"Sure we will." I gave him short wave and stepped off the porch before rolling my coin.

I probably should have gone back to the condo and studied some more before my last final, but it wouldn't have done much good anyway. My mind was not on the books. Bub had gotten what he wanted, left in the middle of the night, and then had his butler give me the certificate to avoid having to deal with me. He came. He saw. He conquered. He was the typical misogynist male. And I was an idiot, because I had known all along. It should have been easy enough to convince myself that it didn't matter, that I didn't really want anything more from him anyway, but I did.

I walked around Limbo City, down near the harbor on Market Street, and got lost in my thoughts. The babysitting detail had grown a little lax since the rebel arrests, and in my experience, ambushes rarely occurred in the morning hours.

The peddlers were setting up shop along the coast wall that lined the Sea of Eternity. I found an open spot between two tent booths and leaned over the wall, resting my chin on my folded arms. The sea sloshed around below, the occasional soul peering blankly up at me. A nice breeze came in with the ghostly turquoise waves, tickling my curls across my face.

"Good to see you're not letting the rebels get the best of you." I jumped at the sound of Holly's voice and spun around.

The feathered Ms. Spirit was dressed in white shorts and a sparkly, peach blouse. A pair of flat sandals laced up her calves. Her blond locks were pinned up in a pretty little nest on top of her head. She leaned over the wall next to me and dangled the vendor bag she carried out over the sea. "I was sure Maalik would still have you under lock and key until Grim was absolutely certain we had eliminated the rebel base."

I frowned at her and rested my arms on the wall again. "Maalik is not my keeper. Actually, I'm glad you spotted me. It saves me the trouble of trying to set up an appointment with Charlie."

"What's on your mind, Lana?" Holly smiled at me.

"I would like to stay at Holly House, but only if you will allow me to pay my own rent. Also, I expect the same privacy rights as your other tenants. I'm no longer seeing Maalik. I'd like him removed from my visitors list, and I don't want him having access to the visitor log to keep tabs on me."

Holly grinned mischievously. "I don't suppose this has anything to do with your slumber party with the Lord of the Flies last night, does it?"

I blushed. "Like I said, I'm no longer seeing Maalik. So it's not really any of his business who comes and goes."

Holly nodded. "Don't sweat it, Lana. Your secret is safe with me." The way she said the word secret sent a chill over me, and I wondered just how many of my secrets she was aware of.

"Thank you."

"I do remember you saying that Holly House was out of your price range though. Won't that present a problem for you?"

"That's something else I wanted to discuss with you. My apprentice is staying with me for a bit, and I was wondering what the protocol is for roommates."

Holly shrugged. "As long as they're clean and follow the rules, I don't see why moving in a few roommates should be a problem."

"Great. I think the rent should be manageable then."

Holly smiled at me. "Good. I like having you at Holly House. And just so you know, I'll be voting in your favor on the Posy Unit proposal."

I tensed, waiting to hear what special favor was going to come with her vote. When she noticed me staring at her, she giggled one of her musical giggles and pressed a hand to her chest. "I'm not as skeptical or suspicious as some of the others on the council. When Grim says you're not his choice as his new second, I believe him. He may be secretive at times, but that doesn't always suggest one is untrustworthy. Wouldn't you agree?"

There it was again, the subtle mention of my secrets. Somehow, I doubted that my tryst with Bub was the only thing on her mind.

"I suppose," I answered carefully.

"I'm headed back to Holly House to do some paperwork. Would you care to walk with me?"

"Sure. Why not."

It was beyond strange to me that Holly was being so friendly, especially if she didn't want anything from me in return and if she didn't believe I was going to be Grim's new second. Politicians just weren't the nice-for-no-reason type in my experience. And as sweet and innocent as Holly seemed, she was still a politician.

We leisurely strolled past the venders, stopping to check out a tent selling frankincense and rosaries. Holly picked out a set of candlesticks adorned with little crystal angels, and I bought a pair of earrings from a Summerland vender. Holly was a council member, so she was drawing plenty of attention, which meant I was too. I could smell the rumors cooking, but there wasn't much I could do about it. I guess somebody had to fuel the rumor mill. Might as well be me.

When we turned off Market Street onto Morte Avenue I noticed two nephilim dressed like civilians following us. Holly sensed my anxiety and followed my gaze.

She placed a hand on my shoulder. "Don't worry. They're with me."

"Nephilim Guard?"

"No, my personal bodyguards. Grim has been monopolizing the Guard for his own purposes." She huffed.

We passed Kevin and the hounds on the way inside Holly House.

"Josie waiting for me?" I asked him.

"Yeah." He blushed at the sight of Holly and gave her a little bow. "Good evening, Councilor."

"Good evening, young reaper. I hear you've joined Lana here as a tenant. I hope you find the accommodations pleasing."

"More than pleasing. It's a beautiful condo. You really have impeccable taste," he gushed.

I rolled my eyes. God, he was such a suck-up. I wondered if that had anything to do with him graduating at the top of his class. At least it was better than Craig Hogan's tactics. A small smile came to my lips at the thought of our last encounter. Karma had taken her sweet time, but she made good in the end. I was just glad I got to be there for the show.

CHAPTER 30

*"A true friend never gets in your way
unless you happen to be going down."*
-Arnold H. Glasow

Josie was waiting at my dining room table when I came through the front door. She had changed out of her work cowl and into a pair of jeans and a gray, long-sleeved shirt that accented her steely gray eyes. Her short black hair was gelled into stiff spikes. A few angled inward and framed her face. It was an aggressively sexy look that I usually liked on her, when I didn't feel like putting a boot up her ass. Her expression was neutral, but her pissy attitude was still obvious. Her legs were crossed and her arms folded tightly under her breasts. It didn't look like an apology was in my future, but I didn't see one in her future either.

"Josie." I threw the leather folder with my fancy new certificate on the table.

"Lana." Josie's expression stayed icy, but I knew her well enough to know curiosity would get the best of her. "All finished with Bub?"

"Yeah. I'm officially certified to protect myself against demons. So maybe I'll be able to leave my own home from now on without being tranquilized in the process."

"Christ, Lana." Josie sighed. "Of all the nights to go out, you managed to pick the worst possible one. I would have darted you myself if I could have. Lucky for you, Warren had already heard what was going down and knew more than anyone that your stubborn ass should have been content to stay in."

I shook my head. "I'm done playing hide and seek with the rebels. I've made it through the training Cindy requested. If you can't accept that and still feel the need to boss me around, I don't know how this whole roommates thing is going to work out."

"Roommates?" Josie blinked at me, and then the corner of her mouth tugged up into a lopsided smile. She quickly hid it with a frown. "I'm not apologizing."

"Neither am I."

Josie narrowed her gaze at me. "It was for your own good."

"I'll decide what's good for me from now on, thank you."

She snorted and snatched the demon certificate off the table. I hadn't really looked at it yet, but she read it aloud for me. "This certificate hereby certifies reaper Lana Harvey as a Demonology Specialist, now proficient in knowledge and skill to identify and defend against aggressive demon threats. Validated by the Lord of the Flies himself." She looked up at me. "Well now, isn't that special."

I winced at the mention of Bub. "Yeah."

Josie's eyes widened at my pained expression. "Oh my god. You slept with him!"

I opened my mouth, but I couldn't get the words to come out. So I pulled out a chair and slumped down at the table across from her. I couldn't tell if she was more impressed or appalled.

"What about Maalik—"

"We broke up," I grumbled.

"Before or after you boned the prince of demons?"

"Before." I closed my eyes and dropped my forehead to the table. "Right before. As in a couple of hours."

"Wow, Lana." Josie gave a short laugh and then cleared her throat. "Are you two an item?"

"No. I don't know. We haven't really talked since."

"Who's the tart now?" She laughed and then paused thoughtfully. "I never really figured you had a type, but it appears you have one after all. You're a sucker for men from Hell."

"Sure I'm not just a magnet for men from Hell?" I asked with my head still pressed to the table. "I mean, it's not like I'm being pursued by anyone else."

"What about Craig Hogan?"

I groaned my disgust. "Swine doesn't count."

Josie giggled and hopped up from the table to go fetch a couple of Gabriel's Ambrosia Ales out of the fridge. She dropped back in her seat and slid one of the beers across the table to me.

"Thanks," I said pulling my face off the table and propping my chin in my hand.

Josie cracked open her beer and took a drink. "So you really want another roommate?"

I nodded grudgingly. "I may need two more, considering how god-awful expensive it is here. I've already told Holly that Maalik is not to pay my rent anymore. I know I'll be getting a bump in pay when I start on the Posy Unit, but not that big of a bump."

"About that." Josie looked a little sheepish. "I don't have the council sponsoring me, but I do have quite a few credentials making me eligible. So I was thinking about joining the Posy Unit with you and Kevin. Is that cool with you?"

"Yeah. Definitely." I was surprised.

Josie didn't generally seem to enjoy working with me, whether we were delivering souls on our ship or taking a class together. She usually regarded me with mild annoyance and lectured me on the rules. That could present a problem if she caught me doing Horus's little side job. Of course, she was probably joining for Kevin's sake. Maybe he would be distraction enough.

Josie folded her arms over the table and tilted her head to one side. "Who else are you considering as far as roommates go?"

"Do you have someone in mind?"

"Well, Jenni's going to have to find another roommate if I leave, unless you want me to extend the invitation to her as well?"

"Hmmm. Yeah. If you and Kevin plan on sharing a room, that could work." I frowned.

"What's wrong?"

"Gabriel's going to be stuck on the couch again."

Josie shrugged. "He's used to it."

I scrunched up my nose. "I just hope he's gentle on the furniture. How much do you suppose one of those white sofas cost?"

"Good point."

We finished off our beers just as Kevin came back with the hounds. He gave us a cautious look as he took off Saul and Coreen's leads. They both brushed by me for a mandatory ear-scratch greeting before curling up on the living room rug for a nap.

Josie stood to wrap her arms around Kevin's neck and gave him a peck on the cheek. "Looks like Jenni and I are going to be following you here."

He raised his eyebrows and looked at me with a smile. "Wow. That's great. We should celebrate."

"I've got one final left tonight."

"Afterwards," Josie said. "Jenni and I already passed our last finals, so it can be a celebration for all of us. I'll give Gabe and Amy a heads up too."

"Sounds like a plan." I grinned.

Things were starting to feel normal again. Well, aside from my little situation with Bub. At least my circle of friends was nearby, and I'd be back to work soon. I was actually looking forward to it. How pathetic was that?

CHAPTER 31

"May God have mercy upon my enemies,
because I won't."
-George Patton

Words could not express my elation. Not only had I managed to pass my mentoring final, but I got an A. It was a miracle... or possibly a mistake. Either way, I'd take it. It was all I could do not to skip down the sidewalk on my way to meet Josie and the rest of the gang at Purgatory to celebrate.

I didn't want to waste one minute of the evening, so I had found an outfit that worked for class, but still managed to be festive enough for Purgatory. I didn't want to have to go home and change after my final. A black pencil skirt fit the bill. I added a white, sleeveless blouse, a black and white checkered scarf, and some strappy black heels. It was genius. All I had to do when I left the academy was add some red lip gloss, and presto! I was party worthy. I was sure that passing my last final had given me a nice glow of achievement as well. I walked down Council Street with a smile, wondering what could possibly make this night any better.

My moment of joy staled once I caught the scent of sulfur. The news of the rebel arrests had really diminished my caution. I tried to relax my shoulders and increased my pace as much as possible without looking too obvious. I secretly hoped it was Bub trailing me, but I should have known better. The rebels had just taken a large blow. They were sure to retaliate, and of course, I would be their target. I was three blocks away from Purgatory when a familiar figure rounded the corner and headed my way.

Craig Hogan's casual attire hadn't change much in three hundred years. He was in jeans and a black polo. The short stubble on his head was so thin that it looked more gray than black. With his splash of gray freckles and pale skin, he looked washed out and more like a soul than a reaper. His eyes locked on me, and he immediately donned one of his fake grins, the kind that said he thought he was made of awesome.

I contemplated walking across the street to avoid him, but I had the shrinking feeling that was the direction my demon stalker was approaching from. I dug a coin out of my pocket, but before I had a chance to do anything, the streetlights flickered and died. A familiar and chilling doom engulfed me, and I couldn't help but notice that Craig didn't seem affected as he neared me.

The impact of the dread spell hit me like a blow to the chest. I hunched over and clutched the front of my blouse, struggling for my next breath as I tried to keep my panic at bay.

"You look terrible, Lana." Craig said with an entirely fake air of sympathy. "Here, let me help you."

I put my hand out to keep him back, but he turned sideways, taking my arm and steering me into the nearest alley. There were a few other reapers out, making their way home from the academy, but I imagined it just looked like Craig was helping me up from a fall. Every ounce of energy was drained from my body. I couldn't even find my voice to call out to them. This was not how my night was supposed to end.

Craig pulled me a ways down the alley, until we reached a recess in one of the buildings that formed a small area for dumpsters. He pried the coin out of my hand and pushed my back up against a brick wall, leaning into me. I turned my face away from him.

"Demon got your tongue?" He laughed, and I could smell the sulfur on his breath. He wasn't gambling with demons. He was sleeping with one. Not that I had any right to point fingers. I was sleeping with one too.

From the corner of my eye, I watched the hell bitch Tisiphone emerge from the opposite alley. The Tinker Bell dress had been replaced by leather pants and a black tube top, and her knee length locks lay in a single braid over her shoulder. She looked more appropriate for the city tonight, and she could have almost blended in, if not for the sticky, black blood running from her eyes. The small concrete courtyard felt even smaller as she fanned her batwings open into a fear inspiring display behind her.

"Miss me?" she purred.

I took a deep breath and focused, trying to remember what Bub had instructed me to do if I found myself at her mercy again. The exercise had been easier in the comfort and safety of his home. My mind grasped for the details. It had something to do with visualizing blue light over certain chakras. I had been visualizing something a little less innocent while he had been pressed up against my backside, running his hands along my body to identify my power points.

Craig reached up my skirt, and I yelped in surprise as he ripped the strap of throwing stars from my thigh. Several bit into my skin, and I felt warm blood trickle down my leg.

"You won't be needing these," he sneered.

I swallowed and closed my eyes, forcing myself to picture the blue light swallowing my chakras.

"What's she doing?" Tisiphone snapped.

Craig pushed me harder into the wall. "I don't know."

"Well, make her stop. I don't like it."

Craig reached up and jerked the scarf from my neck. I opened my eyes when I felt his hand close over my throat.

"Play nice, Lana. We just have a few questions for you."

"Questions?" I asked.

He eased up but kept his hand around my neck.

"Where's the soul Grim assigned you to collect last fall?"

"I collected a lot of souls. You'll have to be more specific."

Craig let go of my throat, and before I had the chance to exhale my relief, he backhanded me across the face hard enough to throw me back against the wall. I stumbled in my heels and slid to the ground.

"Let's not play games, Lana. I've seen the reaper logs."

I looked up at him with wide eyes. "You? You broke into the records office?"

I clenched my teeth together and punched him in the balls. It was a straight shot from my position. Craig bent over with a grunt and placed a hand on the wall behind me. I took that as my opportunity to make a getaway and crawled out from under him. He seized one of my ankles and flipped me over onto my back, dropping his knee into my sternum to pin me to the gritty blacktop while he caught his breath.

"That's right, I took the reaper logs. I tried doing this the easy way first. We could have been in this together, but you just couldn't help but be a bitch. God, you haven't changed a bit." Craig pressed his knee in deeper, forcing the air from my lungs. He snatched my wrists and squeezed until my hands went numb. "This could have been nice. I could have fucked the information we needed from you."

"You wish." I gasped in enough air to spit in his face.

"Now I have to let Tisiphone beat it from you instead."

His eyes widened as his pupils dilated. The thought of killing me was just as exciting as the thought of bedding me. He was an even bigger bastard than I had realized.

The weight of him on my chest started to take its toll, and my vision went spotty. I stopped struggling, because I needed all my strength just to breathe. Craig took that as his cue to jerk me to my feet and pulled me around to face Tisiphone. He slid one arm across my throat and looped the other around my arms, pinning my back against his chest.

Tisiphone didn't look as happy to see me as she had the first time. Her pride had been wounded, and I was sure she was disgusted by the fact that she had to work with a lowly reaper like Craig. She paced in front of me, her barbed whip coiled in a tight loop in one hand. I did not want her to use that thing on me again.

She stepped in closer, sneering mere inches from my face. "You won't be so lucky this time, reaper."

I held my breath and leaned away from her, only to find Craig leering at me from behind. "What are you getting out of this Craig?"

He laughed. "You mean other than the satisfaction of seeing you suffer for being a bitch?" He pressed his face into my neck, breathing in the smell of my hair as he insulted me, like a true psychopath. "In exchange for helping the rebels secure Grim's secret weapon, they're turning over Reapers Inc. for me to manage."

"They really think you could do half as good a job as Grim?" I said, trying not to tremble in his arms as Tisiphone's hot breath brushed against my neck.

"Someone has to run it," she hissed. "Grim will never agree to submit to our ruling. He will have to go."

"And you chose Craig?" I laughed. Craig tightened his arm across my throat, nearly lifting me off my feet.

"I graduated with higher honors than you," he snarled.

"And we all know how you managed that. Guess old habits die hard," I said, my voice strained from his grasp.

"Fuck you, Lana. You're just jealous it's not you."

"They didn't choose you because they thought you were the most capable." I turned in his grasp to look him in the eye. "They chose you because they knew you had no morals. They saw you for the sniveling weasel that you are."

I knew that one was going to cost me. Craig lifted me off my feet with a grunt and turned to slam me face first into the brick wall behind him.

"Oddly enough, we didn't bring you back here to discuss my rise to power," he said through gritted teeth.

"No, we did not," Tisiphone injected. "We brought you here to find out where Grim's been hiding the soul he sent you to collect last year."

"How should I know?" I lied.

Craig leaned into me, pressing my face against the brick wall. I tasted blood and wasn't sure if it was coming from my mouth or nose. Everything hurt.

"Grim wouldn't risk abandoning his secret weapon in the event of his death. He would at least share that secret with one other, namely, his new second-in-command."

I wanted to laugh, but it ached just to breathe. "Grim can't stand me. Why the hell would he make me his new second?"

Craig lifted me from the wall only to slam me back against it. I whimpered. It was a pathetic sound that I had managed to hold in up until that point. They really planned on torturing me until I told them what they wanted to know. I had a sinking feeling that I'd eventually be found in one of the restaurant dumpster after they were done with me.

"Let me have her, reaper." Tisiphone was getting impatient.

I struggled against Craig, not wanting the black-eyed fury anywhere near me. As I did, I felt the small can of angelica mace in my pocket, crushed between my hip and the brick wall. I shouldn't have been in this situation. I was trained to prevent this, although, Tisiphone was a little more demon than any reaper could handle, even one with special training. Craig was another story. I hadn't been prepared to defend myself against my own kind, if you could call Craig my own kind.

Craig turned me around again to face Tisiphone. I held my breath, trying to formulate a plan through my panic. The black-eyed wench uncoiled her whip, and something in me snapped. My instincts went into overdrive, and I screamed. I lifted both of my legs, pulling my knees up to my chest before kicking Tisiphone full force in the gut. The impact slammed Craig against the wall behind us. His skull made a nice thud against the bricks, and his grip on my arms slacked. I pulled free and took off down the alley, running for all I was worth.

I stumbled in my heels, twisting my ankle, and fell to my knees just as I reached the sidewalk. I screamed again, more from frustration than out of pain. The streets were empty. There was no one to call out to for help. I grabbed the corner of one of the brick buildings and pulled myself up, only to drop again when the sharp crack of Tisiphone's whip sliced up my back.

I lay twitching on the sidewalk and watched as Craig descended on me. My hands were shaking, but I managed to shove one in my pocket and retrieved the can of angelica mace. It fit neatly in my palm. Unfortunately, it wouldn't do much good against Craig. A dark little part of me wasn't too upset about that. I wanted to get my hands dirty when I took my revenge on him.

Craig grabbed a fistful of my hair, yanking me to my feet. He pulled me back into the alley, and I let him, trying to get closer to Tisiphone. My body was humming with adrenaline. My breath rushed in and out like I had been running a marathon all day. Tisiphone smiled and swirled her whip in little circles on the ground, taunting me, daring me to run.

"Let's try this again," Craig said, still leading me by the hair. He stopped in front of Tisiphone and twisted me around to face her. I finally managed to catch my breath and looked up at her with a grin.

"Yes, let's." I lifted the mace and nearly emptied the whole can in her runny, black eyes.

Tisiphone opened her mouth, and what came out could hardly be called a shriek. It sounded like a wild animal being strangled.

"What the fuck!" Craig threw me to the ground to go to her.

I rolled away from them and onto my side, scanning the alley for my throwing stars. Craig had dropped them beside one of the dumpsters. My knees were bloody and raw, but I crawled my way over to the stars and stood, unclipping two of them before tearing off down the opposite end of the alley.

I made it to the sidewalk and immediately ducked around the corner, throwing my back against the brick building for cover. They would be following soon, and they were going to be pissed. I didn't have enough time to run, so I tried to still my mind enough to formulate a plan instead.

The bitter taste of blood was heavy on my tongue. I reached up to touch my face. The side Craig had slammed into the brick wall was swollen and sticky with blood. My leg still ached from the bite of the throwing stars, so I strapped them on my other thigh and tore my skirt up the side so they would be easier to get to.

It wasn't long before Tisiphone's high pitched screech was replaced by a guttural growl that vibrated the very ground with her rage. I was beyond surprised that the streets were still empty. How had no one heard that? Perhaps her little doom spell was soundproof or warded others off. I could still feel the weight of her magic and sensed the haze it laid over everything, but it was affecting my mood less now. I wasn't sure if that had something to do with my training or the fact that she wasn't as focused with all that mace her eyeballs were swimming in.

Tisiphone's whip cracked and my back went rigid from the sound. I held my breath and squeezed the throwing stars in my hand until I felt them cut into my flesh. They were sharper with the crystal tips, and I wondered if they would serve me better against the angry fury this time.

My nerves were too shot to wait around the corner for them any longer. Besides, I wanted the element of surprise. It was probably the only advantage I would have. I took a deep breath and launched myself across the alley opening, only slowing enough to aim and hurl the stars in my hand. I didn't wait to see where they landed, but the startled shrieks were satisfying. Especially Craig's.

I sprinted down half an alley and tucked myself into an alcove entrance of some nameless store. I pushed myself back in a corner, wishing Bub had trained me to be invisible. That seemed infinitely more useful all of a sudden.

What the hell was I going to do? I didn't really think I could take them both out with my throwing stars. Did I? Where was MacGyver when you needed him? My ankle was throbbing, so I slipped out of my strappy heels. I'd run faster without them anyway. I was about to drop them when I noticed a small metal box stuck in the corner of the store window. It had to be an alarm system.

"I can smell you, reaper!" Tisiphone sounded close, but I didn't dare peek around the corner.

My heart was doing flip flops. I had a feeling that the dash and throw maneuver wasn't going to work on her a second time. Panic set in, and the next thing I knew, I was smashing my high heels through the glass of the store door. An alarm went off as I poked my hand through the broken glass and unlocked the door. I hurried inside, hoping I had enough time to figure something out before Tisiphone arrived. Surely someone would come to investigate the alarm. Her doom spell couldn't be that good.

I skipped the obvious cover of the checkout counter and worked my way to the back of the dark store, shuffling around racks of musty, secondhand clothing. I imagined the place was where a lot of the Three Fates Factory souls dumped their wardrobes before venturing back to the human realm. Hopefully the racks would buy me a little more time.

I heard Tisiphone before I saw her. The broken glass crunched under her boots. I ducked under a row of fur coats and pulled another throwing star from my thigh. The only window was at the front of the store, but an exit light over the back door casted a dim red glow over the racks of used threads. I nearly bit my tongue off when I caught sight of a scraggly mannequin hunched over on the other side of the coats.

"Come out and play, little reaper," Tisiphone taunted me.

The snap of her whip sent a chill down my spine, making me painfully aware of the salty sweat working its way into my wounds.

Tisiphone inhaled sharply. "I can smell your fear and your pain. It's intoxicating. I can't wait to draw more from you."

I closed my eyes and tried to tap into the state of mind that allowed me to see demon heat signatures. I wasn't sure if it would work without the raskov smoke, but I had to give it a shot. I was running low on options. Tisiphone hadn't moved as far as I could tell, so I focused in the direction her voice had come from.

Sweat beaded across my brow and trickled down into the corners of my eyes. I held my breath until I thought I would pass out, and then it appeared. A huge, pulsing red light swelled up right where the queen of pain had stopped near the shop entrance. The light was such a deep red that it was almost purple. Then it moved closer. I sucked in a startled breath, and before I could fully grasp my next thought, I had snatched the old mannequin. I hurled it towards the back exit and didn't even wait to see if Tisiphone would take the bait before migrating carefully around the racks, back towards the front door.

I stole a glance behind me before coming out into the open. The heat signature had faded from my mind, but so had her doom spell. I did a double take when the black braid over her shoulder coiled itself around and hissed at me. Tisiphone shrieked her frustrations at the mannequin, snapping the plaster torso into pieces with her whip. She spun around, catching a glimpse of me, but it was too late. I was out the front door and halfway down the next alley before she had time to turn on her pretty little heels.

I stopped to catch my breath once I had rounded the next block. Dear god, I was going to have some nightmares about that hair of hers. I would have almost rather suffered through the doom spell than to have witnessed that. I was within a block of Purgatory at this point, and feeling pretty confident that I was going to make it. The relief flooded in, mixing with adrenaline to form a nauseating concoction in the pit of my stomach, which doubled in toxicity when a hand gripped my shoulder and pulled me back into the alley, yet again.

My voice froze in my throat as I laid eyes on Craig. He dug his fingers into my arms, pulling me into his chest. My throwing star was lodged in his eye. It oozed pus and blood that splattered across my face as he screamed at me.

"Where is he, Lana? Where is he? Where is he?" he shouted, over and over again.

I recoiled from him, holding my breath as he pressed his face into mine. He had been terrifying enough before, but now he looked like a crazed zombie. His buzzed head was smeared with blood. It ran down his face and soaked the collar of his shirt. His good eye was dilated and bloodshot and pierced through me like a poisonous arrow.

My blood was frozen in my veins. I couldn't breathe. I couldn't think. I was dangerously close to blacking out, when I finally snapped out of it. I sucked in a shuddering breath and screamed. I screamed like it was the last scream I had left. I screamed like the world was about to swallow me whole, and the only thing keeping it at bay was the breath in my lungs.

Craig jerked away, and then lifted me up and body-slammed me, bouncing my skull on the pavement. My shoulder blades ached, and my head was spinning, but I kept screaming. Craig straddled my legs and then lifted my shoulders and slammed me back to the ground, trying to shut me up. It took him several tries, but my voice finally fizzled out into a raw cry.

My vocal chords were shot, and I was fairly certain I had a few broken ribs. A burning sensation filled my chest, and I wondered if this was what dying felt like. I quit fighting and slumped in Craig's arms. My pulse slowed in my temples and I rolled my eyes up to meet his so he could see the satisfaction in them before they went out. He had done his worst, but I hadn't given in.

"Where is he, Lana?" He shook me again to keep me conscious.

I smiled and put a hand up to his chest. "Wouldn't you like to know," I croaked.

Craig shook me harder and growled his frustrations.

The heat in my chest felt like it was about to melt my heart and lungs, but I laughed anyway. Craig bared his teeth and then reeled his fist back, as if to punch me. I lifted my other arm, pushing him away with both hands, and that's when the fire in my chest blossomed, filling me to the brim. I was no longer solid. It was as if my whole being had turned to molten lava. My hands sunk through Craig's chest like he was made of butter. His mouth fell open, but nothing came out. A big orange hole formed around my hands. I struggled to pull them free, but as I did, Craig was sucked inward. He had been reduced to a soulish form, and I had somehow turned him inside out. His particles dispersed with a sudden pop and scattered into the night with the distant echo of a scream.

CHAPTER 32

"You don't develop courage by being happy in your relationships every day. You develop it by surviving difficult adversity."
-Epicurus

I lay on the pavement, panting and confused, and wondered what the fuck had just happened. I could barely wrap my mind around the fact that I was still alive, let alone the freak incident that had just occurred. A sob slipped out of me, and I covered my face with my bruised and bloodied hands. There was no one around to impress, and I hurt like hell.

The sound of frantic voices caught my attention as they drew near, but I was too exhausted to care if they were friend or foe. Craig was gone. Forever. When I was done crying from sheer terror and pain, I'd cry again from relief.

I hadn't quite made up my mind if I had enough strength to make it out of the alley, when Josie rounded the corner.

"Lana! She's over here," she shouted over her shoulder as she knelt down beside me. "Are you okay?"

I laughed and sobbed at the same time as I reached up to touch her, making sure she was real. A spiral bruise circled up her arm, and a splatter of blood dotted her bare shoulder and chest around a gash across her collarbone. One of the spaghetti straps of her little blue cocktail dress was broken.

"I need a drink," I said, my voice still gravelly from all the screaming.

Josie laughed and wiped a tear from her eye. "You must have passed your final if you're still feeling well enough for a drink after the ass-kicking it looks like you just got."

"As a matter of fact, I did pass." I grinned up at her. "Now help me up."

Kevin and Jenni arrived as Josie pulled me to my feet. Anubis and half the Nephilim Guard weren't far behind them.

"Where are your shoes?" Jenni asked, which for some reason cracked me up. Of all the things to notice, it had been my bare feet.

My fit of giggles became contagious, so by the time Anubis had made it over to join us, we were all laughing hysterically. He gave us a cautious look. "Is everything all right? You look awful."

"I feel awful." I leaned on Josie's shoulder, suddenly aware of my twisted ankle. I was sure it wasn't finished swelling, but I didn't care. I was just glad to be alive.

Anubis frowned and cleared his throat. "Well, the guard and I collected six more rebels in the city tonight, and then we responded to a shop alarm not far from here, where we encountered Tisiphone, the retired fury from Tartarus. I take it you encountered her as well?"

He didn't mention Craig, and I wasn't sure how to tell him what had happened without inadvertently incriminating myself. "Yeah, I guess you could say that." I groaned and glanced over at Josie again.

She looked embarrassed. "We volunteered to help, but I think we got in the way more than anything else," she said.

Anubis cringed, but to his credit, he didn't criticize. Most other gods would have jumped at the opportunity. "It's all right. We'll get her next time."

214

"I sincerely thought she was just another run-of-the-mill demon." Josie winced and rolled her bruised shoulder under the weight of my arm.

"Don't sweat it," Anubis assured her again. "Take care of her." He nodded to me.

I blinked a few times, feeling my adrenaline take a downward spiral. My consciousness wasn't in very good shape, but if I passed out now, I just knew I was going to end up at Meng Po's again.

"Lana, thank god." Gabriel approached us from the opposite side of the alley. He took my free arm and pulled it over his shoulder. "Do we need to go to Meng's?"

"Take me home," I groaned. Josie struggled to hold me up, so Kevin moved in to take her place on my other side. He had a busted lip, but looked all right otherwise.

Anubis nodded, giving my wounds an unsure glance. I tried to smile, but it was too strained to look genuine. "Take it easy," he said, and then signaled the guards waiting in the street to follow him through the alley.

Jenni stepped in towards us, completing our little bruised circle. Kevin rolled a coin and took us all to the front gates of Holly House. We didn't waste any time making our way inside.

Charlie met us at the elevators. He gently scooped me into his arms, relieving Kevin and Gabriel. We crowded into the elevator, and by some miracle, we managed not to bleed all over the shiny glass and metal. My head lolled in towards Charlie's chest, tucking my nose into his armpit. I thanked Khadija that he was wearing deodorant. I was far too tired to move another muscle. Charlie smelled like leather and lemon cake. It was an odd combination, but somehow soothing. I mumbled into his suit jacket as the doors pinged closed.

"What's that?" he whispered, tilting my head back.

I looked up at him. "Now this is what I call room service."

215

He gave me a light chuckle. I was out before we made it to the tenth floor. Visions of sugarplums didn't even come close. It was more like a coma, and when it came for me, I welcomed it.

CHAPTER 33

*"The average, healthy, well-adjusted adult gets up
at 7:30 in the morning feeling just plain terrible."*
-Jean Kerr

I wasn't sure how long my dreamless sleep stretched for,
but when I came to, I was relieved to see that I was in my
own bed.

"Feeling better?" Warren stirred in the corner chair. He
stood and stretched his wings and arms with a yawn before
taking my wrist to check my pulse.

"Playing doctor today?"

He raised his eyebrows at me. "Yesterday too, but that's
one thing I don't have a license for, so let's keep it 'tween us
girls, shall we?"

I twisted my head to the side and popped my neck with
a groan. One of my wrists had been wrapped, and an ankle
too. I felt like one giant bruise. "How long have I been out?"

He scratched his head. "Thirty-six hours, maybe?"

"It's Saturday?" I sat up with a start.

"You haven't missed anything. It's still early," he said,
patting me on the leg.

I sighed and relaxed again. "How are the others?"

"Better off than you, that's for sure. Bruises and scratches mostly. Meng Po sent Jai Ling over last night with some tea. Are you feeling well enough to have some?"

I crinkled my nose, but nodded. The aftertaste would be worth not looking like the walking dead at the placement ceremony.

Josie passed Warren as he left to fetch the tea and took a seat on the edge of my bed. The spiral bruise on her arm had faded to a grayish-green and a few stitches sealed the slash across her collarbone. She wore a sports bra and a pair of cropped yoga pants, and her skin held a dewy pink hue.

"Hey there, pilgrim." She smiled down at me.

"Hey. You breaking in the gym here already?"

She blushed and rubbed a hand over her arm. "Yeah. It helps keep my nerves in check."

I nodded. After a rough day, I found that taking the hounds for a run seemed to calm me down. I imagined the slight run-in with Tisiphone ranked up there with the worst of Josie's days.

"Maalik stopped by yesterday," she said, giving me a curious look.

I groaned and closed my eyes. "What did you tell him?"

"Nothing much." She shrugged. "I told him you would recover and that that was all he needed to know, considering your recent breakup."

I sighed. "Thank you."

"Oh, and I saw something in the paper today that might interest you." She tossed the latest *Reaper Report* in my lap.

The front cover showed another arrest scene with the Nephilim Guard taking a handful of demons and lesser Egyptian deities out of a dilapidated apartment complex.

"Yeah, I remember Anubis mentioning the additional arrests."

Josie pointed to an article highlight along the side margin. "Miranda Giles from the Lost Souls Unit has gone missing."

"Craig's girlfriend?"

"Who?" Josie tilted her head in confusion.

"Craig Hogan," I tried again.

"Sorry, never heard of him."

"Are you kidding me?" I swallowed, remembering how quickly he had popped out of existence in that dark alley. Apparently I had done a lot more than just kill him that night. I was officially freaked out.

Josie looked at me blankly, waiting for an explanation.

"Never mind." I shook my head.

"It hasn't been determined yet whether Miranda is in league with the rebel forces or if she was their new target since they couldn't get to you."

"It's hard to say. I didn't know her well." I shrugged and tried to rub out the goose bumps forming along my arms.

"Thought you'd be comforted by the notion that the rebels might have given up on you and moved on to someone else. Not that I'm wishing harm on Miranda or anyone else. I just think you could use a break, especially since you're not actually going to be Grim's new second."

I laughed. "Damn straight."

I didn't really want to go into detail about how the rebel demons were trying to get to the high priority soul we had harvested last fall. To be honest, I was a little surprised that they hadn't gone after Josie and Kevin as well. They were on the team too, but I had been put in charge. I was also surprised that Josie hadn't asked more questions about our assignment. I was guessing that she didn't think I knew anything more than her, so she had left the subject alone. There were a lot of little things I was thankful she had conveniently forgotten or avoided asking me about.

Josie cleared her throat. "Well, the placement ceremony starts in eight hours, and you still look like death warmed over. I'm not sure makeup is going to cover this much damage."

"Meng sent some tea over." I stuck my tongue out. "Warren should be back with it any minute now. Hopefully makeup will take care of what the tea doesn't, though I'm not so sure the outfit I picked out for the ceremony is going to work now."

"Way ahead of you." Josie grinned and opened my closet door. A soft, blue tunic dress was hung on the inside hook. It had long sleeves and a slinky cowl neck. It looked short and snug enough to pass as sexy, and with a pair of black tights, all my bumps and bruises would be covered. Well, except for the ones on my face. Makeup would have to do there. I frowned, wondering just how long I was going to be working my wardrobe around unsightly injuries.

"You don't like it," Josie said, looking dejected.

"No! It's perfect. Thank you." I tried to smile.

"Well, I'm going to go finish unpacking with Kevin. Jenni is out walking the hounds. We're taking turns until you're feeling better."

"Wow. Thank you. Really. You guys are the best."

"You better believe it." Josie's smile faltered as Warren returned with the tea. She obviously still remembered the taste from last fall when she had been sent to Meng's after Wosyet stuck her in the gut with a syringe full of laced hellfire. The horrific brew wasn't something easily forgotten. This was my third round in a matter of weeks, and I still wasn't used to it.

Josie crinkled her nose and backed out of my room. "I'll catch you later, Lana."

I nodded to her and took the tea from Warren. It wasn't any easier to keep the stuff down this time, but I drank it steadily, hoping I had enough foundation to touch up what it left behind. The side of my face that had taken the most of Craig's abuse still felt like hamburger, but I could tell that someone, probably Warren, had applied some ointment.

I finished the tea and napped away the rest of the morning and good chunk of the afternoon. Josie woke me a couple of hours before the ceremony and I took the longest, hottest shower of my life. Stepping out of the luxury stall felt like a resurrection. After I toweled off and the steam had cleared, I finally took a look at myself in the mirror.

I had been too afraid to assess the original damage, and my reflection confirmed that had been a good move. I looked like hell. Stitches lined the arch of one brow and I was sure my eye socket had been cracked in a few places since I still had a nasty, black and blue shiner. A faint, yellow bruise blotched across my jawline. I sniffled, feeling pathetically sorry for myself.

"Chin up, chica. I got this." Josie stood in the doorway of my bathroom with her industrial makeup case. One of the kitchen barstools was tucked under her arm.

I swallowed and let the tears streak down my face. "You really think this is fixable?"

"Well, it's not like I could make it any worse, right?" Josie centered the barstool in front of the bathroom counter and patted it. I obeyed with a sigh and plopped down in front of the mirror.

She started with a thick white base that made me look even paler than I already was. My skepticism spiked until she blended in a couple blush shades with a sponge. Next she polished my lips with a deep mauve and shadowed my eyes with smoky charcoal hues. The look was a lot racier than I would have normally gone for, but it definitely drew the attention away from the underlying bruises that were still faintly visible.

Josie tilted my chin up to examine me. "Maybe we can do something different with your hair to hide the stitches."

I was pretty set in my ways, and I wore the crystal bands Saul had bought for me to most events. But for the sake of vanity, I would skip them tonight.

Josie sectioned off the front of my chin length curls and styled side-swept bangs over my injured eye. She pinned the rest of my hair back into a French twist. I hardly recognized myself, and I wondered if anyone at the ceremony would either. At least they wouldn't be gawking at me because I looked like I had been hit by a bus. The tea was still working its magic. If I stared in the mirror long enough, I could watch the bruises fade.

When Josie was finished with me, she clapped her hands together and grinned ear to ear. "What do you think?"

"Bravo. I think I can actually show my face tonight." I smiled at her and went to fetch my outfit.

I was actually starting to look forward to the ceremony, and then I remembered that Bub would be there. He had planned it after all. I wondered if he had heard about my latest run-in. I was more than disappointed that he hadn't stopped by to check on me and Maalik had. Even if Bub had used me, I still felt like I had made the right decision by ending things with Maalik. I groaned, remembering that Maalik would be at the ceremony too. This was going to be interesting to say the least.

CHAPTER 34

*"Some drink from the fountain of knowledge,
others just gargle."*
-Robert Frost

The academy held the annual placement ceremony at the city park. The stage was set up on the opposite side of the park from Saul and Coreen's memorial statues, which I was thankful for. The statues just reminded me of all the nerve-wracking secrets I was keeping lately, including Winston. I wondered how he was faring, but with all the attention on me lately, I didn't dare try to visit him.

The placement ceremony drew fewer attendants than the Oracle Ball, but it did allow for soul guests, which the ball did not. Most of the souls who lived in Limbo and worked at the Three Fates Factory kept to themselves, but a few were brave enough to befriend the other locals, mostly reapers and nephilim.

There were about two dozen reapers from the academy seated near the front of the stage, awaiting new placement orders. Josie, Jenni, and I sat in the center of the second row, unsurprisingly blending in with the others in our formal black robes. We'd strip down to our reception clothing after the ceremony. There was a certain way things were done at Reapers Inc., but the ceremony seemed silly and unnecessary to me. I guess some people just needed an excuse to dress up and feel important.

I hadn't heard anything new from Horus, but I was fairly certain I would be making it on the Posy Unit. I had passed my finals, and I knew I could count on favorable votes from at least four of the nine council members. Surely Horus had secured one more for me to tip the scales.

The placement procedure was really a surprise for all reapers involved. Sure, they could submit applications for the units they were interested in, but whether or not they made it on those units depended on several factors. There had to be an opening or substantial need for more reapers in that specialty. There was also seniority and credentials to consider. Sometimes a reaper could be denied the unit they applied for and be placed on another unit that needed them more, and sometimes a reaper could fill out an open application and be placed on whichever unit needed them most, like in Jenni Fang's case. She was a sixth generation reaper who was more qualified than most third generation reapers. I was curious to see which unit she would end up on.

The last of the guests arrived and took their seats just as Grim appeared on the stage, capturing everyone's full attention. Grim was good at drawing attention, but especially so today. He had been pretty scarce during the rebel threat plaguing the city the past few weeks. Half the locals seemed to think him a coward for it, and the other half saw his actions as reasonable and expected, considering his status.

"We are gathered here today to celebrate education and revel in achievement," Grim said, opening his speech. "Words cannot express the pride I feel when I see young reapers taking initiative and improving their status and station at Reapers Inc. So without further ado, let us begin."

I zoned out as he began the long, drawn out process of listing off each individual reaper, along with their every credential and announcing their new placement and rank within their unit.

Each unit had a captain with one or more team leaders. The idea was to create a safety net for the more unpredictable and complicated harvests. Freelance harvesters received a soul docket every morning from Ellen Aries, Grim's secretary, but reapers belonging to a unit took their orders from their unit captain. The harvests were still commission based, but they were assigned throughout the day. When a reaper returned from one harvest, they were given another. Who got the better assignments depended on how proficient a reaper was, or on how much they kissed their captain's ass. I wasn't looking forward to that bit of my new job, and I was pretty sure that lots of ass-kissing was going to be expected from a rookie like me. I was hoping to get around that by proving my efficiency early on. The more souls I went through, the sooner I would find a replacement for Winston and the sooner I could get back to freelance work.

My ears perked at the first mention of the Posy Unit. Grim announced Adrianna Bates, Josie's mentor and the current captain of the Posy Unit. She made her way to the stage to receive a scrolled certificate from Grim.

"Your esteemed services on the Posy Unit will be missed, but are quite welcome on the Mother Goose Unit who look forward to your expertise and leadership as their new captain." Grim shook her hand and motioned her past him.

Well, shit. I had hoped the Posy Unit would be bearable with Adrianna for a captain. Now I was left in limbo, waiting to find out whose ass I would be kissing.

Grim continued on, and I found myself annoyed that I actually had to pay attention now. The ceremony seemed to drag on forever, and of course Josie, Jenni, and I were near the tail end of the list.

"Josie Galla, a seventh generation reaper of noble credentials, who has recently completed training in the art of soul hypnosis and the management of wandering souls, please come forward to receive your certificate for placement on the Posy Unit."

Josie beamed at me before heading towards the stage, while I clapped with everyone else. Even if I ended up with a shitty boss, at least I could take comfort in knowing that Josie would be suffering with me. I relaxed my shoulders and smiled as Josie shook Grim's hand and took her certificate. He gave her a quick nod and waved her by without so much as a blink.

I was rolling around the possibility of Jenni being my boss when Grim announced me. "Lana Harvey, an eighth generation reaper who has recently completed training in apprentice mentoring, the management of wandering souls, and tactical demon defense, please come forward to receive your certificate for placement as the new captain of the Posy Unit."

Instead of the generic clapping, a murmur of surprise snaked through the crowd. I somehow doubted Josie's fancy makeup job was enough to hide the dumbfounded look on my face. My mind drew a resounding blank, and I completely forgot myself. Grim looked like he might call my name again, until Josie shoved me out of my chair and towards the stage. She started clapping with crazed enthusiasm, jumpstarting the crowd's manners. Everyone joined in with more zeal than I had counted on.

My knees wobbled, and I nearly fell on my face as I climbed the steps up to the stage. I took my certificate from Grim in a zombie-like daze. His serious expression never changed, but I could see the satisfied humor in his eyes.

"May your success as head of special projects last fall carry on into your new role of leadership on the Posy Unit," he said, waving me on my way.

I swallowed and hurried out of the limelight. I didn't bother looking over the crowd as I made my way back to my seat. I could feel the eyes crawling over me like so many spiders. There were a few faces I wanted to see, but the looks reserved for them were private.

I was sure Horus was pleased with himself. I knew he had been pushing for my placement on the Posy Unit, but the captain position was way beyond anything I had expected him to accomplish. I desperately wanted to interrogate him to find out just how he had managed it, but that was a conversation that would have to wait. There were too many eyes and ears here.

As if the placement news wasn't shocking enough, Grim's decision to make my demon training public knowledge was another pound of surprise dropped in my lap. I suppose it made my placement as captain more justifiable, but I hardly believed it was a random act.

I had barely taken my seat before Grim continued with the ceremony, announcing the last reaper in waiting.

"Jenni Fang, an ambitious sixth generation reaper of fine repute and unmatchable training and experience, please come forward."

He broke protocol and waited for her to join him on stage before announcing her new placement. Instead of handing her a certificate like the rest of us, he placed a hand on her shoulder and looked out over the crowd. "I am pleased to present my new second-in-command." He turned to Jenni then. "There is not another more qualified or deserving, Ms. Fang. I see great things in store for Reapers Inc. with you by my side."

The expected clapping and cheering followed. Jenni looked mildly pleased and not at all surprised, like Josie and I. I wondered how long she had been harboring that secret and how hard that must have been, and then I remembered the smorgasbord of secrets I was keeping. Instead of reclaiming her seat, Jenni disappeared behind the stage.

Grim waited for the clapping to taper off and then his look grew somber. "It's no secret that Limbo City has been victim to terrorist acts as of late. I'm sure that many of you have already encountered the newly assigned Nephilim Guard who has gone to great measures to minimize the impact of these attacks.

"While arrests have been made, and we are confident that the rebel base hidden within the city has been dissolved, more measures to ensure our future safety have been taken. As of midnight, tonight, unrestricted coin travel within the city will be permanently deactivated—"

A collective gasp rose up from the audience, followed by excited and outraged murmurs.

Grim's voice rose above the static. "A small number of guarded coin booths will be installed throughout the city. I do hope this will not inconvenience Limbo City's fine citizens or guests too terribly, but I assure you, this is a necessary precaution that the Afterlife Council has given much thought and consideration."

That had to be the exhausting work Winston spoke of. Altering the state of such a large chunk of Eternity wasn't something that could be tackled by wiggling one's nose. Grim wasn't wasting any time flexing his new muscle. If he kept this up, we were going to need a replacement a lot sooner than expected. I might have hated Horus for blackmailing me into being his minion, but that didn't mean that he wasn't right about needing a backup soul.

Grim silenced the audience one last time. "There is a final measure of precaution I urge reapers of all generations to look into. The Lord of the Flies, Beelzebub, will be joining the faculty at the Reaper Academy next semester. He will be offering a demon defense course co-developed by Lana Harvey."

Co-developed? That had been unexpected. My heart fluttered at the mention of Bub. I just couldn't decide how I felt about him lately, and it didn't help that I was so unsure of how he felt about me, what with his little disappearing act. I wanted to scan the crowd for his face, but once again, there were too many eyes, and I was the source of enough gossip already.

Taking in the ceremony attendees was easier once Grim finished up with the standard acknowledgements and invited everyone to enjoy the refreshments. Josie and I shuffled out of our seats along with everyone else and handed our robes over to a nephilim attendant for safekeeping. I snuck a glance over the guests. I was more than a little shocked to find Holly Spirit and Cindy Morningstar seated on either side of Horus. It hadn't dawned on me before now that Holly might be friendly with the Egyptian deity. I wondered if Maalik would have been so anxious to accept the condo at Holly House if he had known.

Speaking of the keeper of hellfire, Maalik was seated a few rows behind Horus's little ménage á trois, looking miserable as ever. His jaw was clenched so tightly that it looked like it might break. He caught me staring and looked away just as quickly, opting to gaze unblinkingly at the stage instead. Next to him, Ridwan checked his watch and rolled his eyes. I was sure he found the whole event beneath him.

Josie nudged me towards a table holding an array of finger foods and a big bowl of punch that was more than likely spiked. A drink didn't sound half bad, especially after having my mind blown. I hadn't really absorbed everything yet, and I was hardly in a position to be answering nosy questions from random acquaintances, but I could hold it together long enough for a drink or two. After that, I could politely excuse myself and head back home where I fully intended to drink a whole bottle of wine, eat half a gallon of ice cream, and sleep the rest of the weekend away.

Kevin emerged from the swarm of reapers with a cheer and lifted both hands, prompting Josie and I to give him a double high-five.

"Congratulations!" he shouted over the buzzing crowd.

To my relief, the news about the travel booths and Jenni's placement as Grim's new second was the highlight of the mindless chatter filling the park. I got a few dirty looks, but I was too distracted to care.

I was a little taken back when Josie flung her arms around my neck. "This is amazing! We're all going to be working together! Let's ditch the cookies and go celebrate at Purgatory."

I laughed and hugged her back. I was actually surprised by how relieved I felt. Josie didn't have a problem with my new job title. Screw everyone else.

I wobbled, catching her arm when she pulled away. "Sounds like fun, but I'm really beat. I should get some more rest before we start up this new adventure on Monday. You guys go ahead."

Josie gave me a strange smile. "It's not like you to turn down Purgatory."

"Trust me, if I didn't feel like I'd been hit by a bus, I'd be buying the first round." I caught sight of Bub. "Besides, it might be a while before I can get away."

Josie followed my gaze and turned back to me with a grin. "Good luck," she said and patted my shoulder before tugging Kevin off towards the refreshments.

My view of Bub was suddenly cut off by Maalik.

"Congratulations." His scowl matched my own.

"Maalik." I tried to step back, but he stepped in closer, taking me by the arm.

"I realize that we're through, but that doesn't mean I don't still worry about you—"

"I can take care of myself."

"Clearly," he snapped. "I just thought you might appreciate a little fair warning. Grim's suspicious of you, and he's not the only one. You need to be careful, especially now that you're living with his new second. She's not to be trusted either."

"Well darn, and here I was planning on divulging all my deepest, darkest secrets to her." I folded my arms.

"This is not something to make light of, Lana." He gritted his teeth and pressed himself in another step.

My breath caught in my throat and I looked away. It was hard being this near to him. It was too soon, and I still felt like my little indiscretion with Bub was somehow a betrayal.

Maalik softened at my unease. "I am almost certain that there are still rebel spies within the city. Whatever your feelings towards me are, you must remember that you are valuable to the future of Eternity, therefore you must be more responsible about your safety. If you must visit your *friend*, be discreet and infrequent. If you are caught, you will be finished, and I couldn't bear that."

I sighed. "Okay. Thank you for the warning."

Maalik nodded and released me, disappearing into the crowd just as Bub stepping up beside me.

"Congratulations, Lana," he said, handing me a glass of punch to toast with him.

"Thanks." I frowned. Eyes were on me again.

Bub certainly knew how to make his presence known. While Maalik had nearly blended in with the reapers in his black robe, Bub's silky, maroon suit demanded attention. The collar of his shiny black dress shirt lapped over the collar of his jacket, and a black fedora with matching maroon trim sat on his head.

I gave him a strained smile, and sipped at my punch.

"Are you all right?" he asked quietly, aware of all the onlookers.

"Yeah, considering everything I've been through."

Bub frowned. "I heard. I had an urgent matter to take care of in Pandemonium. I'm so sorry I wasn't there."

"Which time?"

"What?" Bub blinked at me.

"Which time are you sorry for not being there? When I was attacked by Tisiphone? Or the morning after we..."

Bub blushed then. "Lana—"

"You know what, just forget it. Thanks for the punch. Enjoy the party." I tossed back my drink and left, leaving him standing there with an unspoken apology smeared all over his face. I didn't know if that apology was because he hadn't meant to hurt my feelings, or if it was because he hadn't realized I had the kind of feelings for him that could be hurt. Either way, I felt sick and just wanted to be home and out of the public eye.

There was still a few hours until midnight, so for the last time, I used a coin to get back to Holly House.

My mind skipped around like a lost child while I went through my evening routine of getting ready for bed. I wondered where the travel booths were going to be located and how many of them there would be. I wondered how living with Jenni was going to be now that she was Grim's new second and how I was going to sneak out to visit Winston. I wondered how I was going to handle being captain of the Posy Unit. I wondered what the hell had happened to Craig and why no one seemed to care or even notice that he was gone. I wondered about Horus's side job and Tisiphone's whip. I wondered how long I was going to have to wonder about all this crap.

By the time I was finished with all my deep and pressing thoughts, I had changed into a pair of drawstring pants and a tank top, brushed my hair and teeth, and washed my face. Meng's tea had really patched me up nicely. There was still a faint purple bruise around my eye, and the stitches above my brow weren't quite ready to come out, but everything else looked good as new.

I fed the hounds and spent a few extra minutes scratching and rubbing on them. I think it was more to comfort myself than them. Starting Monday, they'd be back to work with me, and I could hardly wait. I had the sinking feeling that everyone was waiting around to watch me fall on my face. I would show them. My mind was made up. So help me Khadija, I was going to be the best captain the Posy Unit had ever seen.

CHAPTER 35

"What is man?
A miserable little pile of secrets."
-Andre Malraux

Thanks to his special training, I could actually smell Bub before I answered the door. My heart couldn't decide if it wanted to leap or sink, but I tried to keep my cool as I faced him.

He had changed out of the suit he'd worn to the placement ceremony and now wore only the black dress shirt and a pair of blue jeans. With the tortured expression on his face, it made him look more vulnerable than any demon I'd ever known.

"So that's it?" he asked. "You're done with me? Just like that?"

"Done with you?" I was baffled. "You were commissioned to train me by Cindy. You've fulfilled your duty. I figured you'd be glad to be done with me."

"You're an idiot," he said, pushing past me and closing the door behind him.

I was angry and hurt and confused. And my nipples were hard. Which for some reason, made me even angrier.

How could he just stand there, looking at me, like I had somehow wronged him?

He took a step closer, and before I could turn away, his hands were on me. One found the back of my neck, and the other grasped my hip. I had a second to gasp, and then his mouth was on mine. He pulled me in, pressing me against his chest until it hurt, until I could feel him hard against my stomach. My moan was smothered by his kiss. I pressed my hands against his shoulders, and he pulled away, his face stained with want and frustration.

Something broke in my mind. Whatever it was that gave a damn about right or wrong or rules. Something cracked me down the center like a dam, and everything I wanted came pouring out into the open.

I bit his bottom lip and took hold of his belt. He slid a hand under my tank top, pressed his palm under one breast, and drove me up against the wall.

I gasped and pushed him back an inch. "Not here."

"Hmm?" He groaned against the side of my neck.

"Not out here. I have roommates."

"Then where?" He untied my pajama pants and circled his thumbs around my hip bones.

I pulled him through the kitchen and down the hall into my bedroom, closing the door behind us. Bub loosened my pants and let them drop to the floor. Then he cupped his hands under my ass and lifted me, tossing me on the bed. He peeled off his shirt and jeans before climbing on top of me and pinned my hands over my head as he kissed his way down my neck and over my chest.

I arched beneath him, my pleasure boiling as he took my nipple into his mouth through my shirt. He teased me through the thin fabric until my hips spasmed against his chest. When he rose up between my legs and entered me, I was almost embarrassed by how fast I came. And then I came again, and again. After he finally found his release, I was spent and beginning to feel all the aches and bruises that hadn't quite finished healing.

The leftovers of my injuries and Bub lying on top of me reminded me of how Craig had pinned me to the ground. I almost felt guilty for how satisfying killing him had been. It made me feel rotten and twisted for finding that much joy in such a destructive act, and it was only made worse by the fact that I wished he was still alive, just so I could kill him again. I hated that the memory was spoiling my fun.

"Lana?" Bub reached to wipe a tear from my cheek. I hadn't realized I was crying. I turned my face away from him.

"Sorry." I laughed. "It's just been a rough few weeks."

"Tell me about it." He rolled off me and nuzzled in against my back, peppering my neck and shoulder with soft, careful kisses.

"I'd rather not. In fact, I'd really just like to forget most of it."

Bub stopped kissing me. "Even the time spent with me?"

"No." I grinned. "The time spent with you is the only thing I'd like to keep."

His goatee tickled my skin as he grinned against my neck. Not a moment later he was snoring, and a moment after that, so was I.

CHAPTER 36

"In three words I can sum up everything
I've learned about life: It goes on."
-Robert Frost

I woke from a dead sleep with alarms going off in my head and slid out from under Bub's arm as quietly as possible. I tugged on a pair of jeans and a tee shirt before Winston had a chance to ring the doorbell.

It was something I couldn't explain, but anytime I was near the kid, I could feel him like a gong echoing in my head. I was going to kill him if Grim didn't first. He knew better than to leave his secret hidey-hole.

Bub was still tangled up in my sheets, and I hated the thought of leaving him there, but this was an emergency. I gave him a gentle peck on the cheek and snatched a work robe from my closet before racing out the front door, just in time to slap Winston's hand away from the bell.

"Hey," he whined as I steered him away from the condo.

"I have company. You can't be dropping by like this. Are you crazy?" I snapped as I led him back towards the elevators.

"It's been over two weeks, and the only face I've seen day in and day out is Grim's. Do you have any idea what that's like?" He jerked his arm out of my grasp.

We loaded into an elevator and I pulled my robe on. Winston's hair was dark, but he was just a little too tan to pass as a reaper. I pulled his hood down further over his face, hoping Charlie wasn't feeling too conversational tonight. Winston frowned up at me and then pressed the emergency stop on the elevator.

"What the hell are you doing?"

"What the hell am I doing?" he snapped. "It's two in the morning. Coin travel is deactivated. So what the hell are you doing?"

"Shit." I ran a hand through my hair. "How the fuck am I supposed to get you home?"

Winston sighed and shook his head at me. He grabbed my hand and flipped a coin in the air. We were sucked out of the elevator, and I all but fell on my face when we spilled out onto Winston's front lawn.

"God damn it, Winston! A little warning would have been nice." I wobbled and blinked a few times, adjusting to the light. In the realm of the secret throne it was always day. Grim thought it added an extra measure of safety.

"Sorry, but you weren't exactly listening, and we had to move fast. I can only freeze time for so long."

"Freeze time? And I thought you said coin travel was deactivated."

"You think that old buck of a banker is the only one who knows how to bespell coins?" He grabbed my hand and pressed the coin he had just used into my palm. It was larger than the typical coins used in Limbo and a dark, charcoal gray color.

"Does this work anywhere or just in the elevator?"

"Anywhere, but it will only bring you here, and you'll have to be very discreet, of course."

"Of course." I frowned. "Does Grim have one of these too?"

"Do I look stupid?" Winston scowled at me. "No, and he's not getting one. I have to deal with that bastard enough as it is. With the deactivation order, he'll be forced to cut back his visits to once a week, and I can't wait."

"What about Horus?"

Winston's scowl deepened. "He doesn't get one either. You're the only one I care to see on a regular basis. Speaking of Horus, I have something for you to give him on your way home. He'll be waiting for you in the alley where you killed Craig."

I almost swallowed my tongue. "How do you…"

He sighed again. "That much power doesn't go unnoticed. You're just lucky that Tisiphone was there to blame the disturbance on."

"Why doesn't anyone else seem to notice he's missing or even remember he existed?"

"Because you didn't just kill him, you undid him. I'm tapped into the power that created him, so I still experience an echo of his existence." Winston shrugged. He couldn't have cared less, but it was still unnerving that he had so much to hold over me. I was feeling the need to be careful with him suddenly.

"I'm finished with school and the demon training, so if you want, I can bring you a box of life support tomorrow."

"It can wait. You're starting a new job Monday, and I hear it's a big one. Congratulations, by the way."

"Thanks."

He handed me a padded, black envelope. "Give this to Horus."

"When exactly did I become your messenger?"

"Would you rather I deliver it myself?" He raised an eyebrow.

"No." I frowned and turned the envelope over to reveal a gold wax seal with an Egyptian ankh embedded in it. "What is it?"

"A permission slip for a field trip." Winston laughed. "If it was any of your concern, I wouldn't have sealed it."

I rolled my eyes. "I'll see you next week."

"The coin will drop you off in the travel booth half a block from the alley where Horus is waiting for you."

"Super." I flipped the coin and left him standing there on the sunny lawn.

The trip to the travel booth felt different than regular coin travel. I popped up in the little glass booth and waited for my eyes to readjust to the darkness. A nephilim guard glanced up at me long enough to press a little clicker in his hand. A camera anchored to the booth flashed. I frowned and waited for my sight to clear again. I wondered if this was a process I would get used to or if I'd just go old-school and start doing more walking around the city. Maybe I'd get a bike.

I left the booth and hurried down the block towards the alley where I was to meet Horus. It seemed a little ridiculous. I had just been named as captain of a specialty unit, and now I was playing messenger for a spoiled soul.

I glanced over my shoulder before ducking into the alley. My steps slowed as I ventured further away from the street, and my mouth went dry. This was a bad idea, and I suddenly hated Winston for it. My chest tightened at the sight of my dried blood on the ground and splattered over the brick wall. I swallowed and hugged myself, wishing I had told Winston to deliver the envelope himself. I didn't need this bullshit.

A heavy hand rested on my shoulder. I turned suddenly and kneed Horus in the groin. I had been so lost in the sour memory of the alley that I hadn't heard him sneak up behind me. So it was an accident. Mostly.

"By the dog, Lana," Horus groaned, squatting down to brace his arms on his knees. "It's just me."

"We're in a dark alley, and you really thought sneaking up behind me was a good idea?" I put my back against the brick wall and folded my arms. "Maybe try saying my name next time. Even a whisper will do. I might not be so inclined to kick you in the balls."

Horus glared up at me. "You have something for me?"

I pulled the envelope from my robe and threw it on the ground in front of him. "Are we done here?"

He frowned up at me. "You know, you never even bothered to thank me for your new job. I thought you'd be especially pleased that you were named captain."

"The only reason I have this job is so that I can do your dirty work, and now that I'm in a higher position of power, if I get caught, the penalty will be that much worse. So if you were expecting me to kiss your ass for the additional workload and stress you've forcefully injected into my life, think again."

"You're not even the least bit excited about your advancement?" Horus snorted. He picked up the envelope on the ground and stood.

"Can I go home now?"

He sighed and nodded. "I'll be in touch."

"I'm sure you will." I pulled the hood of my robe up and hurried out of the alley. The streets were empty at this hour, and even though I knew no one would be popping up out of thin air to attack me, I still felt uneasy. I wasn't sure I'd ever feel comfortable walking alone at night again.

Charlie gave me a strange look when I arrived at Holly House. He was a perceptive guy and was probably wondering how I had left without him noticing. I gave him a small nod and headed for the elevators before he had a chance to question me.

I tiptoed back into the condo and hung my robe in the hall closet. I wasn't sure if the others had made it back from celebrating yet, but I didn't want to wake anyone. The hounds were curled up on the living room floor. They stirred and Coreen lifted her head to sniff the air before nuzzling in closer to Saul. I slipped back into my room. The sight of Bub lying naked on my bed brought a grin to my lips. Truthfully, I had been a little worried that he might not be waiting for me when I got back.

I stepped into the bathroom and quietly stripped out of my jeans and tee shirt before patting my face down with cold water at the sink. My nerves were still a little twitchy, but they were settling. I looked up at the mirror with a sigh, truly grasping my exhaustion and relief.

"One day at a time," I told my reflection. "We'll get through all this and laugh someday." I raised an eyebrow, knowing that the laughter was more likely to be induced by madness at the rate I was going.

"Lana?" Bub stirred in the bedroom.

I clicked off the bathroom light and crawled back in bed with him. He curled an arm around my middle and pulled me in tight against his chest, nuzzling his chin against my neck.

I grinned and closed my eyes. Cuddling with a demon had to be somewhere near the top of my list of most crazy things that I was least likely to ever do. But tonight, it felt like the perfect kind of crazy. Who knew what the morning would bring? I didn't anymore. And for once, I didn't care. It was time to stop worrying so much and start enjoying some of the crazy life was throwing my way.

ACKNOWLEDGEMENTS

Holy cow. This book took forever to finish. I'm sure it had absolutely nothing to do with the fact that I've moved several times, gotten married, had a baby, and juggled a few graphic design jobs on the side. Nope. Couldn't be that.

To my awesome readers, who have continually asked when this book would be finished, thank you. I'll admit it. Life got so hectic at times, I actually forgot I was writing it. If you hadn't kept reminding me, this book would still be under construction. You pulled me through. You are the reason I still fancy myself a writer. You rock.

Justina Roquet, my beautiful, brainy seester, thank you for your editing expertise, yet again. School may be out for the summer, but you kept your red pen out of storage just for me. You're the best!

Thanks also goes to my supportive husband, family, friends, and the cupcake girls. You make me feel like a rock star, even on my worst days. And finally, thanks to my online followers. Some of you make me feel like a maniacal cult leader, but I kind of like it.

If I've missed anyone, go ahead and send me an angry email at angela@angelaroquet.com and I promise to thank you from the bottom of my heart next time.

ABOUT THE AUTHOR

ANGELA ROQUET is a great big weirdo.
She collects Danger Girl comic books, owls, skulls, random
craft supplies, and all things Joss Whedon. She's a fan of
renewable energy, marriage equality, and religious
tolerance. As long as whatever you're doing isn't hurting
anyone, she's a fan of you, too.

Angela lives in Missouri with her husband and son. When
she's not swearing at the keyboard, she enjoys painting,
goofing off with her family and friends, and reading books
that raise eyebrows. You can find Angela online at
www.angelaroquet.com

If you enjoyed this novel, please leave a review on Amazon,
Goodreads, or wherever possible. Your support and
feedback are greatly appreciated. :)

Catch up with Lana in book 3, *For the Birds*,
now available in print and for Kindle.

CPSIA information can be obtained at www.ICGtesting.com
Printed in the USA
LVOW08s1516060416

482439LV00001B/220/P